D0953783

CITY OF THIRST

CITY OF THIRST

The Map to Everywhere:
Book 2

by Carrie Ryan & John Parke Davis

Illustrations by Todd Harris

Little, Brown and Company
New York   Boston

Little, Brown and Company

Hachette Book Group
1290 Avenue of the Americas, New York, NY 10104
Visit us at lb-kids.com

Little, Brown and Company is a division of Hachette Book Group, Inc.
The Little, Brown name and logo are trademarks of Hachette Book Group, Inc.

The publisher is not responsible for websites (or their content) that are not owned by the publisher.

First Edition: October 2015

Library of Congress Cataloging-in-Publication Data

Ryan, Carrie, author.
City of thirst / by Carrie Ryan & John Parke Davis ; illustrations by Todd Harris. — First edition.
pages cm. — (Map to everywhere ; book 2)
Summary: "Master Thief Fin from the Khaznot Quay and suburban schoolgirl Marrill from Arizona reunite on the magical waters of the Pirate Stream to seek a mysterious and legendary wish machine"—Provided by publisher.
ISBN 978-0-316-24084-0 (hardback) — ISBN 978-0-316-24083-3 (ebook) — ISBN 978-0-316-24081-9 (library edition ebook)   [1. Adventure and adventurers—Fiction. 2. Pirates—Fiction.   3. Friendship—Fiction.   4. Magic—Fiction.   5. Maps—Fiction. 6. Fantasy.]   I. Davis, John Parke, author.   II. Harris, Todd, illustrator.   III. Title.
PZ7.R9478Ci 2015
[Fic]—dc23

2015008673

10 9 8 7 6 5 4 3 2 1

RRD-H

Printed in the United States of America

For Esmé and Audrey
No walls are too high.

Contents

My Friend Fin
By Marrill Aesterwest

I, Marigold Mae Aesterwest, have a secret. I may seem

Trust me, you don't.

like an ordinary neighborhood girl to everyone at school.^

But what no one would ever suspect is that I have sailed the

Even made-up places get capitalized.

P   S

pirate stream! As my friend Ardent the wizard says, the

P   S

pirate stream is a river where the water is pure magic,

and it touches all worlds at some place and time. And

Karny and I

Karny and me ^are the only ones from our world who've

Seriously, Marrill?

ever been on it!^

    P   S

    This summer I sailed the pirate stream on the good ship

Underline ship names.

the Enterprising^Kraken, with Ardent and his captain, Coll,

who is just a little older than me but is an awesome, awesome

Shouldn't this be pirates?

sailor and the ship is crewed by the pir^ats who have too many

Run-on sentence. Also, this makes no sense.

legs and also the Ropebone Man who is the rigging.^ We had to

Okay, this makes no sense.

fight pirates and charm trees ^and gather the pieces of the

Is this supposed to be "Been There"? That's actually pretty cute.

Bintheyr^Map to Everywhere before the evil wizard Serth

could put them together and open the gate to the Lost Sun of

????

Dzannin, which would destroy the whole ^P ^S pirate stream!

But the best thing about the ^P ^S pirate stream is my friend

Fin. No one notices him, and no one can remember him except

Wow, it's almost like he's imaginary?

me. Fin is a master thief who can steal anything, but he's not

like a bad thief, even though he does hang out with pirates.

Fin needs help finding his mom and figuring out where he

came from, and I wish I could be there to help him. He's my

Really, sweetie, maybe you should try

best friend and I miss him a lot. *talking to the other kids in*

your class. You might like them?

The best thing ever would be to go back to the ^P pirate

☹

^S stream (other than Mom getting well again). But if I

This is not a word.

ever can, that means something superbad has happened,

Real subtle, M.

because our world has too many rules. Too much magic, and

How about your homework?

we would break apart. So all I can do is think about Fin and

Underline ship names.

Ardent and Coll and the <u>Kraken</u> and hope they are doing okay.

Marrill, this was a <u>math</u> assignment, not creative writing.
I can't tutor you if you don't even try, you weirdball.

                                        —Remy

CHAPTER 1
The Message on the Stop Sign

Karnelius J. Mousington was not, as a rule, a cat that appreciated being ignored. He tugged on his leash, drawing it tighter around Marrill's arm and breaking her concentration. She flapped a hand at him to be still. Her eyes, meanwhile, stayed fixed on the three little boys standing before her, the youngest of whom casually held an object that didn't exist.

At least, not in *her* world it didn't.

"I've never seen anything like it," Tim said. His cheeks flushed as he passed it to her.

Marrill tried to keep her fingers from shaking as she turned it over in her hands. It was a net, sort of; or more like a spiderweb made out of soap film; attached by a single thread to a thin glass rod. It looked so delicate that she was afraid it might vanish if she gripped it too hard. And yet, from what Fin had once told her, it would hold up against the force of a hurricane.

The Hatch brothers looked up at her, waiting expectantly. This was the third time today they'd called her out to the empty lot at the far edge of their neighborhood, promising to have found the lost treasures of Atlantis, unearthed by the recent flash flood. Up until now, those "treasures" had been half an old tire, two glass bottles, and a shinier-than-normal-but-not-really-that-shiny rock.

Normally, she would make up stories for them, like how an old cow's bone was really the remains of a baby dragon, or how a rusted coffee tin was the power core of a crashed alien spaceship.

But this time, she didn't need to make it up.

"It's a cloud-catching net," she explained.

She chewed her lip. Back on the Pirate Stream, it wouldn't have been unusual to come across a cloud-catcher. She'd seen a whole stack of them in the Naysayer's frozen tower of junk, in the CrystalShadow Wastes.

But the Pirate Stream was an endless river of pure magic, full of marvelous magical things and crazy, magical places. *This* was Arizona—it was about as unmagical as places got. Cloud-catching nets weren't exactly common here.

Marrill stared at the gossamer net, excitement and fear and confusion all mixing together into one explosive ball inside her. "Where *exactly* did you find this?" she asked.

"Down in the ravine. There's tons of good stuff there. Come on, we'll show you!" The middle Hatch took off across the empty lot, his brothers close behind. It had rained just a few hours before, a good-sized storm for the desert, and puddles still spotted the ground. Marrill snatched Karnelius up and chased after them across the damp earth.

The "ravine" in question was really more like a big, steep ditch running down the back of the lot and ending in a narrow culvert under the road. It was usually bone dry, but after the morning's rain, a thin trail of water now meandered its way down the middle—the last gasp of the flash flood.

The Hatch brothers led her to a snaggle of metal piled up against the entrance to the culvert. "We found it there," Ted said, pointing. "Check out all the treasure!"

"Hmmmm…" Marrill set Karny down, ignoring his protests as she poked cautiously at the debris. The more she uncovered, the more confused she became: a cracked nightmare shield, still snarling to keep the bad dreams away. A broken fishing pole with a prollycrab carved onto it. And something that looked suspiciously like a used hope crystal. Things that existed only on the Pirate Stream.

Marrill's pulse quickened as she dug deeper. A hunk of what looked like jellyfish jelly shifted to one side and fell, revealing the bottom of an old, dented stop sign wedged against the side of the big pipe. And scrawled across it, in thick black letters, were the words:

"What in the world..." she mumbled, clearing away a tangled mesquite branch to yank the sign free. She read it again, then flipped the sign over. On the back, an image had been sketched in the same dark writing: a series of jagged triangles, inscribed in a circle, all resting on the back of a dragon.

A fist of uneasiness curled in her stomach. Someone,

somehow, had sent her a message: She was needed on the Stream!

But there was no going back to the Stream; Ardent had made that clear when they'd parted. Her world followed rules, while the Stream's magic knew none. Too much contact between the two and her world could be ripped apart.

Marrill swallowed, her throat tightening. *The Stream will touch your world again,* Ardent's final words sounded in her head. She could still remember the deathly seriousness in the wizard's voice. *But if it's close enough for you to stumble upon, something has gone terribly, terribly wrong.*

"What's the Pirate Stream?" Tim asked, peering over her shoulder. "Do you know pirates? Have you been holding out on us?"

Marrill shook her head slowly. "Oh, no...uh...this is just a note from Remy," she said, pulling out the first name that popped into her head.

"Your babysitter sent you a message on a stop sign?" Tom asked.

Marrill let out a strained laugh. "I know, right? She's so weird! Anyway, this is just her crazy way of reminding me to do my homework. On pirates."

She struggled to grip the cumbersome sign in one hand and tugged on Karny's leash with the other. Unattended, her cat had poked his way into the tunnel-like culvert to investigate. "Come on, you fuzzy beast," she mumbled into the darkness, pulling on the leash again.

A low growl was the only response. She sighed and set the sign aside so she could crawl into the dim tunnel to retrieve her cat.

The sudden darkness surprised her. It was so dark, in fact, that she could barely make out her cat's outline up ahead, his tail bristle-brush straight and his fur in full-on puff. He let out a low, angry hiss.

Goosebumps ran across her skin. Something was wrong.

"Karny?" she whispered softly. Carefully, she laid one hand on his back. "You okay?"

A woman's voice spoke, loud and fast and so close it made Marrill jump. "The Iron Tide is coming. You must stop it! Stop the Iron Ti—*MREAEEEK!*"

Karny bolted forward and pounced. There was a brief scuffle with something she couldn't see. Then silence.

"Hello?" Marrill whispered.

She was greeted with a *mrrrp* and the brush of fur against her wrist. Fur and something cold. She snatched her cat up by the ruff of his neck and dragged him back into the light.

Karny hung limply in her arms, glaring with his one eye. A bloated, white-and-brown thing dangled just as limply from his mouth.

"Eww, it's a frog!" one of the Hatches cried.

It was, indeed, a frog. Its big white belly glistened up at her, marked in the middle with a weird pattern of dark lines.

"Oh, Karny," she sighed. She pried the poor thing from her cat's jaws, hoping against hope it wasn't too injured for her to help.

"Who was in there?" another Hatch asked. Marrill shivered, remembering the voice. She glanced back into the culvert. If anyone was in there, she couldn't see them.

But there *was* something familiar in the air. It was the smell of salt, and the ozone scent of energy, and the feeling that anything could happen all rolled into one. A rush of nostalgia flowed through her. It was the smell of the Pirate Stream—the scent of magic.

"No one," she muttered to the Hatches. "I was yelling at Karny, that's all."

Marrill snatched the stop sign and Karny's leash with one hand, still hanging on to the frog with the other. "Better get this guy some medical attention."

The youngest Hatch jumped up onto his toes, eyes bright. "Ooh, can we come help?"

"Um...didn't I just hear your mom calling?" she countered. She didn't think the Hatches were quite ready to handle whatever the Stream might have in store.

As one, their eyes went wide. "Awww, but things were just getting good!" the oldest protested. Marrill shrugged in fake sympathy. Shoulders stooped, they trudged up the bank toward their house.

As Marrill made her own way home, the frog twitched in her palm. She wasn't an expert in amphibians, but she'd spent enough time rescuing and rehabilitating various animals to recognize a broken leg. "You poor thing," she cooed. "We'll get you fixed up soon." He opened his mouth to croak but no sound came out.

It wasn't easy to balance an angry cat, an injured frog, and a stop sign, but eventually she reached the house and slipped through the front door as noiselessly as possible.

But Remy, it seemed, had the ears of a bat. "Marrill, that you?" she called over the sound of the TV blaring from the kitchen.

Marrill winced. "Yep, I'm home!" She crept toward the hallway, trying to stay out of her babysitter's line of sight.

"Your dad called."

Marrill froze, her heart squeezing tight. "Um, yeah?" The tips of her fingers began to go numb and she gripped the sign against her hip to keep from dropping it. The frog opened his mouth again. This time, Marrill was grateful he hadn't found his voice.

The sound on the TV dropped a few notches. "He said visiting hours end at seven, if you want to call your mom before surgery tomorrow."

Marrill glanced toward the clock on the far wall. It was 4:50. Plenty of time to take care of the frog and—

"That's Boston time!" Remy added.

Marrill kicked herself. If it was 4:50 here, it would be 6:50 in Boston. Only ten minutes left! She scrambled toward her room. For all the traveling she'd done with her parents, she never had gotten used to the time changes. It just seemed so weird that something as basic as the *time* could be different from one place to another.

"Pizza'll be here in half an hour!" Remy shouted just as Marrill slammed her door. She dropped the sign on her bed and unhooked Karny's harness. Grabbing a pillow, she raced to her desk and flipped open her laptop. With one hand, she logged into her video chat. With the other, she gently nestled the frog onto the pillow, then pushed it out of sight.

Her dad answered almost immediately, his image filling the screen. He sat on the edge of a bed, the computer balanced in his lap. In the background, she could see the telltale signs of a hospital room: tubes and cords and the glow of various monitors. Her heart squeezed at the sight of her mother in the middle of it all.

"Hi!" Marrill waved, forcing a smile. It felt like something heavy was sitting on her chest. "How are things going out there?"

Her father clasped her mom's hand tightly before responding. Immediately, Marrill knew something was wrong. The weight grew heavier; it became impossible to breathe.

Karnelius jumped up onto her desk, strolling toward her and bonking her chin. She nudged him out of the way.

"Everything's fine, Petal. I promise." But then her mom's smile wavered, and Marrill felt something inside begin to crack. Her mom glanced at her dad.

And just like that, it came. "The surgery tomorrow is going to be a little more extensive than we expected," her father said. "It's not uncommon, apparently, and the doctors say there's nothing to worry about. They'll just...want to keep her here a little longer than we anticipated."

"What?" Panic edged into Marrill's voice. "How long? Why?" Her eyes began to burn, and she wiped at them furiously.

Karnelius, no longer held back, strutted across her keyboard and positioned himself directly between her and the screen.

"It's nothing you should worry about, honey," her father said as she pushed her cat aside. "It's just precautionary. But they said to expect a week at least."

A week?! Her throat closed in, suddenly choking her with fear. "Can I..." Marrill had to swallow so her voice wouldn't crack. "Can I come out there?"

Her parents glanced at each other and Marrill already knew the answer. "We don't want you worrying, sweetie," her mom said.

"And we don't want you missing classes and falling behind," her dad added.

"But I wouldn't really miss that much school," Marrill protested. "It's a long weekend."

"And you should spend it there, making friends," her father added gently.

Marrill knew what they really meant. They had to keep

her mom's stress level low. And Marrill being scared and upset would only make things worse.

Which meant she had to stay here, in boring Arizona. Away from her mom. She bit her cheek.

Karny crouched on the edge of her desk, staring at the injured frog. His tail thrashed from side to side and she shoved him away from the poor creature. He let out an angry *MROW* and jumped to her bed.

"I've already spoken with Remy and her parents," her father continued. "Everything's set for her to keep looking after you."

Her mom leaned forward, her smiling face filling the screen. "I promise we'll be jumping off cliffs again before you know it."

Marrill tried to search her mom's eyes to see if it was true. Something rustled nearby, distracting her. She cut her eyes toward her bed. Karnelius sat there glaring, angry at being deprived of what he clearly considered to be his rightful prey. Scornfully, he stalked to her bedside table and batted a loose pen to the floor.

"Karny!" she hissed. Ignoring him, she turned back to the computer. Up in the corner of the screen, the clock flashed. It was almost five—seven Boston time. Visiting hours were nearly over. This was the last time she'd talk to her mom before the surgery.

"Mom…" Her throat felt painfully tight as she tried to search for the right words. If she were there in the hospital room, she could rest her head in her mother's lap and let her mom stroke her hair. Just that touch would be enough to reassure her. Just to be able to close her eyes and feel the solidity of her mom's presence.

Just to be able to pretend that everything was going to be okay.

But now there was too much distance between them. There was nothing for Marrill to hold on to. She gripped the edges of her chair, wishing there was something she could do to make her mom better. Wishing she really *was* back on the Pirate Stream, where she wasn't so useless and unimportant.

"Mom, I'm scared," she whispered. As hard as she tried, she couldn't keep tears from escaping down her cheeks.

Her mom leaned forward, expression serious. "So am I, baby," she admitted softly. "But it's okay to be a *little* afraid. You just can't let it control you. And you have to believe everything will be all right." She smiled. "Now, before I have to go, is there anything else exciting going on?"

Marrill's eyes darted to the sign on her bed, then to the skysailing jacket Fin had given her, hanging on the hook behind her door. A smile twitched at her lips. *Well,* she thought, *a river of pure magic may be touching our world again....*

"Nothing big," she said instead. Before she could add anything more, a large crash interrupted her.

She spun in her seat, ready to swat Karny away from the frog again. But he wasn't on the bedside table. Because the bedside table wasn't beside the bed. Instead, it was in the corner. Cowering. Its drawer rattled as it trembled in fear.

That isn't right, Marrill thought. She blinked. Then she froze.

On the floor in front of the table, next to an uncorked and almost empty crystal vial, lay a wet, tattered piece of parchment, swirling with inky images.

"Everything okay, honey?" her dad asked.

"Um…yeah…" Her heart began to pound. The crystal vial filled with magical water from the Pirate Stream had been Fin's last gift to her. The bedside table, which up until today had shown no signs of life whatsoever, looked ready to bolt for the door. And that parchment, which had been blank for nearly six months, was the legendary Bintheyr Map to Everywhere.

Marrill quickly turned her laptop so her parents wouldn't see the animate table tiptoeing its way across the room. She pasted on a smile. "Karny knocked over some water, better clean it before it stains! LoveyoubothgetbettersoonMombye!"

"Water doesn't stain," her mom called.

Marrill was about to close the computer, but she cringed. Her mother's voice raked at her heart. "You know I love you, Mom, right?"

Her mother laughed. It might have been the most perfect sound in the world. "Never as much as I love you. Good night, dear heart!"

And the connection was cut. Marrill dove for the Map.

Ever since her return from the Pirate Stream, it had been nothing but a useless scrap of blank parchment, no matter how often she'd wished for it to be more.

But now... now dark lines seemed to reach up for the surface of it, like the tentacles of a sea monster rising from the deep ocean. She tilted her head, searching for some sort of pattern. And then her eyes widened in recognition. It was a map of her neighborhood, with a bright red X a few miles up the road. In the abandoned parking lot where she'd first stumbled across the *Enterprising Kraken*.

Marrill scarcely even wanted to think of the possibility. But her hopes were already flying as high as a kid with sky-sails soaring on the winds of Khaznot Quay.

Because it could only mean one thing. She could go back. She looked at the sign leaning against the end of her bed.

YOU ARE NEEDED ON THE PIRATE STREAM MARRILL

Her heart thundered with excitement. In fact, she *had* to go back. What other choice was there? The woman's warning from the culvert echoed in her head:

The Iron Tide is coming. You must stop it!

Unfortunately, doubt crept in, too. The last time she'd been on the Stream, she almost hadn't made it home. If she went back, she might never return.

The bedside table crept close, nudging her knee with a corner like a dog nosing at its master's hand. She absently trailed her fingers across its surface. One of its legs twitched and thumped as she traced the edges of a knot in the wood.

But would it really be all that risky? After all, she still had the coordinates from the Map that led her home last time. They had worked once, and so long as the Stream touched her world, they ought to work again. And if the Stream was close enough that she could get *to* it, then it was close enough to get *back* from too, right? She could return to the Stream, fix whatever needed fixing, and be home before anyone grew too worried. Especially with her parents being out of town!

Marrill took a deep breath. Ever since returning from the Stream, she'd tried to live a normal life. She'd gone to a regular school for the first time. She'd helped out at home, taking on extra chores to keep her mother's stress level low. She hadn't complained when her parents left her behind to go to Boston for her mother's treatments. She'd even managed to make a few friends. But none of them like Fin. Or Ardent, or Coll.

And now the Stream needed her. She had to stop the Iron Tide, whatever that was.

Biting her lip, she glanced at the collage of pictures on her bedroom wall. In the center was her favorite: she and her mom holding hands as they jumped from a cliff into crystal-blue waters. Moments before, her mom told her that sometimes in life, you just had to dive right in.

Marrill pushed herself from the bed, snatching the Map from the floor. "It's settled," she declared, swiping her fingers through the air in determination. "Karnelius, grab your leash. Mr. Frog, pack your things. Fin's jacket, get ready to fly again. We're going back to the Pirate Stream!"

CHAPTER 2
The Perpetual Stowaway

Fin landed on the street with a squish. It was like falling onto an old sponge. He flapped his arms, struggling to keep his balance. Mushroom towers leaned over him, bobbing in a stale breeze. Dank sogginess filled his shoes and soaked into his socks.

He didn't care for Belolow City. The thieving was terrible. For one thing, the goo that constantly seeped from the 'shroom towers made them impossible to climb, as he had just found out. Not to mention this world's sickly green sun, which put everything in a bad light (literally: he hadn't gotten away with a single "innocent misunderstanding" since they'd arrived that morning). Good thing he could always slip around the mushroom caps and be forgotten, or he'd have been in slime-mold jail for sure.

And then there was the moisture.

Belolow's "famous" moisture was...aggressive. Fin could constantly feel drops of it running *up* his leg, gathering in pools behind his knees and threatening a full-on invasion of his waistband. He swatted at the back of his calves and gave silent thanks that he'd soon be headed out on the Stream. He slogged his way down toward the murky pool where the *Kraken* was anchored, shaking his hand to fling away some of the clinging slime as he went.

Once again, he hadn't found the first trace of his mother. Another dead end, just like every other place the *Kraken* had stopped in the last six months. He wasn't one to give up, not when it came to something as important as figuring out who he was and why he was so...forgettable. But he was really starting to wonder if he would ever find her at all.

Lost in thought, he never saw the girl coming. One minute he was squelching through the bog that passed for a marketplace here, doing a little dance to keep his armpits dry. The next he was sprawled on the wet ground, dankness rushing up the back of his shirt to puddle on his shoulders.

"Ay, watchit," he grunted. A girl around his age rolled to her feet nearby, clearly as stunned as he was. Which wasn't weird; no one ever noticed him. He'd have been jostled to death long ago if he weren't so good at avoiding *them*.

And that was the odd part—that he hadn't avoided *her*. Dodging people was second nature, even when he wasn't paying attention. He shook his head and hopped to his feet. *Must be the light,* he figured as he gave her a once-over.

She was a thief, no question, though she'd done a respectable, Quay-worthy job with the disguise. Most anyone would have taken her for a standard-issue street urchin, what with the dark, knotted hair, dirt smudged across her chin, and unmatched shoes. It was the details that tipped him off: The beds of her nails were clean. Her ears were still pierced from wearing earrings. And he just barely caught the glint of silver from inside the cuff of her tattered sleeve. She was no beggar, that was for sure.

As if to confirm his impression, shouts of "Thief!" and "After her, go!" filtered through the air, coming from somewhere amid the stewing market crowd. The girl tried to make for an alley, but a thick tangle of fern-fences and dangling moss blocked her. She glanced back, worry on her face.

Three angry-looking guards cleared their way through the street, sweat streaming down their snouted faces. Passersby began to mill about, watching.

Fin smirked. Many a time, he'd been in the girl's position. It would be good to observe another professional in action. He might learn something. And who knew? Maybe he'd even help, if he was so inspired.

Of course, if it were him, he would just slip up to some unsuspecting mark, call them the thief, and disappear in the confusion. By the time things got cleared up, no one would even remember the kid they'd originally been chasing. He crossed his arms to watch.

Then the girl did something truly strange. She caught Fin's eye. And she winked.

He could scarcely contain his shock. No one ever caught his eye. Or noticed him at all, really. Not unless he was doing something especially bad. Which, in a rare turn of events, he currently wasn't.

"Here he is, boys!" she cried, stabbing a finger at Fin as the guards swarmed around them. "We got that thief right here!"

"What?" Fin blurted. That was his line!

The first guard squinted at them both. "This yat thief-is?" he said in the distinctive Belolow drawl. He seemed as confused as Fin was.

"For sure," the girl said. "Don't you remember? I was right next to you when you saw him!"

"Arp," a second guard said. "Very familiar looks-she." He shifted from one leg to another, squishing unpleasantly. "But thinks-I the thief was a girl?"

"Whoa whoa whoa, bloods," Fin protested. "You've got it all wrong. I haven't stolen anything!" He looked up. "Important," he added. "Today. In the last hour. I didn't steal whatever you boys are after, is what I'm trying to say."

The girl scrunched up her forehead and pursed her lips.

"Noooo," she said, drawing out the word. "It was definitely a boy. Don't you remember the black hair?" She leveled her gaze at Fin with a look that seemed to say *Go with it*.

Fin threw up his empty hands in front of him. "No way."

The first guard rounded on Fin. "Thief," he growled.

Fin took a step back, his heart thundering against his ribs. He couldn't believe what was happening. "Wait now, not me! It was her!" he said, waving frantically.

"Nice try, kid," the girl said. She winked at him again. "But these guards saw the thief clearly. And it couldn't have been me. Because they've never seen me before in their lives."

Fin swallowed. Was that nervous sweat or just Belolow funk he felt gathering on his forehead? "But that's not—" He was about to say *possible*, but the word stuck in his throat. Because it was possible. Totally and completely. Hadn't he just been thinking about all the times *he* had pulled this exact same con?

That was when it hit him. The girl was forgettable. Like him. It suddenly made sense. That was why he hadn't noticed her when she ran into him. She wasn't noticeable. Like him.

He sucked in a breath. Never in all of his life had he met someone like him. Someone forgettable. He hadn't even considered someone else like him *existed*.

"Wait!" Fin cried, reaching for her. His fingers brushed her sleeve. But she slipped out of his grasp, backing into the gathering crowd as the guards closed in.

"Hey, wait!" Fin cried again as a guard's hand closed

on his arm. It was too late; the girl had already disappeared down the sodden street. As if she had done this a million times before. Just like *he* had.

Fin tucked his free hand into his thief's bag and looked up at the guards. He had to follow her. And that meant losing these tinheads, fast. He snatched a tiny glass pebble from the bottom of his bag, something he'd been saving for just such an occasion. Pulling it out, he crushed it between his fingers. Smoke poured from his palm, coalescing and growing into the figure of a massive giant.

"Arp!" a guard cried. "A mist-man is!"

The crowd watched, every head tilted back in awe as the smoke giant grew larger and larger. Every head except for Fin's, that is. He slipped from the guard's grip as easily as he slipped from all of their minds. That was his very last Puff-Decoy. He hated to see it go, but it never failed to distract.

Fin charged after the girl, through the spectators and toward the docks. At this point, he didn't care about stealth, only speed. The soggy ground slurped at his shoes as he ran.

He was out of breath by the time he hit the pier. It didn't take him long to figure out where the girl had gone; a ship had already pulled free of her mooring and was headed out toward the middle of the harbor, where the open Stream spilled into this world. Sure enough, the girl stood at her stern, staring back toward shore.

He hadn't seen the ship when they'd first arrived. If he had, he'd have recognized her immediately. The design was unmistakable, even though this ship was much smaller and sleeker than the great galleon he'd once seen drawn in moving ink and sailing across the face of the Bintheyr Map to Everywhere.

Fin had no doubt. This ship had the same look, was maybe even from the same fleet, as the ship the Map had shown him. The ship that carried his mother.

"Wait!" he screamed with all his might.

The girl saw him and waved with a huge smile. "Thanks for the distraction, brother-fade!" Her voice barely carried across the distance, but sounded like she meant it. Did she think he'd helped her on purpose?

Quickly, he scanned the docks for the *Enterprising Kraken*. He found her nearby; the jetty wobbled like old gelatin beneath his feet as he ran to his ship.

"Ropebone Man, full sails!" he shouted to the rigging as he hit the deck. "Pirats, weigh anchor!" He leaned forward, bracing for the ship's movement.

Nothing happened. The *Kraken* bobbed softly, but otherwise stayed put. A trio of rodents glanced up from where they sat in the shade of a bulkhead, tossing tiny teeth toward a copper cup.

"Let's go!" Fin shouted to them. He stomped his feet, trying to spur them into action. They just yawned at him, then scampered off to lounge elsewhere.

A quiver passed through his body, frustration and desperation and sorrow all twisted up as one. It was no use. Of course they didn't follow his commands. He was a stranger. The *Kraken* had forgotten him, just like everyone else did.

Fin let out a long, shaky breath and dragged himself slowly aft. Rumor vines looped around the stern railing, whispering his own words back to him as he watched the girl's ship pull farther and farther away.

"Who are you?" Fin said to no one. The vines echoed him:

whoareyouwhoareyouwhoareyou

He closed his eyes in defeat. The only person like him he'd ever met, on a ship like the one the Map had shown him. It was the lead he'd been waiting for, and it was sailing out of reach.

The girl's ship turned broadside as it headed out to the open waters of the Pirate Stream. A jagged metal symbol was emblazoned on its side, looking pale and ill in the green light. Fin squinted, hoping it might mean something. But before he could fully make it out, the horizon reached up and swallowed the ship whole. It had made the Stream. The girl was gone.

The green sun's rays turned even more sickly as the sallow orb crouched toward the horizon. The day was ending.

Around Fin, rumor vines echoed his sniffles, until it sounded as though the entire ship were weeping. Inside, emotions twisted against each other like serpents. Wriggling with glee at having met someone else like him. Squeezing with misery that he had no idea how to find her.

The *Kraken*'s hatch slammed open, spilling light out across the deck. A lumbering shadow shuffled forth, a lizard-like head and four arms lurching toward him, a thick tail trailing behind. The Naysayer let out a throaty belch and twisted one finger into his earhole, scratching his backside with another. A watering can dangled from a third hand, and a half-eaten prollycrab from the fourth.

As he neared the stern, the old monster frowned. "Quit your whiney-vining," he said, brandishing the watering can. "I'm fixin' to water ya."

whiney viney quit your fixin

several of the mouth-shaped buds echoed back.

Fin wiped his sleeve across his nose. "It's just me," he said.

The Naysayer let out a honk of surprise, which the rumor vines gleefully parroted. He glared at the garden and then back at Fin. "Which one are you again?"

"The forgettable one," Fin moped.

"That don't narrow it down," the Naysayer grunted back.

"Try somethin' new and make yerself useful." He shoved the watering can into Fin's hands before wandering off.

With a sigh, Fin lifted his eyes, searching the darkening sky for a star. The one his mother had pointed out to him. The one that meant someone out there was still thinking of him. But tonight, it was hidden by the clouds.

As he raised the watering can, it smacked against his thief's bag, which jangled, jogging his memory. He grinned. He'd totally forgotten the one thing he did have!

Carefully, Fin slipped his hand into his bag and pulled out a circle of silver. The girl's bracelet. The thing she'd kept hidden beneath her sleeve. The one she hadn't even noticed him slipping off her arm when he grabbed for her in the crowd.

He chuckled to himself as he tossed it in the air and caught it again. The girl had been a pretty great thief, he had to admit. But *no one* skinned the Master Thief. Not without getting skinned themselves, anyways.

He held the bracelet up to the dying light. Etched in its center was the same symbol he'd seen on the side of her ship. Only he could see *this* one clearly: a dragon underneath a circle filled with what looked like mountains.

And just like that, despite everything, hope swelled in Fin's chest. For the first time since Marrill left the Stream, he had a lead.

CHAPTER 3
Fangs, and Other Car Troubles

Marrill's plan started off perfect. First she waited until her dad called to say that her mom was out of surgery and the doctors were optimistic (phew!). Then she told him she'd been invited to a camping trip over the long weekend—to a place out of cell phone range, of course. As concerned as her parents were about her making friends, there was no way he could say no.

After that she'd tucked a note explaining she was okay

and would be back soon. She totally expected to make it home in time to destroy it, but just in case....

Now all she had to do was get past Remy. With a natural skepticism and a reputation to protect as the best babysitter in the school district, the older girl had made it her personal mission to prevent a repeat of "the desert incident," as Marrill's weeklong disappearance over the summer had become known. Marrill's parents had never said as much, but she was pretty sure that was why they'd hired Remy in the first place.

Still, Marrill wasn't worried. Now that her dad had signed off, even Remy couldn't say no. It was just a matter of walking up to the old parking lot to "get picked up for the trip," and she'd be off sailing the Pirate Stream again!

"Wait...weren't you walking up toward that parking lot right before *the desert incident*?" Remy asked. And that was when things started to fall apart.

Ten minutes later, Remy's car pulled into the old abandoned strip mall, Marrill in the passenger seat. "You can just drop me off over there," Marrill said, pointing toward the cracked sidewalk running along the strip of empty stores. "I'm sure the other kids will be here soon."

Remy's frown deepened as she steered into a parking spot. "Are you sure this is the right place?" Disbelief hung in her voice.

Marrill nodded, trying to act natural. "We're supposed to all meet here, and Mrs. Mullen will come pick us up."

She shifted Karny in her lap, making sure his harness was tightly secured, as the car ground to a halt. With the other hand, she grabbed the backpack from the floor between her feet. Inside she'd stuffed Fin's jacket, a change of clothes, and an old guinea pig cage lined with grass, holding the frog.

Remy wasn't buying it. "And you brought Karnelius why, again?"

"So, uh, you wouldn't have to feed him?" A gust of wind washed across them as Marrill pushed open the door. "Thanks for the ride! See you next week!" The words came out in a tumbled rush as she leapt from the car.

"Not so fast, kiddo." With impressive coordination, Remy snagged the back of Marrill's pack even as she shifted into park. A second later, they both stood in the empty lot, staring at each other. In the distance, thunder rumbled. Storm clouds were building on the horizon, and coming fast.

"Mrs. Mullen will be here soon, promise. You should go," Marrill urged. "Really."

The wind tossed Remy's long blond ponytail. "Not one chance I'm leaving you out here alone. Not one." Her statement was punctuated by another low grumble of thunder.

Marrill winced as rain began to fall, pelting the parking lot. Karny hissed, tail fluffing in anger. She scooped him up and tucked him into her arms. "Oooh, it's starting to come down," she said. "You go ahead home. I'll just wait for everyone in there. She jabbed a thumb toward an abandoned store. Behind the dirty glass, the name ROSEBERG'S still hung in sun-faded red letters.

Remy's head shook so hard it nearly popped off of her shoulders. "If you think I'm leaving you in a crusty old death trap during a storm, you're insane. There are flash floods, Marrill. Flash floods!"

Above, the sky boiled black, making Remy's fears seem somewhat reasonable. But then, a flash flood was exactly what Marrill was banking on.

"Oh, it's nothing." Marrill had to raise her voice over the growing wind. "Just a sprinkle! When we lived in Costa Rica, this much rain fell, like, every day!" She blinked as a huge raindrop fell straight into her eye.

Remy was having none of it. "Marrill Aesterwest, you'd better—" But she didn't finish. Her eyes grew wide, jaw dropping as she stared at something over Marrill's shoulder.

"Oh my... shooting stars!"

Every atom in Marrill's body vibrated as she turned. Her lips curled into a smile; she half expected to see the *Enterprising Kraken* sailing into the handicapped spots once again.

Instead, a three-story-tall wall of water pounded toward them. Its top frothed and curled and danced with the golden glow of magic. Deadly, powerful magic.

"The Stream is here!" she yelped.

"Into the car, now!" Remy screamed. She snatched Marrill by her backpack, shoving her and Karnelius inside and scrambling in after them. She'd barely gotten the door shut when the wave hit.

The impact came like a giant had picked up the car and tossed it into a lake. Metal groaned under the force of the water. Remy wrapped her arms around Marrill, tucking her against the seat. Marrill, in turn, tucked Karny against her chest. All they could do was hold on.

"We're going to be okay," her babysitter reassured her. "It's only a flash flood. The water will drain away as fast as it came. We just have to hold on, and, you know, think buoyant thoughts." Her voice trembled even as she tried to laugh.

But Marrill knew that sinking was the least of their worries. Because the water all around them had that familiar golden sheen. The one that said any minute now, the car could catch fire, or start singing, or turn into a log or a cloud or a sandwich, or all of these things at once.

A tingle buzzed along the back of Marrill's neck. It was the sensation of possibility—of pure magic. Karny hissed, the tip of his tail twitching. He struggled out from underneath her and leapt onto the dashboard.

"Does it taste like Thursday in here to you?" Remy asked. "Why does it taste like Thursday?" Her voice grew suddenly panicked. *"Why does Thursday have a taste?"*

Marrill pushed herself up and looked around. They were floating now, at least. But the desert was gone. A wide, endless expanse of golden water surrounded them. As she watched, a small wave crested across the hood and rippled around the base of the antenna. In a flash of light, the aluminum rod exploded into a swarm of tiny squid-shaped birds that zipped around the car like chattering hummingbirds. Karny batted at the window after them.

Remy's jaw dropped. Her entire body trembling, she clenched the steering wheel as if that might help. "Wh-what just happened?"

Marrill held out her arms weakly as the car shuddered around them. "Welcome to the Pirate Stream?" she offered.

Remy just stared at her, eyes wide. "Where did the everything go?" she whispered.

"Okay," Marrill said, trying to think. "The good news is we're still alive. And human." Just then, the whole car buckled and shook. A groan of metal came from all around. In front of them, translucent scales popped out along the surface of the hood. "The bad news is that we might not stay that way...."

Overhead, the sunroof folded upward, forming into a point that looked suspiciously like a shark's fin. Marrill grabbed Karnelius and held him close. She turned to face Remy. "No matter what happens, don't let the water touch you! And hold on tight!"

Remy shrieked as the hood popped open and long, curving fangs sprouted out. The carpeted mats turned squishy and soft beneath their feet. Long rows of narrow teeth snaked from the doorframe. The car was turning into some sort of creature, and they were sitting in its mouth.

The walls of the car ballooned, growing translucent as the metal stretched and thinned. Larger than a hot-air balloon now, the car-creature billowed out around them, bobbing along the surface of the Stream.

Remy screamed again. After a second of restraint, Marrill gave in and screamed as well. From somewhere behind them, back in what was now the inflated body of the beast formerly known as Remy's car, a deep, hollow moan sounded right along with them.

It vibrated through Marrill's body, swishing her stomach and making the world swim. It was a pitiful sound, fierce and lonely. Marrill felt a stab of sympathy for it.

But that feeling only lasted a moment. Then everything shook, and she tumbled onto her back. Thick, nasty-smelling fluid coated her arms and fouled up her hair. Remy smashed into her, elbow smacking Marrill's hip and making her grunt with pain.

"We're going down," Remy yelped. "Hang on to me, Marrill!"

"I can't get *off* of you!" Marrill yelled back, rolling around on what was now a big, spongy tongue. The creature was moving. They were diving into the Pirate Stream!

"Everything's going to be fine," she said, trying to reassure herself as much as Remy. It was like being inside the body of a giant jellyfish. One with a set of nasty, curved teeth. But so long as the thing kept its mouth closed, they might be safe. "Coll says the Deep Stream is really a bunch of different rivers, all around and on top of each other. So maybe diving is just following a different branch?"

"I have absolutely no idea what that means," Remy fired back.

Karnelius squirmed in Marrill's arms, letting out a loud *MROW*. She pulled him against her shoulder for comfort. "It's okay, Karny," she whispered, kissing his head.

"Oh yeah, this is definitely okay," Remy said. Marrill looked over at her and grinned. The older girl's eyes were wide, her blond hair plastered to her forehead with monster spit. "So, so not okay," she muttered.

Marrill held her chin up with pride. "I think you owe me an apology for my math assignment."

"I don't feel that way," Remy said sternly. "Math is math, Marrill. But yeah, I guess you were telling the truth about the whole magic-river thing. Now, how are we getting out of here?"

The creature turned its head one way, then the other, but all Marrill could see through its translucent skin was golden water, spiraling and eddying as they sliced through it.

Suddenly, a violent jerk threw them backward, sending Karny skittering off her. Around them, the creature began writhing as it zoomed upward. Marrill's ears popped as the gold water gave way to blue sky. The creature let out a loud bellow as it was yanked up and out of the Stream.

"Hold on!" Remy cried, pulling her close. The thing lurched to a halt, swinging back and forth, but no longer rising.

"The kids in *The Lion, the Witch and the Wardrobe* didn't have to deal with this stuff," Remy pointed out. "Why couldn't you find a nice magic wardrobe to walk through, huh?"

And then the jaws opened, and they crashed onto the hard wooden deck of a ship.

"Ooooowwwww," Marrill moaned, rolling onto her back. Overhead, the creature swayed, hanging by a weird flipper foot from a tangled net strung from a tall mast that reached up into the sky. High above them, a black flag flew. A black *pirate* flag.

"Shanks," Marrill groaned.

A moment later, a band of men, and things that looked sort of like men, and things that really didn't look that much like men at all, surrounded them. Each was more menacing than the last. Their skin was dark from the sun; at least the ones that had skin, rather than fur or scales or *whatever* those pink spiky things were. Their clothes were tattered along the seams from the harsh days at sea. Each held a weapon at the ready. Not even *one* of them was smiling.

"Hi?" Marrill tried. "Nice to meet you?"

Several of the pirates stepped aside, and a man strode forward to glare down at her. He was tall and thin. His close-cropped pants and vest were made of gleaming leather. Almost every inch of visible skin bore either a scar or a tattoo.

"I think this is yours," he said, holding Karny forward

by the scruff of his neck. Even her angry, cantankerous cat seemed to give up in the man's grip.

"Please don't kill us," Remy gushed beside her. "I've got the ACT in, like, a month, and I was just starting to look at colleges...."

But Marrill had to smile. Because this wasn't just *any* random wicked pirate captain.

"Stavik!" she cried as she pushed herself to her feet. And before he could protest, she launched herself at the dragon-leather-clad Pirate King.

+ + +

"So..." Marrill tented her fingers together in front of her, a gesture she'd picked up from Ardent. It meant he was contemplating something weighty. She hoped it looked the same when she did it.

She let the word trail off, hoping one of the pirates might jump in and she wouldn't have to admit that she really had no idea what to say or where to begin. They sat around a scarred wooden table in Stavik's cabin, Marrill across from Stavik, with the pirates all gathered around but seated just a little back from their boss. Each cradled a glass of strong-smelling amber liquid. Marrill clutched her mug of warm milk the same way. Beside her, Remy sat with arms crossed, shaking slightly.

"He looks mean," she hissed to Marrill.

"He's the Pirate King," Marrill said. "He's *supposed* to look mean. But inside he's really a kitten."

"Kittens have sharp claws," Stavik snarled. "And pointy little teeth." The pirates looked at each other nervously. "First oneaya who calls me a kitten loses a finger," Stavik warned. The pirates stared back down at their mugs.

"Don't worry, he owes me one," Marrill whispered to Remy. "After all, I did break his crew out of a spell and save them from a sinking ship. Pirates actually have a pretty strong code of ethics." *I assume,* she mentally added.

Remy narrowed her eyes, giving Stavik what Marrill knew all too well was her I'm-watching-you look, but she kept quiet.

"So..." Marrill started. "The *Purple Serpent*'s a nice ship," she said, looking around. "Is she new?"

The pirates in the room went completely quiet, all eyes swiveling toward Stavik. Marrill wondered if perhaps the Pirate King was still a bit sore about losing his last ship, the *Black Dragon*.

She cleared her throat and tried a different approach. "I mean, uh, how's... pirating?" The pirates exchanged glances, and she thought she heard a "Not bad" somewhere in the crowd, but Stavik said nothing. He just kept his cold eyes glued on her, face frozen in a sneer. Marrill took a deep sip of milk and tried to gather her nerve. "Seen the *Enterprising Kraken* around, by any chance? Coll the sailor, Ardent the wizard, another guy you probably don't remember?"

There were a few grunts of recognition, but still Stavik's expression didn't change. Not even an eyelash twitched.

"Anyway," Marrill continued, "I'm trying to find them. It's important."

Slowly, Stavik leaned back in his chair, the dragon leather of his pants creaking as he lifted his feet and placed them on the table. "The *Kraken*, yeah? Rings a bell. Strange ship, lots of brainbroke goings-on going on. Rats with spare legs and decks that don't stay put and whatnot." He shrugged. "Brig wasn't half bad." Around him, the pirates murmured in agreement.

Marrill nodded eagerly. That was her *Kraken*! "Do you know where she is?"

Stavik lifted a shoulder. "I know a lot of things."

Marrill beamed. "Can you take me to her?" she asked, almost breathless.

The Pirate King pretended to examine his fingernails. "I can do a lot of things," he said. His eyes met hers. "Question is, why should I?"

Marrill bit her lip, her stomach twisting. He had a fair point. After all, they *had* just sort of popped up out of the Stream, lodged in the mouth of a sea monster. She wasn't really in much of a position to make demands. "It's *really* important?"

"I got a whole slew of important stuff on my to-do list." Stavik shrugged. He snapped his fingers at the pirate hovering behind him. "What do we have on tap tomorrow?"

The pirate's eyes grew wide, his nose turning an alarming shade of red. "Uh…" He looked around the cabin nervously, then swallowed. "We, um, got a thing. The one with the thing. You know the thing I'm talking about?" He cringed, like he was bracing to get smacked.

Stavik just grinned and laced his hands behind his head. "Well, there ya go. 'Fraid I'm all booked up."

Marrill sighed. It was almost as bad as trying to get something relevant out of Ardent. *Fin would know what to do*, she thought. After all, he'd gotten along with thieves and rapscallions for years. Of course, Fin would just leave the room and let them forget about him, then swagger back in like he knew exactly what was going on. He'd be calm and confident and just a little bit groveling.

It wasn't exactly her strong suit, but she let out a slow breath, trying to focus. *Be confident, be confident,* she told herself.

Beside Marrill, Remy laughed. "Can't find it, huh?"

Marrill stared at her babysitter. "What are you doing?" she hissed under her breath.

Stavik's smug smile faltered. Every eye in the room swiveled toward him. He pulled his feet from the table and slammed the front legs of his chair to the floor. Marrill struggled not to cringe. The scars on his face turned purple and danced as he spoke. "Believe me, I know *exactly* where the *Kraken* is."

Remy raised an eyebrow. "Oh, *obviously*."

The pirates around the table shifted, uncomfortable.

Stavik ran his tongue over his teeth, a knowing look in his eyes. "Totally doesn't know," Remy said with an exaggerated flip of her ponytail.

Marrill held her breath, trying not to imagine what walking the plank would be like.

After what seemed like eternity, the Pirate King leaned back. "All right," he said. "Set course for the *Enterprising Kraken,* mates. Full sails."

CHAPTER 4
Here There Be Pirates

I've never seen anything quite like it," Ardent confessed. He was clothed in a white dressing gown with big purple slippers, and the wind whipped his beard through the air behind him. His robe and hat, still drying from washing out the Belolow funk, fluttered above their heads on a line strung up special by the Ropebone Man.

Fin snatched the silver bracelet back before the wizard could forget where he'd gotten it. "You must have seen that symbol *somewhere*," Fin pressed. With his thumb, he traced the raised outline of the dragon, the arcs of the circle above it.

The *Enterprising Kraken* skated across the Stream, surrounded by clouds. This branch of the magic river spouted up through empty air, like riding on a rainbow. Fin had no idea why they weren't currently falling, and he liked it that way.

Ardent shook his head. "The Stream is a large place. Endless, really. Do I know most of it? Possibly. More than nearly anyone else who ever lived? Obviously. But even I can't know *all* of it. Wherever this came from, it is either obscure, or isolated, or very, very secluded."

Fin nodded, pretending he knew what those words meant. "Soooo…" he said. "How do we go about tracking it down?"

Just then, a flat wobbly creature that looked like a cross between a manta ray and a flying pancake swooped straight toward them, hissing and chirping as it came.

"I said we don't want any!" Coll shouted from the ship's wheel. He waved at it with a long wooden pole they'd brought out for just this purpose. The creature gave a disappointed chirp and swooped back into the clouds.

Fin shook his head and turned back to Ardent. The wizard looked at him suspiciously. "How do we track it down?" Fin repeated.

"Track what down?"

Fin threw up his hands. "The symbol! We have to track down the symbol and find my mother!" Ardent opened his mouth, but Fin cut him off. "Before you ask, my name's Fin." He could already tell the wizard had forgotten him. *Again*.

Ardent frowned. "We're not accepting stowaway applications, I'm sorry to say. We're full up at the moment." He rolled an eye toward the Naysayer, who was slouching down toward the lower decks.

Frustration tightened the muscles along Fin's shoulders. "It's *me*," he said. Ardent stared at him blankly. "There are posters all over the ship to remind you?" Fin snatched the nearest one from the mainmast and thrust it at the wizard. It was tattered and torn from exposure, the ink smeared where he'd misspelled something and tried to cross it off. A circle-face smiled a big thick swoosh of a smile beneath two misshapen eye-dots.

Ardent squinted at it. "Is that you? I thought that was supposed to be Ropebone!" He laughed. "Coll, guess what?" he shouted toward the quarterdeck. "Those signs are pictures of this boy, not Ropebone!"

Coll came closer and squinted at the image. "I thought it was a dinghy. I really thought you made this to remind me to haul in the dinghies."

Fin scowled furiously. Okay, so he wasn't a good artist like Marrill was. But there were still her originals. "Also the drawings pinned to your sleeves," he reminded them. For the umpteen millionth time.

They both looked down. Only dirty scraps of sail clung to Coll's shirt. "Oh yeah," he grunted. "Must have lost it back in the Skeleton Garden."

Fin's eyes whipped to Ardent, who was licking his. The entire thing, Fin realized, was stained gray. "Toadbutter," the wizard said with a scowl. "Definitely toadbutter. When did I have toadbutter?"

Fin ground his teeth. "It says I'm part of the crew. That I helped defeat Serth, and I'm Marrill's friend, and—"

Ardent's expression softened into a smile. "I wonder how Marrill's doing. I miss her, don't you, Coll?"

"She definitely livened things up," Coll agreed. "Remember that time she threw the pepper shaker into the Stream and it turned into a kraken?"

Fin closed his eyes. It was like he'd never existed to them. As if he hadn't been the one who'd thrown the pepper into the Stream. As if he hadn't rescued Coll from the Gibbering Grove, or tricked Serth into diving into the Stream and saved the whole world.

As if he didn't miss Marrill way more than they did.

"You guys are *never* going to help me, are you?" he asked.

Ardent frowned and placed a hand on his shoulder. "We're on a quest to find a dear friend of mine, young man. A friend who may be in grave danger. I'm afraid we can't just stop to help every stowaway, no matter how much we might like to."

"But—" Fin stopped himself. It was no use. He could convince them to help him—remind them of Marrill and of what the scraps said, and that he wasn't just *some* stowaway. They would believe him. And they would want to help him. They really would.

And then two seconds later, they would forget all over again. It wasn't their fault. Everyone did. Because he was no one.

"Never mind," he whispered. He turned away and headed quickly for the stern before the tears could form.

Back by the rumor vines again, Fin let the emotion well up in his chest. If only Marrill were still here. *She* would have helped him. She would have made Ardent and Coll stay on track.

He reminded himself, again, that she was gone forever. That it was a good thing she was back home with her family, and a good thing that she had taken the Map to Everywhere with her to keep it safe, no matter how much he needed it.

His hand strayed toward the familiar weight in his hidden shirt pocket. The Key to the Map, the piece that controlled it, safe where he'd stashed it. But what good was it without the Map itself? He forced his fingers into a fist, then dropped his arm to his side.

Fin closed his eyes, feeling the earlike leaves of the rumor vines waving across his knuckles. "I wish Marrill was here," he whispered to no one.

the vines softly whispered.

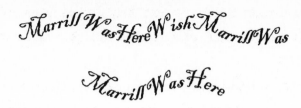

Marrill Was Here Wish Marrill Was

Marrill Was Here

After a long time, he opened his eyes again. That was when he noticed the other ship.

She was dark and low-decked and racing up the arch of glowing water behind them. And if she had been just a bit larger and a touch better made, he'd have thought for sure that she was Stavik's old ship, the *Black Dragon,* risen up from where they'd sunk her so she could chase the *Kraken* once more.

Then he caught sight of the black flag flapping from her mizzenmast gaff, and he understood why she looked so familiar. "Pirates," he mumbled under his breath. Then the thought hit him harder.

"PIRATES!"

PIRATES PIRATES PIRATES!

the rumor vines cried, the cacophony of their shouts almost deafening.

In moments, Coll, Ardent, and the Naysayer were all beside him. The ship was coming straight for them. And the narrow ribbon of water they were sailing left no way to escape.

"Maybe...we could...just let them pass?" Ardent offered.

"Sure," said the Naysayer. "Just find us a nice stable-looking cloud to pull off on and I'll lean out and wave 'em around."

Coll's voice broke the moment. "Prepare to be boarded!" he barked. "Get the nets ready, Ropebone! To arms, you pirats! Ardent, get your best wizarding ready. Looks like we'll need a healthy dose of it today."

The rumor vines took up the call.

toarmstoarmspiratspreparetobeboarded

Ardent cracked his bony knuckles as the pirats scampered back and forth, sealing hatches and securing lines. Fin saw one strapping an empty can on as a breastplate. He swallowed and looked back to the pirate vessel.

As she drew closer, the ship looked even more like the *Black Dragon*. He squinted. Sure enough, the man at her bow moved with a familiar swagger, and his leather tunic bore a familiar cut. Apparently, Stavik had found himself a new flagship.

She was lower than the *Kraken*, and he couldn't quite get a good look at the men on her deck. But he could tell from their voices that they were preparing to board.

He stroked his chin, considering the situation. Being boarded by pirates was bad, as a general rule. Even if those pirates were your friends. And especially if none of your friends ever remembered you.

On the other hand, it occurred to him that getting Ardent and Coll to follow the forgettable girl's ship would be near impossible; they had their own leads to chase, their own quests to fulfill. Stavik, meanwhile, would track a ship like a sweathound on a deer with perspiration problems, so long as there was the slightest hint of loot involved. And Fin was very good at hinting.

Fin grinned. Maybe this wouldn't be so bad after all. He'd have to talk the pirates out of taking the *Kraken*, sure, but that was another thing he was good at. And talking his way *onto* Stavik's ship would be twice as easy.

This was it, he decided. He was leaving.

The thought came suddenly, but surely. He had to go. As the pirate ship came abreast of the *Kraken*, Fin took one long, last look at the ship that had been his home for the last six months. It hurt to leave, especially remembering the good times he'd had there with Marrill. He wouldn't see her again, he knew, but maybe one day he could come back, after fixing whatever was wrong with him and finally becoming memorable, and rejoin the crew of the *Kraken*.

But until then, it looked like a pirate's life for him. As the boarding hooks clinked onto the railing and the pirates drew to jumping distance, Fin raised his hand in the traditional thieves' greeting. "Hello, fellow shady-fellow," he began. But the words caught in his throat.

Because one particularly small pirate stepped forward.

A small pirate wearing a backpack and clutching a big, one-eyed orange cat.

"Fin!" she cried, waving.

His jaw dropped. He blinked, rubbing at his eyes. It couldn't be real. "Marrill?" he whispered.

"Fin!" she shouted again. Without hesitation, she thrust her cat into Stavik's arms, grabbed a rope, and swung between the two ships. Before he knew it, Fin found himself face-first in an enormous hug.

Deep inside Fin, all the frustration of being forgotten, all the fear of never knowing who he was, all the sadness from being alone—all of it just exploded and disappeared in a single moment. A lone tear rolled down his cheek. For the first time in what may have been his entire life, he felt like he had come home.

"You came back," he whispered. He threw his arms around her. "You came back!"

Marrill pulled away from him, a huge grin plastered on her face. Her eyes were bright and watery. She squeezed his hand. "I came back," she said.

Fin just nodded. They were riding a rainbow of magic across an endless clear sky. Flying manta-pancakes warbled all around them, and the sun shone bright on the deck where his best friend now stood beside him.

Maybe wishes came true after all.

CHAPTER 5
The Colloquy of Pickled Pate

Marrill couldn't help herself. She pulled Fin in for another hug. "I missed you so much, Fin." Her throat tightened with happy tears. She wanted to pinch herself to make sure this was all real. She couldn't believe she was back on the Pirate Stream. That she was back with her best friend.

Closing her eyes, Marrill took it all in: the salty, slightly effervescent smell of the Stream, the rocking of the waves, the snap and squeal of the *Kraken*'s rigging.

It was like being home again.

"I never would have pegged you to turn pirate," a mellow voice teased. Marrill looked up to find a tall, narrow boy leaning against the nearby mast, his arms crossed loosely in front of him. A wide smile broke across his face.

"Coll!" Marrill cried, launching herself at him.

If the usually taciturn captain of the *Kraken* was surprised, he didn't show it. Instead he wrapped his arms around her. "Welcome aboard. We could use a good first mate. Been shorthanded for a while." Beside her, Fin cleared his throat. Coll glanced at him. "Brought a friend, huh?" he added. "Hope he knows how to sail."

Even Fin's frustrated sigh made Marrill smile. A smile that grew even wider to see a damp purple robe, a sagging, pointy-tipped hat, and the bony old man wedged into them. "Well, these pirates really aren't the most efficient, are they?" Ardent mused. "The legendary corsair Glasskin Jill would've had the ship boarded and half the crew tied to the rafters at this point."

He tugged his bushy white beard and leaned out dangerously over the railing. "Any day now!" he shouted to the other ship. "Some of us have plans, you know!"

"We ain't here to board ya, old man," Stavik growled up from the deck of the *Purple Serpent*. "But keep talking like that and the plan may change."

Just then, Remy shoved him aside. A chorus of gasps sounded from the pirate crew; several even cringed. "Marrill Aesterwest, get back here this minute!" she shouted, fists against her hips in fury. "You do *not* run off like that! Magic stream or no, I. Am. Your. Babysitter!"

At the sound of Marrill's name, Ardent's shoulders straightened. He spun around to face her, flipping the tip of his purple cap out of his eyes to get a better look.

"Marrill?" he whispered. She waved. He stared at her for a shocked moment. Then his face split into a grin. "It *is* you!" He held his arms wide for a hug.

Marrill bounded into him. The wizard let out a muffled "Oomf" as she threw her arms around his waist. "Well, this is certainly a delightfully unexpected..." He trailed off and pushed her back a step.

"You're here," he said. "On the Stream," he added.

She nodded, her smile growing wider. Her heart nearly burst with happiness. She was back with her crew. Back where she belonged.

Ardent's lips tightened with concern. "But you shouldn't be. I mean, you shouldn't be *able* to be," he said softly. "Not that I'm not glad to see you. Of course I am, but..."

Marrill took a deep breath. "It's not good, I know. But I was needed here, right?" She looked from Fin to Coll to Ardent. They each nodded, especially Fin.

But at the same time, they all seemed genuinely surprised to see her. Genuinely confused that she was there. She saw no hint that they had actually *sent* for her or told her to come back. Which meant they hadn't been the ones to write the message on the stop sign. But then, who had?

Beneath her, the deck of the ship lurched, sending her off balance. She remembered to bend her knees slightly, as Coll had once taught her. "The Stream is touching my world again," she began. "Which you probably figured out, since I'm here and all. But there's more." Quickly, she recapped everything, from the cloud-catching net to the stop sign to the weird voice in the tunnel and the Map's awakening.

Ardent stroked his beard. "The Iron Tide," he muttered to himself.

Just then, a slick bald head covered in stringy hair shoved straight into the middle of their group. Seconds later, the stout purplish-blue body followed. "One side, scoot, clear out, ain't ya got better places to be?" the Naysayer grumbled. He jostled past Coll and bumped Ardent with a thick shoulder. A watering can dangled from one of his four hands.

Marrill couldn't help grinning. "Good to see you, too, Naysayer," she chirped.

He paused, looking her up and down. "Oh," he said. "Huh. Where've you been?"

Marrill laughed. "Well, I was—"

"Not interested." He swatted her out of his path with one heavy hand and shambled over to the railing. Then he snorted. "And what a great job you all did getting rid of those pirates we were so worried about. I bet they're just swinging them boarding hooks to come over and give us a big hug good-bye. But you guys keep jawing—it's fine."

As if to emphasize the point, several sharp multi-hooked

metal grapples sailed through the air toward the *Kraken*'s railing. Marrill looked to the *Purple Serpent*. She should have known better than to trust pirates!

"You should have known better than to trust pirates," Fin said as they all raced to the railing.

shouldhaveknownbettershouldhaveknownbetter

the rumor vines echoed from their garden.

Marrill rolled her eyes as she struggled to unhook a barbed grapple. "I know!"

"Thassit, lads," Stavik snarled from the other side of the water. The *Purple Serpent* weaved like a water-skier across the ribbon of Stream, tied to the *Kraken* by several lines. With one arm, the Pirate King held a furiously struggling—and furious—Remy. "Pull them ropes tight! Don't let the whale escape! And you, stop biting me!"

"Nice fella," the Naysayer grunted. "Anyone needs me, I'll be in the hold, practicing my surrenderin' speech."

Behind Marrill, Ardent seemed distracted. "Was there anything else about the Iron Tide?" he asked. "Anything at all?"

Marrill tugged harder at the grappling hook. "No, it was just this voice out of nowhere warning that it's coming and we have to stop it." She stumbled as the grapple popped free in her hands. She did her best to lob it back at the *Serpent,* but the shot went wide. It splashed into the Stream, erupting into an explosion of bright autumn leaves. Marrill was sure she smelled eggnog. Her mouth watered. "Have you heard of it before?" she asked.

Ardent shrugged. "The voice? Unlikely, though I do tend to hear them often." He hesitated, ear cocked to the side, shook his head, and continued. "More relevant, I have heard of the Iron Tide. It's mentioned rather prominently in the first verse of the Meressian Prophecy."

Marrill's heart skipped a beat. "The Meressian Prophecy?" she squeaked. Behind her, a tangle of rumor vines caught up the phrase:

prophecyprophecyprophecyprophecy

She forced herself to be calm. The Meressian Prophecy had ended when the mad oracle Serth had fallen into the Pirate Stream, taking the Key to the Map to Everywhere with him. The Key that could transform the Map into a gateway to the Stream-destroying Lost Sun of Dzannin. With Serth and the Key gone, the Lost Sun was locked away for good. There was no need to fear the Meressian Prophecy anymore.

Another boarding hook flew past them and slapped onto the deck, trailing a long line with it. Ardent frowned. "Bad weather out. Let's continue this discussion in my cabin. There are a few things I've discovered that I believe you'll find most illuminating!"

"Um, Ardent?" Coll growled, jabbing his head sharply

toward the growing web of lines. Already, a zealous pirate was crawling hand over hand toward the *Kraken*. "More pressing concerns?"

The wizard almost looked surprised. "Oh, yes. I'm sorry to say it, but I fear we've no time for a pirate battle today." At the flick of his fingers, the grappling hooks turned soft and wobbly like gummy worms. The pirates yelped as the lines they were tugging suddenly came free. Marrill stuck her head over the rail just in time to see the overenthusiastic boarder scrabbling up the side of the *Serpent* as her mates struggled to haul her in.

"Could have done that all along," Coll muttered.

Ardent shrugged. "Yes, but where would the fun have been in that? Alas, now this Iron Tide situation requires our attention instead." He whirled on one heel and headed toward his cabin. "To the Learnatorium!"

Fin caught Marrill's eye. "Let's go see what he's on about," he said, motioning.

But Marrill still had some loose ends to tie up. "Um, my babysitter and cat are on the *Purple Serpent*," she said to Coll. "Could we maybe get those back?"

"I'll take care of it," Coll sighed. He ambled across the deck as though he were any normal sixteen- or seventeen-year-old boy strutting down the hall of his high school. With a little "Hup!" he hopped over the railing, just as a rope slung in from above to grab him and carry him across the water to the *Serpent*. Seconds later, the clang of metal on metal and the grunt of a struggle echoed through the air.

"See?" Fin said, grabbing Marrill's hand and tugging her aft. "Under control. Now let's go!"

Marrill's concerns fell by the wayside as Fin pushed open the door to the wizard's living quarters, which occupied most of the back of the ship. Ardent's cabin was a hopeless mess. And still, it was an incredible one. Overstuffed book-cases lined the walls, shelves filled with baskets of oddities. There was an entire army, no bigger than Marrill's palm: tiny bagpipers, Lilliputian warriors, even a few miniature ponies thrown in. There were jars of various flavors, some enticing, like "sunset eve," others revolting, like "swamp-strainer's morning breath" or the mysterious but ominously labeled "toeskunk." Boxes wrapped with rope and stenciled with warnings were piled in one corner, and books covered almost every available surface.

In the middle of it all, Ardent tossed his way through a big chest. Marrill tried to pretend the fangs lining its lid were fake. She slipped off her backpack and collapsed into a chair that scooted itself into place at the central table. Fin stood awkwardly a moment, then rolled his eyes and dragged a stool noisily across the floor next to hers. He sat with an audible huff.

Ardent didn't seem to notice. "I confess," the wizard continued, "that your message about the Iron Tide is of particular interest to me. You see, my old companion Annalessa was hunting for Serth when she disappeared. And in order to find him, well, she may have been trying to decipher parts of his Prophecy."

At the mention of the wizard Annalessa, guilt tugged at Marrill's insides. She remembered Ardent's portrait of Annalessa, her sharp-but-pretty features emblazoned on one of the cards he always carried with him. Annalessa's disappearance was the reason Ardent had been chasing the Map to Everywhere to begin with . . . and apparently he was still looking for her. Marrill had been so focused on her own problems, she'd totally forgotten about Ardent's. Her heart broke a little to think about it.

"So you tried to figure out the Prophecy, too? To try and find her?" Marrill offered.

Ardent nodded. "Which brings us to the Iron Tide." He leaned so far into the trunk he nearly disappeared. Marrill could swear she saw the lid salivating.

But then the wizard stood straight, holding up a sheaf of metal plates bound together by string. "Found it!"

"Um, before we get too far into that," Marrill said, "I was hoping you could maybe help me with something?" She pulled open her backpack and tugged out the guinea pig cage. The grass inside was a bit crumpled and the frog appeared rather disgruntled, but otherwise he seemed to have made the journey intact.

She let out a relieved breath and set the cage on the desk. "So Karnelius has this thing about amphibians," she started.

"Who doesn't?" Ardent said under his breath.

"Right?" Fin agreed.

The wizard shot him a confused glance. "Usually. Who are you again?"

Marrill cleared her throat. "He's a friend. Anyway. There was an accident at home and the frog was injured and I was hoping..." She bit her lip, remembering the way he'd once healed scratches on her hand. The way she hoped he could heal her mother someday. "Can you fix him?"

Ardent bent and peered into the cage. "You didn't mention it was a speakfrog!"

"A speak...frog?" Marrill asked.

"Quite so," the wizard said, pulling the little guy out and holding him up into the light. "They're rather good little messengers. You simply tell the frog what you want him to say, and he goes and says it."

"It's a frog," Marrill repeated. "That talks."

"Well, technically, it's a salamander that only *looks* like a frog," Ardent said. He cupped his other hand over the creature. For a moment the air warmed. Marrill tasted honey and thunder.

The moment Ardent set the frog back on the desk, it began to screech. "The Iron Tide is coming. You must stop it! Stop the Iron Tide before it spreads beyond the docks and *oof*. Hey, watch where you're—oh wait my frog get back here you little—" The voice stopped and the room was silent.

Marrill stared at the frog. It crawled back into the cage, fluffed up a patch of grass, and settled in.

"So yeah," Marrill said. "That was the voice I heard. And that was pretty much the message."

"That dovetails nicely into what I wanted to show you," Ardent said, grabbing the metal plates he'd pulled from the chest and slapping them down on the table next to the cage.

Marrill leaned over them. *The Colloquy of Pickled Pate*, the first one read. Chiseled underneath the words was a portrait of a squat man with a jutting lower jaw and enormous nose. The metal gleamed like oil in the candlelight.

"Spiff," Fin said beside her. "What is it?"

Ardent puffed himself up. "This, my young let's-just-assume friend, is one of the most ancient stories I've seen on the Stream. It's at least seven thousand years old, judging from the style of the engraving and the scent of the magic residue still lingering in the crevices."

Marrill squinted at a number scratched in the corner. "Also it's got the date written on it," she pointed out.

Ardent snorted. "Notoriously unreliable. But yes, that is also a clue." He waved his hands over the plates, and they dutifully spread themselves out in a neat row across the table. Marrill leaned over them and read the words aloud:

The Colloquy of Pickled Pate

Oh, Pickled Pate, ware hay ye been?
I been ta tha place war tha water bend

Oh, Pickled Pate, ware did ye goe?
I went me to tha shattered
archey‑pelly‑goe
Oh, Pickled Pate, what hay ye seen?
I seen tha city ware tha wall does stand
War thay sing o' tha king o' salt an sand
An I seen tha comin' at creepin' stride
O' tha doom whut fears me,
O' tha IRON TIDE
Oh, Pickled Pate, yer good and sauced
Ye's pickled too much, yer brain be lost

"Huh," Fin said.

"Huh," Marrill agreed. It mentioned the Iron Tide, all right. But it just seemed like nonsense.

Ardent folded his arms and nodded knowingly. "Indeed. Quite amazing. I'm sure you see the significance?"

Marrill thought hard. "Ancient people didn't know how to spell?" she offered.

Ardent waved his hands dismissively, and the plates reassembled themselves into a neat pile. "Yes, well, you have to think about the bigger picture, obviously," he said. "You see, our friend Pickled Pate may have been the first, but I've collected hundreds of stories just like this one, spread out across history, from all sorts of different places and people. And all essentially the same."

Fin nodded. "Used to hear that type of thing all the time at the Khaznot Quay. Some sailor gets lost on the Stream, vanishes, comes back all addled and babbling about crazy places and such."

"Indeed," Ardent said. "That's exactly why this escaped my notice until recently. 'A bunch of swoggle sold by drunkards and madmen,' as Coll would say. But all of *these* stories have a few important things in common."

"The Iron Tide?" Marrill volunteered.

Ardent nodded. "Just so. Stories centuries, even millennia apart, and every single one has the same three things: the city on the wall, the King of Salt and Sand, and escape from the Iron Tide. Often as though the Tide had been right on their heels! And every single person refused to return to the place where they'd seen it, for fear that the Iron Tide would destroy them."

"Now, I'm as excited about boring old legends as no one, obviously," Fin said. "But how do we know this is real? I mean, no one's ever seen this Iron Tide thing, right?"

Ardent shook his head. "No, indeed not. And yet all the missing sailors seem quite insistent that the Iron Tide *is* coming, sometime in the future." He tented his fingers together and looked very seriously down his nose at Marrill as if she, and not Fin, had spoken. "That leads me to conclude that the

Iron Tide was a bit of the Prophecy yet to be fulfilled. And if the Stream is touching your world again, and the Map has warned you of it, well, that seems to confirm the idea."

"And I'm guessing there's no way the Iron Tide could be something really cool and great like a flotilla of marshmallows sailing a river of whipped cream?" Marrill asked.

"To be fair, no one quite knows exactly *what* it is," Ardent offered. "But *doom* is a word often associated with it."

Marrill gulped. She stared down at the image of Pickled Pate. The big nose sagged over his puffed lower jaw, etched onto the shining surface of the story-plates. As if he were locked eternally in metal. In small script, she noticed something written along the bottom that she'd missed the first time:

Bewayr yer folks and bewayr yer kin for tha TIDE be comin' tho I know not when

Marrill shuddered. It gave her the willies.

"Yes," Ardent continued gravely. "Whatever the Iron Tide may be, it will almost certainly bring great destruction to the Pirate Stream...and anything in its path." He stared off into the distance for a long moment. "So," he said with a clap, "who wants to go looking for it?"

CHAPTER 6
Lost Key, Found

Fin followed Marrill and Ardent onto the main deck, blinking in the sunlight. Around them, the *Kraken* sailed across golden seas once more. Big puffy globs of foam floated on the water, the only trace of their jaunt through the clouds. A salt wind whipped past, carrying the tingle of magic and the scent of raspberries.

"Get me down!" a voice cried from the rigging. Fin looked up to see a blond-haired girl with a ponytail and an extremely unhappy expression dangling from the rigging by her heel. "Marrill, tell this *jerk* to get me down!"

The jerk in question stood at the *Kraken*'s wheel, guiding her deftly through the swells. "Pirates are taken care of," Coll offered as they approached. "They figured it was worth giving up the attack to get rid of *that* one." He jabbed a finger at the dangling girl.

Fin couldn't help but laugh. Marrill looked less pleased. But he could still see the tips of a smile playing at the edges of her lips. "Mr. Ropebone Man, would you mind letting my babysitter down?" she politely called. "Remy's a friend."

With a squeal of pulleys, the rope holding the girl lowered gently. A strange flash of jealousy shot through Fin. The living rigging actually listened to Marrill. The feeling caught him off guard; as much as he wished he were memorable, he had never felt so jealous of her before.

Then again, the last time they'd all been together, Marrill had been with the crew longer than he had. Now, *he* had been with the *Kraken* far longer than she had ever been. It didn't seem fair that after all this time, he could still be forgotten so quickly, and she remembered so well.

The moment Remy's fingers brushed the deck, she scrabbled onto her hands and knees and lunged toward Coll. Unfortunately, the rope was still tightly wound around her ankle and the ship caught the eddy of a new current, the deck pitching steeply as the sails filled. Remy fell hard against Coll's chest. He wrapped an arm tight around her, grabbing the wheel with the other to keep from falling.

"Well, looky there. Cap'n Kid caught himself a cheerleader," the Naysayer snarked as he lumbered by.

"I'm not a cheerleader." Remy stepped away from Coll, her face still bright red. "Um. Thanks."

Coll shrugged and mumbled, "No problem. Try keeping your knees soft. It helps with balancing." He coughed and composed himself as he turned back to the wheel.

Ardent cleared his throat loudly to get the captain's attention. Coll rolled one deep amber eye in their direction. Fin could just see the sailor's tattoo, peeking out from beneath his collar, a coil of dark ropes that he knew from experience moved around Coll's body depending on where they were.

"What," Coll said. It wasn't a question.

"We need to go somewhere," Ardent announced.

Coll shrugged. "We are going somewhere. We're always going somewhere."

"Well, yes," Ardent said. "But I mean somewhere specific. Specifically, the one place that every legend of the Iron Tide has in common." He looked to Marrill knowingly. "The very place Pickled Pate, and all the other sailors like him, disappeared: the Shattered Archipelago."

"The Shattered Ark-i-pell-ah-what now?" Fin asked.

"Archipelago," Ardent repeated. "A series of islands next to one another. It's mentioned by Pickled Pate as well as some of the more ambitious travel guides, and even then only rarely. It's said that at the islands' heart lies a great, all-consuming whirlpool, hungry to drag down any ship that ventures too near."

Coll pressed his lips together. "Great." Unhappiness dripped off the word. "Will we be going there for some fool reason that's likely to get us all killed?"

"We're hunting the Iron Tide, a mysterious force that may threaten all of the Stream," Ardent explained.

Coll nodded. Fin noticed his grip on the wheel growing ever tighter. "Sounds about right. And there'll be no talking any of you out of it?" His gaze swept over them.

Marrill and Ardent shook their heads furiously. Fin shrugged; he wasn't exactly sure this was a great idea. But then again, Coll never really much noticed what *he* thought.

"Fine," the sailor sighed. "How do we get there?"

Ardent looked away sheepishly. "Well, navigation is really more your specialty, to be honest...."

"Well, darn," Coll drawled, "I guess the ship-eating whirl-pool of death will just have to wait for our *next* vacation." He placed one hand on the wheel and leaned back in his traditional sailing posture, scanning the horizon. "We're three days out of the Cuttlefish Khanate," he said. "We can ask about it there. I'm sure the cuttlefish have an excellent sense of direction."

"Three days?" Remy said. "We're stuck here for three days?"

"Oh, before we even get started!" Ardent said. "I fear it may be a lot longer before we've solved *this* mystery. Assuming, of course, we find a way back for you at all—"

Coll tapped him softly on the arm, shooting his eyes toward Remy's terrified expression. And Marrill's heartbroken one. "Oh. I mean, I'm sure it will all work out again...." the wizard added weakly.

"I'm sorry," Marrill said to Remy. Her voice was so low and sad, Fin could scarcely hear her. Tears welled in her eyes.

Fin shuffled his feet awkwardly. At first blush, three days to hang out with Marrill making mischief on the *Kraken* sounded pretty awesome. But not with her and Remy this worried.

Tentatively, he put his hand on Marrill's shoulder. "It'll be okay," he told her. "You brought the Map to Everywhere." He pointed to the rolled-up parchment sticking out of her waistband.

"It's blank," she whispered. She pulled it out, showing off the empty canvas. "It's been this way ever since we got back to the Stream."

The weight of the crystal sun hidden in Fin's shirt pocket suddenly seemed to grow a thousand times heavier. He swallowed. "I guess if we had the Key, we could use it."

Marrill forced a watery smile. "It's okay, Fin," she said, mistaking the reason his voice sounded so strained. "You had to toss the Key in the Stream. You really did." Her reassuring tone made him feel even worse. Especially when she gave him another hug. "At least I still have my best friend."

Fin winced at the words. He extracted himself from her and stepped back. "I hope you mean that," he told her. And then, before he could talk himself out of it, he reached into his breast pocket and pulled out the secret he'd been hiding there ever since she left.

At first, everyone just stared. The rays of the crystal sun gleamed in Fin's palm. Instinctively, his fingers curled through the wavy arms.

"Um, what is that?" Remy asked.

"The Key!" Marrill gasped.

The back of Fin's throat wobbled. His hand shook. The last time anyone but him had seen the Key to the Bintheyr Map to Everywhere, they'd been facing off against Serth on the *Black Dragon*. Fin had pretended to throw the Key overboard, and Serth had scrambled after it, plunging to his death in the Pirate Stream.

"I switched them," he told them. He shrugged impishly. "Turns out a tentalo stuffed with hope crystals can look an awful lot like a glowing, sun-shaped crystal. I was going to tell you all back then, after I used it, but…"

He paused mid-sentence. He was used to talking his way out of trouble. It was what he did. And yet, for once, the words didn't come. He struggled to find a way to explain how he had to look out for himself, how no one else would. How even if Marrill had stayed, he couldn't count on her. Everyone forgot him, eventually.

But all of that just got jumbled in his mouth. Coming up with excuses was so easy. It didn't make sense that telling the truth to someone he loved was so hard.

"So...this strange kid found the Key?" Coll asked. "I don't get it."

Fin smiled weakly. That was the upside to being forgettable: No one remembered him long enough to judge him.

No one except Marrill, anyway. "Oh, Fin..." she sighed. It was the most painful sound he'd ever heard. Because it made him feel something he'd never had to feel before with her. Shame.

Ardent stepped forward and lifted the Key from Fin's palm. He examined it from all angles then bit one of its rays and winced. "Ith real," he sputtered, rubbing his jaw. "Well, I daresay this will make things easier. If more troubling." He gave Fin a once-over. "Where did you say you picked this up again, young man?"

Fin shuffled his feet. "Um...the Khaznot Quay?" he offered. When in doubt, he figured, it was always a good call to blame thieves and pirates for things. His eyes cut over to Marrill, then darted away before she could catch them. In that glimpse of a second, she looked confused, heartbroken even.

Ardent nodded sagely. "Well, they do say you can get anything there." He snapped his fingers, and a table scooted across the deck toward them. With a flourish, Ardent plucked the Map from Marrill's grip and unrolled it.

"Now, how to use this," the wizard muttered, staring back and forth between the Key and the Map.

"Touch the Key to the Map and ask it what you want to find," Fin mumbled. The wizard looked at him with a puzzled expression. "I mean, that's, uh, what it said in the instructions. Which it totally had. Before I lost them." He gave his most innocent shrug and smiled.

"So...what's this all about?" Remy asked next to him.

"That's the Bintheyr Map to Everywhere," Marrill whispered, gesturing at the parchment unfurled across the table. "It's supposed to show you wherever you want to go, if you use it right. If you use it wrong, it's a gateway to a lost sun that shoots laser beams and wants to destroy the universe."

"Great," Remy said. "Glad I asked."

Ardent held the Key over the Map. And suddenly, the crystal began to glow like the sun it so closely resembled. Almost instantly, islands and continents and forests and cities bubbled up from the center of the parchment and slid across its face, bumping into one another and rearranging themselves into proper configuration.

The inky lines on the Map swayed and flowed as Ardent waved the Key over it, following each movement like a school of minnows darting back and forth just below the surface of a pond. New continents sprang to the surface, then dropped away again.

Then, with a deep breath, he dipped the Key toward the now-roiling parchment. "Okay then, Map. Show us the way to the Shattered Archipelago."

Across the face of the Map, the images whirled and flew so fast Fin couldn't even follow them. It was as though he were falling into the Stream itself. He braced himself as a familiar nausea ran through him. "I forgot about this part," he managed to gurgle.

"Wuff," Coll let out.

"This is seasickness," Remy groaned. "Is this seasickness?"

"I see sickness," Fin offered.

The ink turned into a swirl, and the swirl turned into a spiral. At first Fin thought it was broken. But then the edges cleared, and misshapen lumps bubbled up, dotting the image. The spiral wasn't just an effect of the Map, Fin realized. It was a *place*.

Ardent glanced toward Coll. "Any clues?"

Coll stepped forward, squinting. He scratched at the knotted tattoo that snaked up the back of his neck. "Hmm," he said. "I don't know where this is, exactly...but..." He scratched at the tattoo again. It moved, ever so slightly, beneath his fingers. "Yeah, I think I can get us there."

Next to him, Marrill clapped her hands together and let out a shout of joy. "We're on our way!"

"Yay?" Remy said. "That's good, right?"

But Fin couldn't take his eyes off the Map. Something twisted in his chest. The last time he'd used the Map, it had shown him the galleon that carried his mother. The one that made him recognize the forgettable girl's ship.

It would be easy for him to snag the Key and Map when no one was looking. Slip away and use it to go after his mom. No one would even remember him. It would be as clean a job as there ever was.

Except for Marrill. He glanced at her and she beamed at him. "We're adventuring together again. Isn't it amazing?" she squealed, her eyes bright. "And now I know we can get home again." All, it seemed, was forgiven.

And he knew right then, there wasn't a job in the world he would take if it meant hurting her. "Yeah," he said, letting her excitement wash over him. "It's spiff news."

Suddenly, it felt as though the temperature dropped by forty degrees. Perhaps it had, Fin realized, as a puff of air escaped his lungs in a cloud of frost. Beside him, Marrill's teeth began to chatter, and scales of ice began to climb a nearby mast.

"Ardent," Coll said, his voice both cautious and assertive. The wizard had the Key firmly pressed against the Map. But it showed him nothing. Just the scribbled image of a bird, the Map's Compass Rose, circling forlornly over the empty Stream as if searching for something even it could not find. "I'm sure it doesn't mean anything," Coll offered.

Without a word, Ardent snatched the Map from the table, turned on his heel, and stalked toward his cabin. The moment the door slammed behind him, the temperature on the ship returned to normal. Ice-ringed yards overhead defrosting in a shower of raindrops.

"Whoa," Remy said. "Things. Just. Got. Real."

Fin furrowed his brow at Marrill. "What was he trying to find?"

Marrill repeated the question, loud enough to catch Coll's attention. The captain shook his head. "Annalessa."

⊣⊢ ⊹ ⊣⊢

Fin spent the rest of the day trailing after Marrill as she gave Remy the grand tour. Whenever he could, he kept a sharp eye on Ardent's cabin. The wizard still had the Map and Key in there, after all. Fin's fingers itched to hold the sun-shaped knob again, to see the great galleon and his mother drawn in ink.

But even as Coll changed their course to head for the Shattered Archipelago, even when the open Stream grew banks that sprouted long arms that tossed spitballs at them as they sailed past, the door to Ardent's cabin remained firmly closed.

Now it was night, and the ship creaked lightly as she skimmed along the surface of the Stream. And though everyone else had gone to bed, the deck didn't feel too lonely. A few pirats working the night shift squeaked up in the rigging. Four and a half moons shone overhead, their silver reflections punching holes in the golden water. And Marrill was here on the Stream.

He'd finally gotten his best friend back.

"I don't think Ardent's budging anytime soon," Marrill said behind him. Fin jumped in surprise, then twisted himself quickly, trying to hide it. She shook her head as she made her way across the deck, one hand hidden behind her back.

"I wasn't going to swipe anything," Fin protested.

She raised an eyebrow. "I didn't say you were, weirdo. Here, I brought you something." She revealed what she'd been holding behind her: a brown, raggedy-looking coat, just exactly Fin's size. A string trailed from each sleeve.

"My skysailing jacket!" he cried, grabbing it eagerly. "You brought it back to me!" He slipped it on. It had grown a little tighter since he'd given it to her, but even after all this time, it still felt natural.

He laughed, tugging on the sleeves and flexing the sails, and Marrill laughed with him. They stood shoulder to shoulder as their smiles faded, staring out across the night-glistening Stream.

"Can I ask you something?" Marrill said at last.

Fin braced himself and nodded. He had a pretty good idea what the question would be.

"Why didn't you tell me about the Key?" The look on her face felt like a knife in Fin's gut. This was the problem with being remembered, he thought: People didn't just forget when you let them down.

He still didn't know how to explain, but deflecting wasn't going to work this time. "I was afraid."

Surprised, she cocked her head to the side. "You? Afraid? Come on. You've stared down evil oracles and played touch-tag with krakens!"

Fin shrugged. "Well, yeah," he said, with exaggerated swagger. "I mean, when you put it like that, I *am* pretty heroic." She swatted him on the arm. He laughed, but heat infused his cheeks. He only wished he *felt* heroic. "I just wanted to find my mom so bad," he said. "And figure out what's wrong with me, and fix it. And you were going home, and I was afraid that once you were gone…once you *are* gone, I'll be alone again."

Marrill was silent. For a moment, the only sounds were the squeal of the sails shifting and the shush of the bow cutting through the golden waves. Then she threaded her fingers through his and the warmth of her touch flowed through him. He'd forgotten how nice it was to be touched by a friend, and not just by angry guards.

They spent half the night talking, catching up about their lives. He hugged her awkwardly when she told him about her mom's illness getting worse. She patted his shoulder reassuringly when he told her about the forgettable girl and her ship.

"So all we need," Marrill said, leaning across the railing, "is some way to find your mom and some way to fix mine. Then you can be memorable, and my mom can be okay, and we can sail off to wherever we want, whenever we want!"

"Don't forget the Iron Tide," he reminded her.

She grinned. "Come on, exploring ancient prophecies, fighting world-destroying dangers? That's all part of the fun!"

Fin had to laugh. Her excitement was so contagious he couldn't help but get swept up in it. "Yup," he said. "All we need is some kind of wish machine, and we'll be in good shape."

CHAPTER 7
A Problem of Unusual Gravity

Laaaaaaaaannnd HO!"

Marrill woke with a start. Coll's voice echoed down the spiral staircase, bounced around the empty cabin, and careened across to the lower decks. Apparently, they'd arrived at...wherever it was they were going.

She jumped from the bed (the *Kraken* had given her a big, soft cushion this time, surrounded by lush Arabian carpets and warm, dimly glowing braziers), quickly changed into a set of clean clothes from her backpack, and threw open the door. Outside, Fin leaned against a doorframe, waiting for her. "Welcome to waking! Nice of you to show up!" He tossed a plummellowich her way. She took a grateful bite as she knocked on Remy's door.

When no response came, she carefully cracked it open. Remy was snuggled deep under the covers. White snowdrifts piled softly in the corners, and her walls wavered and glowed like the aurora borealis. "Mfyou comfhing?" Marrill asked, mouth full.

The lump of covers that was her babysitter barely moved. "Still the weekend," came the muffled reply. "I get five more minutes."

Marrill swallowed the glob of plummellow. "Oh, sure," she said, carefully slinking back.

"Don't do anything stupid until I get there," Remy called after her.

"Totally." Quietly, Marrill closed Remy's door, then raced on tiptoe after Fin, who was already on his way to the staircase. Their giggles echoed down the hallways as they climbed toward the main deck. A second later, they broke through the hatch, out into the sunlight, and into a world so bizarre it made Marrill's head spin.

Half-formed islands swam all around them, as if someone had broken a continent into pieces, shaken them up, and tossed them like dice into the Stream. An upside-down mountain stuck up from the wash of golden water ahead, its narrow peak widening as it rose until its large, root-covered base waved in the air. A mushroom-covered marsh bobbed beneath a tower of rock that drifted freely overhead. All around, disconnected chunks of ground floated inches or feet or miles apart, each one totally different, as though they had no relation to each other whatsoever.

"Shanks," Fin breathed. Nearby, a fog bank dissipated, then suddenly reappeared.

Marrill's steps faltered. "Where are we?"

"The Shattered Archipelago," Ardent announced from the forecastle. The wizard surveyed the landscape through a long spyglass. He rounded toward them, one eye looking so huge through the end of the telescope that Marrill had to laugh.

Ardent set the spyglass aside and tucked his hands behind his back in his favorite storytelling stance. "Do you remember me telling you once that too much raw magic would tear apart a completed world like yours?"

Marrill nodded. It was hard for her *not* to remember, with the Stream being so close to her world again.

Ardent waved a hand at the tangle of twisted landscape. "I suspect that is precisely what happened here. That this was once a world—or maybe even worlds—detached from the Stream, like your own. Only somehow, somewhere deep in the past, they got, well, sucked onto the Stream, for lack of a better term. And these islands are all that remain of the collision."

Off the port side, a pillar of mossy rock let out a belch

of steam, erupted into molten lava, then re-formed, complete with moss again. "As you can see, that event left the islands themselves with some...unusual properties," Ardent continued. "I recall a story of one islet where things broken would mend themselves without warning, and another where a ball thrown into the air might stop there, or start moving again, for no reason at all."

"Weird," Fin said.

"Oh, look, a local!" Ardent chirped.

"He's with me," Marrill reminded the wizard.

"Of course he is!" Ardent turned back to surveying the Shattered Archipelago. "It's best to be careful in a place like this," he said absently. "You never know what you might find. Or what might find *you*."

Marrill looked out, too. The water moved oddly here; there was a current, pulling everything sideways and forward. The beginning, she realized, of the whirlpool.

"Check it out!" Fin stood with one foot up on the bowsprit, pointing. Marrill made her way next to him, stopping just shy of the railing.

The lushest, greenest meadow Marrill had ever seen stretched out before them. Or more accurately, stretched *up* before them. Because it was vertical, towering straight into the air.

"GRASSBERG!" Coll bellowed. "Full stop!" he called to the rigging. At his command, the Ropebone Man trimmed the sails, and pirats scampered along the yardarms adjusting knots. Despite their efforts, the *Kraken* floated closer, her momentum unslowed.

Marrill leaned out, feeling herself oddly drawn to the field-cliff ahead. Like it was pulling her forward. Like she could just fall into it. And then, sure enough, she slid right over the ship's rail and tumbled through the air.

"Yahh!"

A second later, she thudded onto soft ground.

"Marrill!" Fin cried, from somewhere above her. Shaking her head, she sat up, trying to get her bearings. Grass blades tickled at her palms and the back of her knees. In front of her, a sheer cliff of glowing water stretched up from the ground. Now it was the Pirate Stream, not the field, which jutted straight into the air like a shimmering wall.

She braced herself, expecting the water to come sloshing down on her in a tidal wave. But the Stream simply sat there, rippling and eddying. She could even see the current of the whirlpool, still dragging the ship along its lazy spiral. Other than the fact that the water was vertical, which water generally was not, everything was normal. It was just like someone had taken the world and stood it on one side.

"Huh?" she said aloud.

"Marrill!" Fin cried again from above. She looked up just in time to see him tumble by and thump to the ground beside her. "I really should have seen that coming," he muttered.

"Uh-huh," Marrill mumbled. Her eyes were stuck on

the *Kraken*. It floated above them, coming down the water-wall toward them like a spider coming down its web.

Marrill blinked. The world wasn't turned on one side, she realized. *She* was.

"I said full stop!" Coll's voice bellowed. But the *Kraken* was still sailing forward—or falling down, as it now seemed—straight on top of them!

Marrill rolled aside, moments before the *Kraken*'s bowsprit pierced the ground where she'd been sitting. The ship shuddered to a halt, teetering in the air.

"Hmmm." Tugging his beard, Ardent paced the railing, looking down on them. Only, he was totally sideways to them, defying gravity just like the water of the Stream, just like the rest of the *Kraken* itself. Marrill had to crane her neck to look up at him.

From somewhere in the pockets of his robe, he produced a small yellow ball, then let go of it. It flew sideways, straight to the *Kraken*'s deck, as if it had been tossed through the air rather than dropped.

Ardent caught the ball as it bounced, then stepped forward, holding it out over the railing, and let it go again. This time, it dropped straight down like it should have. Fin snatched it with a grin.

"We seem to have a problem of unusual gravity," Ardent offered. "Indeed, unusual gravity is precisely the problem!" He grinned, clearly pleased with himself. "Quite interesting when you think about it," he added.

"Less thinking, more fixing!" Coll shouted. "There's a storm blowing in from the Stream. We need to get clear of this . . . *meadow* and get out of here before it overtakes us!"

Marrill craned her neck, looking up past the *Kraken* to the horizon. Sure enough, dark clouds were gathering there, and moving in on them rapidly. The Shattered Archipelago was a maze of chaos already; she didn't want to think about what it would be like in a hurricane.

She looked around quickly, hoping to find something—anything—that would be useful. The grassberg wasn't huge, she realized, just big enough really to run from one end to the other. On one side, the Stream reached up endlessly; on the opposite side, the ground dropped away, and past that, the sky waited, as if she could just walk into it. Other loose islets floated freely through the air there, drifting on the rising wind from the storm. Not far away, a river floated past, curling and twisting in on itself like a snake.

"We're drifting," Marrill murmured to herself. She looked at Fin. "The current is moving the whole island!"

He held up a hand and sat still for a second, clearly feeling for the movement. "Huh," he said. He pointed to the waterline. "I guess this grassberg doesn't go too deep."

Just then, a loud groan filled the air as the ground—or the *Kraken*—shifted. Her bowsprit scraped through the earth. Overhead, the ship tilted precariously to one side.

"Um, not to be a worrywart, but is the Stream about to fall on us?" Fin asked.

He was right, Marrill saw. It wasn't just the ship that was tilting; it was *everything*. The wall of Stream water was leaning in, threatening to topple on them. The horizon full of dark clouds, which had been straight overhead, was now slowly moving, like the sun traveling across the sky.

Marrill gulped. She knew the Stream wasn't really falling on them; they were falling on *it*. But one way or the other, ship and land were crashing into each other. And for the kids stuck in the middle, well, if they didn't do something fast, it wouldn't be pretty.

"Okay," Fin said. "Way I see it is we either climb the bowsprit to get back onto the ship or run for the far side of the island. Thoughts?"

She took a deep breath and focused. Getting clear of the grassberg wasn't enough. It would still crash on the *Kraken* if they didn't do something to push the two apart.

"Come on, Marrill, decision time!" Fin shouted, waving for her to join him.

Marrill took one last look around, biting her lip. On the Stream-side, she caught sight of the edge of the island, lifting free from the water. The island wasn't anchored at all, she realized. It was free-floating in the air, and the *Kraken* was pushing on one side, flipping it around.

Suddenly, she figured out what to do.

"Jump!" she yelled to Fin. He looked at her like she'd lost her mind. But Marrill knew how to make this work. She started bouncing into the air, each time slamming back down against the ground with all her might. "The grassberg is flying!" she said. "We just have to knock it free from the *Kraken*!"

Fin shook his head, but he took her advice. He, too, started jumping as hard and furiously as he could. Together, they bounced like lunatics on a trampoline. Marrill just hoped the force of their combined weight would be enough.

Above them, the *Kraken* protested loudly, as though it were being wrenched apart. Marrill's stomach churned as the world seemed to shift around them.

"Aaaiiiiii!" she cried. The cold shadow of the ship fell across her shoulders. With one more giant leap, she pushed down with all her might, striking the earth as hard as possible.

A scraping whine filled the air. Her heart pounded in her ears. And then

everything

went

still.

She risked a glance to the side. Fin crouched next to her, eyes wide. Cautiously, she searched for the *Kraken*, but the ship was nowhere to be found.

"Where did it go?" she asked Fin. He shook his head, mouth open.

Something tickled the top of her head. She glanced up,

and came face-to-face with Ardent. He was dangling, upside down, from the tip of the *Kraken*'s mainmast. Because the entire *ship* was upside down.

Or rather, she and Fin were. The Pirate Stream was above them now, a golden expanse of water where the sky should have been.

"Well done, First Mate Marrill," Ardent said. "Clever last-minute thinking. With your help, and perhaps a little magical oomph from someone notoriously talented in such things, we seem to have dislodged the grassberg quite neatly."

Marrill looked around. Sure enough, only a ragged edge of rapidly blooming flowers marked where the field had once met the magic water. Marrill's nerves dissolved into relief and amazement. She was standing on the underside of a flying island.

But before she could get too comfortable, thunder grumbled in the distance. There was still a storm coming in.

"You might want to disembark now!" Ardent suggested, some urgency in his voice. Past him, Marrill could see the whirlpool current was picking up pace as the *Kraken* moved deeper into the Shattered Archipelago. Between that and the rising breeze, the ship had gained speed, threatening now to carry the wizard out of reach.

"We better go," she said to Fin. But there was no answer. Marrill glanced behind her. He'd crawled to the far edge of the islet and was hanging his head down over the side. *Up* over the side, she reminded herself.

"Fin!" she shouted. "Come on! They're leaving us!"

"I found something," he called.

The *Kraken* had just about cleared the end of their little island. "Hurry!" Ardent pressed. Marrill glanced back to the *Kraken*. "Jump now if you're jumping!"

"Fin!" Marrill yelled. "We have to go!" She braced herself, ready to spring up to the ship. Ardent reached out to catch her.

"Be careful," he cautioned. "Remember, when the gravity flips, you'll be falling, and I won't be able to stop you. The wind and I are no longer on speaking terms."

She gulped. It was a long way down. Or up, from this perspective. *On three,* she told herself. *One.* She looked back again. Fin now hung half over the ledge. *Two.* He wouldn't make it.

Three!

She dropped her hands. "Oh, circle around!" she cried to Ardent. "I've got to get Fin!" She turned and raced across the grass.

"She says to circle around." Ardent's voice came from below her. "Well, I don't know. Something about there being fins. Grass sharks? Not in this climate, I wouldn't think."

She reached the edge just as Fin was disappearing

entirely. She was certain he was going to fall. "Fin!" she snapped, snagging the edge of his coat.

He looked back at her. Even though he was hanging out in the open air, his dark, rough-cut hair stayed in place on his forehead. The ends of his coat didn't seem to be dangling down, either. It was as if he weren't hanging at all.

He smirked and stepped forward, dropping over the edge entirely. Marrill's heart jumped. But he didn't fall.

"Looks like the upside's another downside!" Fin quipped.

Marrill shook her head. "Weird," she said. "But come on, we've got to get back to the *Kraken*."

Above her, still sailing upside down, the *Kraken* had started to turn, tacking around a beach that scattered into a billion grains of sand and then re-formed, complete with sandcastles. But the ship was obviously struggling against the current, which must have been stronger than Marrill realized. She didn't want to think about being stranded here.

"Check it out," Fin said, pointing. Marrill rolled her eyes, but did as he asked.

She felt an odd dizziness as her head passed over the edge of the islet, and suddenly what had been down was up again. For her head, at least; her legs were still lying in the grass of the meadow. To her eyes and mind, the sky was overhead now, but her legs and feet still felt pulled toward it.

She shook her head to chase away the sensation and looked around. The underside (upper side?) of the island was all dirt and loose rock. In the center stood a large pillar of black stone with four flat sides and a pointed top—an obelisk, Marrill recalled. It was clearly ancient. And most significantly, in big letters that seemed to burn with hidden fire, a message had been carved on it. The first words stood out above all the others:

BEYOND THIS POINT
CONTINUITY CANNOT BE GUARANTEED

CHAPTER 8
Beyond This Point Continuity
Cannot Be Guaranteed

Fin stared at the letters that glowed like coals on the face of the obelisk. He had no idea what "continuity" was or why he might want a guarantee. "What do you think it means?" he asked.

Marrill pulled herself over and crouched next to him. The wind whipped up, snatching at the sleeves of his coat, running like fingers through his hair. "Oh, I know this!" she said. "It's like, with a TV show..." He arched an eyebrow at her. He was pretty sure a tea veesho was a type of drink you snorted through your nose, but he had no idea how it related.

"Never mind," Marrill said. "Continuity means, like, how everything happens in order and is the same from one moment to the next. Like, in a timeline."

Fin arched an eyebrow. "So stuff might happen out of order if we go any farther?" She looked just as puzzled as he felt. But there was more to the message. They made their way closer, until the words became clear:

BEYOND THIS POINT
CONTINUITY CANNOT BE GUARANTEED
TAKE HEED TRAVELER

AT THE HEART OF THIS BROKEN WORLD
LIES THE SYPHON OF MONERVA
THE LEGACY OF THE SALT SAND KING
THE GREAT AND POWERFUL MACHINE

BEWARE
THE SYPHON GRANTS WISHES
—T. D. W.

Fin turned to Marrill. "Do you see what I see?" he asked. The look in her eyes told him she did.

"The Syphon grants wishes." She reached out and tapped one of the letters lightly, like she was afraid it might be hot.

Fin knew a syphon was something that sucked away liquid; Stavik had once hired him to "syphon" four hundred gallons of stumblefruit juice out of the hold of a merchant ship, using only an eight-foot-long straw and a particularly thirsty guzzlecrow. The memory made him smile, but he couldn't exactly picture that crow granting wishes. Especially not after all that stumblefruit juice.

But perhaps this wasn't that kind of syphon. Perhaps this syphon was something else entirely. "'The Great and Powerful Machine,'" Fin read aloud.

"Do you think it's real? A machine that grants wishes?" Marrill asked. "I mean, that's what it says, right?"

The rational part of Fin's brain told him not to get his hopes up. But the impulsive part of his brain told him to ignore that. And impulsive was his favorite brain part, at least when he didn't think too hard about it.

Excitement jittered up from his toes to the tips of his ears. He nodded.

"My mom," Marrill said, grabbing his arms. He could feel her shaking. "Fin, I could wish my mom better!"

"I know!" he said, grabbing her back. "And I could..." His mind spun with possibilities. He could wish to find the girl. Scratch that—he could find his own mother. Scratch that, even; he could wish to never be forgotten again!

The thought overwhelmed him. Together, he and Marrill bounced up and down, vibrating with energy. Their stomping caused the ground to shift underneath them.

Fin stopped, splaying his feet to keep his balance. He'd completely forgotten they were on a floating chunk of earth, bobbing loose and free through the skies.

"Maybe we're flying a little ahead of the wind, as the Quay folk say," he pointed out.

Marrill held an arm out to steady herself. "Right. Good point...if that means what I think it means." She smiled at him. "Maybe there's something else here...."

She circled the obelisk, scanning the surface. Then she froze, eyes wide. Alarmed, Fin scrambled to her side. But when he saw what she was staring at, his breath caught in his throat. Without thinking, his hand went to the silver bracelet in his pocket, thumb tracing the symbol on its surface. The same symbol was carved into the black stone.

A dragon under a mountain-filled circle.

"I've seen it before!" Marrill said, pointing. "This same symbol was painted on the sign that told me I needed to come back to the Pirate Stream."

Fin couldn't believe it. "I've seen it, too!" He pulled out the bracelet and showed it to her. "I stole this from the forgettable girl." Marrill's lips tightened at the mention of stealing, but she said nothing. "The same symbol was on the side of her ship," he added. He stepped forward and placed his palm against the smooth black stone. "I think there's a connection between this symbol and my mom."

Marrill sucked in a breath. "What does it mean?"

Fin had absolutely no idea. "And how does the Syphon of Monerva tie in?" They stood together, staring at the obelisk. Warmth spread through Fin's chest. It was nice to know he didn't have to face these questions alone.

"We should probably worry about getting back to the *Kraken* first, huh?" Marrill suggested.

He smiled. "Probably." He half jogged, half bounced his way to the edge of the islet, still high on the thought of the Wish Machine and the possible connection to his mom. As he reached the edge, the breeze picked up, carrying on it the scent of rain and an acrid taste, almost as if he'd bitten his lip or gotten a nosebleed.

"Fin," Marrill whispered behind him.

He tented his hands over his eyes. "Wait a tick," he said. From up here, he could finally see the great whirlpool in all its glory. It was enormous; a huge spiraling swirl of glowing water, as if a giant had pulled the drain plug on the whole Stream. Islets tumbled around it and over it, some floating on the surface, some flying through the air, some leaping like whales and diving deep once more. But no sign of the *Kraken*.

"Fin!" Marrill said again. He turned. She stood paralyzed, staring out at the growing storm. Her features were pale, her hands trembling.

On the horizon, a spear of red lightning punctured the clouds.

Fin gulped. The last time he'd seen red lightning, it had brought terror with it. A ghost ship made of wrought iron, her crew cut from shadows. Her Master, clad head to toe in black metal. The memory of Serth's voice skittered like spider legs across his brain: *Fear the Iron Ship. Steer clear the Iron Ship.*

He shook his head. The Iron Ship was gone. It had sunk into the Stream, taking its crew of walking shadows and its cruel, armor-clad Master with it. Nothing could survive that.

Could it?

"We should get out of here," he told Marrill. "Like, now."

A huge gust of wind interrupted his thought, catching him off balance. Marrill ducked her head and braced herself. Beneath them, the floating island shifted and lurched forward, slowly drifting out over the Shattered Archipelago. As the storm came on, the wind picked up even more, buffeting them and pushing them faster with each furious gust.

He made his way carefully back toward the edge, instinctively rocking on the balls of his feet to let the wind pass. It was fierce, to be sure. But Fin had grown up skysailing on the gales that blew off of Khaznot Mountain. Compared to them, this was a cinch.

"What do you see?" Marrill called. She took a hesitant

step toward him, then had to catch herself against the stone obelisk as another strong gust hit them.

Unfortunately, he still couldn't find the *Kraken*. Then it occurred to him: The grassberg was flying. What if the ship was actually *beneath* them? For all he knew, they could be floating above another island of soft pillows or a jungle made of convenient ladders. He needed to get a better look.

"Hold on," he told Marrill. "I'm going over!" And with that, he slung himself right over the edge of the floating islet.

Fin's head swam as the gravity twisted. His momentum shif

    ted as what was

               down   up

                      became   again.

The force of his fall snapped

him tightly around the edge of the islet, onto the grassy meadow once more.

Fin blinked, reorienting himself. The Stream was overhead now. They'd drifted closer to the central whirlpool already; between the swirling current and the growing storm, the islands of the Shattered Archipelago swarmed around it like bees around a hive. And there, weaving among them, he caught sight of the *Kraken*'s mainmast. She was farther out than he'd expected, tacking her way around the outer rim of the great whirlpool to keep from getting sucked in. But she was headed back their way.

"Right, they're coming around to us!" he shouted up to Marrill. "We just have to hold on until they get here...."

Underneath, they passed over the ruins of an ancient building, formed from some kind of smooth mud he didn't recognize, sticking out from the Stream on a pinnacle of clay. A moment later, and they were past it, crossing over a lonesome chunk of tundra, covered in crooked arctic scrub and sending puffs of frost into the air.

"Blisterwinds," he murmured. They were picking up speed. When the *Kraken* got here, here they wouldn't be.

He headed back to Marrill, this time   flipping

an awesome

somersault

as he jumped over the edge of the islet.

Down became down once more, and the whole grassberg tilted when he landed.

Marrill looked more terrified than impressed. She clung more tightly than ever to the stone monument, the wind flicking at her hair. Behind her, the dark clouds cracked with carnelian light.

"The *Kraken*'s circling for us, but we're headed out over the whirlpool," he told her. "And if they get closer, they'll get sucked in."

Marrill shivered against the breeze. "So what do we do?"

Fin shrugged. If only he had his skysails, he might be able to wing them down to the ship. But his jacket was still on the *Kraken*; he hadn't exactly been planning on getting sucked off the ship by a floating meadow when he'd gotten dressed that morning. "No idea," he confessed.

Marrill chewed her lip. "Okay, think." She looked up. "The *Kraken* is going *around* the whirlpool, right?" Fin nodded. "And we're cutting across the middle?"

"We can run into them on the other side!" Fin cried, finishing her thought. She nodded. Thunder boomed in the distance.

"Back in a tick," Fin said. With a quick turn, he dropped back

over

the edge, and down became up again. Beneath him, the storm clouds unfolded like a quilt across the upside-down sky. He shook his head and stumbled. Changing gravity was a bit of a head rush.

A moment later, he was able to take stock of the situation. They were moving out over the whirlpool proper now; the water swirled above him like an inside-out tornado. Before long, they'd be straight over the center, and headed on toward the other side.

The *Kraken*, meanwhile, had already passed behind them; he could make out Ardent waving his hands frantically on the deck. The ship was racing between the bobbing islands, cutting her way around the outside of the whirlpool, already so far in that Fin could practically hear Coll cursing from here. But there was no way they would reach the other side by the time Fin and Marrill did.

Not unless Fin found some way to change the islet's direction, anyway. A little to the right, and maybe they could make it. But how could they steer a flying chunk of grass and rock?

His thoughts were interrupted by the flare of red lightning, slashing up through the air to smash into sparks on the golden water above. Fin looked up. At first, what he saw didn't register. Just a darkness, low and fast at the edge of his vision. And then he understood what he was seeing.

She was deep and black, just like he remembered her. All jagged edges and cold metal, a rusty razor scraping across the surface of the Stream. His chest clenched. She was too far away yet for him to make out the shadow crew, nor could he see the cruel shape of her Master. But it was the Iron Ship, no doubt. And it was headed straight for them.

The ground seemed to tremble beneath his feet as he remembered her smashing through the stern of the *Black Dragon*. Her awful crew of shadows spilling forth to do battle with Serth's weeping pirates. Fire leaping from her bow as she circled the *Kraken*.

"Shanks," he muttered.

Without waiting, he launched   himself   over

the edge

of the island

feeling

gravity

reverse

as he came down again on the top. The island rocked beneath him with the force of his landing. Marrill hugged the obelisk. Her lips were tight, eyes wide, her hair flying wild in the wind. Clearly she'd seen it, too.

"But it sank," she protested. "In the Pirate Stream. We watched it go under."

Another shaft of lightning crashed down. The first fat raindrop sploshed cold against Fin's cheek. "Yeah," he managed. Instinctively, he bent his knees to keep from falling as the island swayed beneath his feet.

Then it hit him. *The island rocked beneath his feet.* It was *still* moving from the impact of his last jump. If he could move it that much that easily, maybe they could move it even more together. Enough, even, to change its direction.

"All right, I've got an idea," he told Marrill. "We moved the island before from jumping on it, right?" She gave him a confused look. "We can do it again, and move it over to the *Kraken!*"

"Say what now?"

He waved her over to him urgently. Reluctantly, she let go of the carved stone and teetered toward him, bracing against the wind and growing rain. He reached out for her hand as she crept close.

"Think of it like flipping a coin," he told her. "If you put it right over your thumb before you flip it, it goes straight up and comes straight back down. But if you put your thumb just barely under one side..."

"You can shoot it across the room!" Marrill squeaked. "Fin, you're a genius!" He smirked, even as he edged them around the side of the island, trying to choose just the right spot. "Okay," Marrill said. "We can do this. We just have to figure out how fast they're moving, how fast we're moving, and the distance each of us has to cover in the same amount of time. Then we take, um...the...uh, radius of the circle...and divide by..." She screwed up her eyes. "Hypotenuse...a train leaves Denver..."

"Or we could just eyeball it," Fin suggested. He looked down, over the edge. They were out over the whirlpool for real now; any misstep and there was nothing between them and swirling death. He could just make out the *Kraken*, racing around the outer edge of the spiral, trying to catch up. And in the distance, the Iron Ship.

Rain dripped through his hair, running down his nose. It was now or never. "Ready?" he asked. Before she could even answer, he leapt off the side with all his might, dragging her with him.

She screamed.

"Cannonball!" he shouted.

The shifting gravity tugged them
down,

a

r

o

u

n

d

back down,
and
SMASHED
them
feetfirst into the soft grass of the field.

The whole island shuddered with the impact,

and turned

spinning

end

over

end.

Up   up. Sky   clouds.
became   became   became   became
down   waves

Marrill shrieked. Fin tumbled one way, then the other.
He couldn't tell what the gravity was. Or if it was.

He fell through the grass (up the grass?), over the edge (around the edge?) and over the rocky ground (under the rocky ground?). He snatched for the obelisk as the islet flipped again.

Gravity no longer mattered; now it was just a struggle to keep from getting thrown off. He clung to the stone, questioning his life choices, his legs flung out toward the moving horizon. In one bold moment, he dared a look over his shoulder.

Sure enough, they'd changed directions. They were going to meet the *Kraken*. All he had to do was hold on, and then...

"Whaaauuahauhaut nowwoowooowww?" Marrill's voice came from somewhere that could have been below, or maybe above, him. Fin gulped. He'd honestly figured they would just play this part by ear.

"Maaaarriiiiiillllll!" Coll's voice carried up to him. Fin's stomach lurched as he looked toward the Stream, but he could see the *Kraken*, slicing across the swirling water toward them. They were nearly there. But he had no idea how to get off the twirling island.

"Throowwwussssroooopes!" Marrill shrieked nearby. "Rooooppebooone!!!"

"On it!" Ardent's voice came. In the next second, Fin caught a glimpse of the Ropebone Man, whipping his corded arms toward them. One headed nearly straight at him. But it was too short to reach. Then the island flipped end over end once more.

On the far side, he could see the entirety of the whirl-pool, swirling and sucking. He could see the storm, rolling in fast. And the Iron Ship, cutting in through the edge of the Archipelago. The island flipped once more.

And suddenly, a tangle of ropes shot out everywhere. As each rope neared the island, the strange gravity pulled it in, holding it tight in the air. Marrill was already sliding down one toward the ship. Fin gulped and jumped for another. He snagged it and held tight.

The next thing he knew, he was falling.

"Yaaaaahhh!!!!!" Fin screamed. The rope pulled taut, swinging him over the *Kraken*'s deck.

The ship rocked and turned sideways as the current pulled on her. The rope tossed him about. He struggled to keep hold. But just as he thought he couldn't take any more, a thick hand grabbed his ankle and held on to it. Then another. Then another. A second later, he was scrambling and kicking across the tilting deck.

"This what you were looking for?" the Naysayer yelled to the rigging. Fin threw his arms around the monster. He'd never been so happy to see the old lizard.

"That's him!" Marrill's voice sounded. Overhead, she lay suspended in a net made from rigging, snagged safe and sound by the Ropebone Man. They'd made it.

Sort of, anyway. The *Kraken* twisted and turned as it surfed the growing current. Lightning crashed all around them, turning the whole world bloody. The Iron Ship was almost on top of them. Her black metal prow sheered through the surf. The Master stared coldly from her bow. Red energy danced between his fingers.

Fin swallowed and scrambled to his feet. Suddenly, he wasn't sure escaping the grassberg had been such a good idea. All he could see was spiraling water, whirling around the abyss that was the heart of the Shattered Archipelago.

AT THE HEART OF THIS BROKEN WORLD LIES THE SYPHON OF MONERVA

The obelisk's words suddenly took on new meaning. Sailors like Pickled Pate had been vanishing here, and reappearing, for ages. There was only one place they could have gone.

"It's here," he breathed. "The Wish Machine is down the whirlpool."

"Haul the ropes, pirats!" Coll shouted. "We have to get away from the whirlpool!"

Fin leapt forward. "No!" he screamed. "Go in! Go in! Marrill, the Syphon is down the whirlpool!"

"Do it!" Marrill cried. "The Iron Ship is coming!" Just across the water, the Master of the Iron Ship raised his hand, preparing to attack.

Fin looked to Ardent. The wizard braced against the

mast, grinding his jaw with worry. His bearded chin nodded toward Coll.

From his perch on the quarterdeck, the sailor nodded back. "All hands, brace yourselves," he shouted. "We're going down!"

Red lightning seared the air as the *Kraken* turned into the current. Fin clung fast to the Naysayer. And in the scariest thing that happened yet, the Naysayer didn't fight him. Because up ahead, the water gaped open, waiting to swallow them whole.

CHAPTER 9
Worst Roller-Coaster Ride Ever

Marrill felt like she was on one of those log rides at a theme park, shooting through a tunnel made of water. Except that getting splashed with *this* water could mean turning into a five-headed penguin with a Swedish accent and tap shoes.

"Brace yourselves!" Coll shouted as the ship sliced its way downward, surfing down the flume. Marrill tightened her grip on the ropes around her, rocking in her cradle of netting. Below her, more ropes dropped, wrapping around each of the crew.

"Oh no, not again!" Remy cried, swatting at the rigging. But then, without warning, the tunnel dipped. The ship dropped out from underneath them. For a moment, Marrill was suspended in midair. It was a sensation she was getting *way* too familiar with.

"Never mind! Hold me tighter, Mr. Rope Man!" Remy yelped. The words were lost in a shriek as the ship bottomed out and twisted violently to the left.

"Nguh," Marrill gasped as her insides flattened and rearranged themselves. Everywhere she looked was the glow of water. It roared and sloshed as it spun around them. Or as they spun around it—it was difficult to tell the difference. It was like they were being sucked down a tube of air cut straight through the heart of the Stream. And that tube was starting to narrow.

Adrenaline spiked Marrill's system. Her heart stuttered as the water closed in around them. As scared as she was of the Iron Ship, this didn't seem much better. Because if the tunnel grew too narrow, the mast would be the first part to go and her with it.

She scrambled across the ropes on her knees, but now that she faced forward, things weren't getting better. Dead ahead, the tunnel seemed to end at a solid wall of water. And the *Kraken* was stuck in a permanent free fall toward it. The ship would shatter on impact.

"Pull her up, Coll! Pull her up!" Ardent shouted.

"That's not a direction ships go!" the sailor shouted back. He yanked the wheel back and forth, as if that could do anything to slow their descent.

Marrill dropped flat and grabbed a rope, bracing for impact. Next to her, pirats clung to the booms desperately, their twin tails whipping in the breeze.

But on the deck below, Ardent seemed unperturbed. He stood at the bow, arms wide and knees slightly bent. The tip of his hat flapped behind him like a wind sock. "Heeeeere weeeeeee goooooo!" he boomed.

Suddenly, a force like an invisible hand crushed down on her. It smashed her into the ropes, making it impossible to breathe. She wasn't even sure her heart continued to beat.

The *Kraken*'s weathered boards groaned. From somewhere in the rigging around her came a snapping sound, followed by several pops. Her hammock jolted, dropping a few feet before it went tight again.

"Hold together, old girl," Coll urged the ship. "You can do it!"

Marrill added her own silent pleas as the Pirate Stream crashed around them. Everything turned to gold. The buzz of magic sang through her veins, setting her hair on end. She clenched her eyes and gritted her teeth, feeling like her insides threatened to turn into outsides.

Then came another loud **POP!** The sky opened up

over her. The ship skidded across the surface of the Stream sideways, like a rock skipping across a lake. Thankfully, the horrible, crushing force eased. Marrill could finally draw the breath she'd been desperate to take for what felt like hours.

"All hands, report!" Coll called as the ship's movement stabilized into something approaching normal. Pirats squeaked and scampered around her, racing along the yards to check for damage.

Cautiously, Marrill cracked an eye. The giant, whirling tunnel of water was gone. As were the floating islets of the Shattered Archipelago. All around, the Stream was oddly smooth and calm. Even the sky was a clear, bright blue.

"Everyone okay down there?" she asked as she scrambled across the netting toward the mast. A rope wrapped around her waist and lowered her gently to the deck. "Thanks," she said to the air. The rope patted her on the shoulder before disappearing into the rigging.

Fin stood near the bow, his hair sticking up wildly. "That was better than the Quay during hurricane season!" he said, grinning.

Next to him, Remy clutched the railing, her cheek pressed tightly against the wooden balustrade. The babysitter nodded, but didn't release her grip as she slowly straightened and looked around. "Um, guys? Where did the other ship go? The scary one?"

Marrill glanced behind them—no Iron Ship. Which

should have been a relief. But for some reason, it just made her more uneasy. The Iron Ship was *back*, even though they'd watched it sink into the Stream. If it could survive that, it could definitely follow them down the whirlpool, scary tunnel or no. At any second, it could pop up beside them. There was no way they were safe.

The Naysayer pushed his way onto his feet beside her. "Great piloting, Cap'n," he snarked. Karnelius scowled furiously from the cradle of one thick arm. "Can't decide what was better, eating the deck or tasting it come up again every three seconds. I've half a mind to get off at the next port and be done with the lot o' ya."

"Then it's your lucky day," Coll said, staring straight ahead. Marrill turned to follow his gaze. And her jaw dropped.

In the distance, an impenetrable range of impossibly high mountains blocked the Stream. Impenetrable, that is, except for a broad gap between the two tallest peaks. And in that gap, across a vast expanse of junk-filled marsh, a massive wall stretched up so tall that even from way out here, Marrill had to crane her neck to find the top.

It reminded her of the Hoover Dam, but much, much bigger. And while the Hoover Dam was nothing but smooth concrete, this wall was covered in buildings, all stacked on top of each other, a haphazard, sprawling vertical city.

Its streets were labyrinths of long ladders and mazes of pulleys and slides. All across it, gears of various shapes and sizes stuck out, half-buried in the wall. Along its base, a flotilla of docks stretched into the marshes, bobbing with each wave. And at the very tip-top, high above the city, silhouetted by thick clouds of black smoke rising from somewhere behind the wall, a lone sinister tower stretched crookedly into the sky.

"Meh," the Naysayer said. "Not really my speed."

"What is this place?" Marrill breathed.

Ardent was perched on the forecastle, staring at the spectacle before them. *"I seen the city where the wall does stand,"* he recited. "That, I wager, would be the place poor Pickled Pate went all those millennia ago. The place where he saw the Iron Tide."

"Fascinating," Coll said drily. "Don't suppose anyone else noticed all the broken ships?" He waved his hand toward the marsh. Sure enough, what Marrill had first taken to be random junk was actually the remains of a small navy's worth of vessels. Ships of all shapes and sizes and states of disrepair bobbed in the muted glow of the Stream water, from gargantuan galleons that dwarfed the *Kraken* to tiny one-man rowboats. "That's what'll happen to us if the Iron Ship catches us. I vote we head for land, fast."

"Seconded," Remy chirped. She looked around nervously, as if unsure she actually got a vote. Then she frowned. "Though it looks like the current is taking us that way regardless."

Coll pressed his lips together. "A captain controls the ship, not the current," he informed her, calling for half sails.

Overhead the pirats hauled the lines, and the Ropebone Man gave the sails a bit of slack. "But yeah," he added reluctantly, "it is pretty strong here."

Fin fidgeted uneasily next to Marrill as they threaded their way through the floating graveyard. "Is no one else worried about how that rusted heap of metal sank and came back from the dead?" he asked. "I mean, I'm not crazy, right? We *did* sink that Iron Ship six months ago, right?"

Coll looked down from his perch. "Where'd you hear a story like that, sailor?"

Fin crossed his arms. "I was there."

"So you're a pirate, eh? One of Stavik's, I'm guessing. Don't know why I trusted the old bafter to honor the trade." He leaned over the wheel and glared at Fin. "How many of you are there on board?"

Fin bristled, puffing up his chest. "I'm *part* of *this* crew!" he growled. Marrill was a little taken aback. She knew how much being forgotten bothered Fin. But she wasn't used to him being quite so angry about it.

"Hey!" Remy barked, pointing at Coll. "Eyes on the road, buddy. We've got a junkyard to get through before that devil ship comes after us." Coll slunk back, chastised. Fin started to chuckle but stopped when the babysitter rounded on him. "And you…" Her frown slipped into a puzzled expression. "Um…Marrill's friend. Whoever you are. Yeah. Don't cause trouble. We've got enough of that as it is."

He grumbled under his breath as he stared over the railing. Marrill touched his arm, feeling bad for him. "What happened to the sketches I made of you? The ones I gave Coll and Ardent so they would remember?"

Fin lifted a shoulder but didn't look at her. Instead he focused on the ship graveyard, eyes tracing the carcasses of old hulls as the *Kraken* weaved its way closer to the wall. "Ink fades. Just like memories."

Marrill tried to think of what to say, but she couldn't find the right words. For the first time since returning to the Stream, something felt off—the silence between them uncomfortable in a way it had never been before.

It almost seemed like Fin was mad at *her*, but for what she didn't know. Going home? Not coming back earlier? She bit her lip and glanced at him. The fact that people remembered her?

She leaned her shoulder against his. "Maybe if this Wish Machine thing is real, we can make everything right again."

"Here's hoping," Fin said. "Or should I say, here's wishing?" He waggled his eyebrows.

Marrill couldn't help giggling. It was nice to have her best friend by her side again.

CHAPTER 10
The Grovel and the Great City

As the *Kraken* threaded its way through the floating graveyard, Fin's eyes skimmed each broken hull they passed, looking for the now familiar symbol. He kept the forgettable girl's bracelet close in his pocket, and already he'd developed the habit of tracing its dragon-under-circle outline with his thumb.

The obelisk in the Shattered Archipelago had borne the same symbol; it couldn't be a coincidence. With luck, the answer to what it meant lay ahead.

He shook his head, snapping back to the conversation. Marrill was eagerly explaining to the others what they'd found on the grassberg and about the Wish Machine. "So, do you think it could be real?"

Ardent stroked his beard, looking skeptical. "It's possible, of course," he mused. "In a sense, all magic is just granting wishes—that is, taking the raw potential of the Pirate Stream and forcing it to be the reality you want it to be. But the more you want, the more magic you need to make it real. To *truly* grant a wish, you would need to harness more of the Pirate Stream than any wizard I've ever heard of could manage."

"But it *could* exist, right?" Marrill pressed.

Ardent laughed. "It could, yes. Back in the days when all of creation was still unformed, the Dzane could do such a thing. But the Dzane are long gone." He patted Marrill gently on the shoulder before wandering off.

Fin remembered the word: *Dzane.* The first wizards, who had made the Pirate Stream and the Bintheyr Map to Everywhere. Of course, they'd also made the Lost Sun of Dzannin, which could destroy anything and everything. He wasn't sure he wanted to know what else *they* could do.

Still, the possibility that the Wish Machine might be real caused his heart to flutter. He could tell Marrill felt the same; she grasped the railing next to him, leaning forward as though it would get them to their destination that much faster. "So, do you think it might be somewhere in that city?" she asked him.

"If we believe the obelisk, it's got to be somewhere around here," he said. "And I'd say the fact that there's a city down the whirlpool at the heart of the Shattered Archipelago is a pretty good sign."

She bit her lip and glanced over her shoulder, clearly worried. Behind them the Stream was an empty expanse, the sky above it clear and blue. "If the Master of the Iron Ship doesn't get us first."

Fin shrugged. "In all the stories I've ever heard, the Iron Ship's never been seen in a port. Once we dock, I'm sure we'll be safe." It was a lie, of course; at this point, he didn't know if they'd be safe from that ghost ship *anywhere*. But if it made Marrill feel better, what was wrong with bending the truth a little?

Her shoulders visibly relaxed, and she smiled. "It is pretty neat, huh?" she said, gesturing at their destination.

She was right. The closer they drew to the Wall, the more impressive it became. Its face gleamed in the sun, a brilliant labyrinth of polished stone and sparkling glass and the occasional dull gleam of black metal. The entire city was completely vertical. Buildings atop buildings atop buildings, a patchwork quilt of stacked skyscrapers stretching so far up that the highest towers were practically lost from view.

All across it, the giant gears jutted out like shelf mushrooms growing on an old tree, half visible, half buried in the Wall. Some seemed carved from glass; others were steel and bronze; still others seemed to sag and rise with each breath

of the wind. A few of them stayed motionless, hosting lush, dangling gardens and rows of carefully buttressed buildings.

But most of the gears moved. Some spun so fast they blurred into a whir. Others, so slowly that there were still buildings atop them being ground into the Wall as the gears turned into it. The rubble from those structures tumbled down like waterfalls, only to be caught by long ropes and cranes before they could reach the mass of docks floating below.

Fin realized with a shock that the whole city was sinking. If he looked at one place long enough, he could see the buildings sliding down the face of the Wall, only to be picked apart and carried back to the top again. The city was a maze of motion and commotion, constantly falling, and constantly being rebuilt from the top once more. Only the gears, anchored into the Wall, remained constant.

Fin shook his head. Of all the wild places he'd seen on the Pirate Stream, he'd never come across something so marvelous.

But as they sailed closer, the city didn't look quite so spectacular. As amazing as the higher parts were, the bottom had been picked clean. Fin could make out huge frames where beautiful windows had once been hung, a few shards of colored glass still stuck around the edges. In one place, he saw an outline that had once been a grand marble fresco. All the way down to the waterline—and no doubt beyond—the remains of amazing buildings had been stripped down to bare dullwood supports.

He whistled. "Look at this boneyard."

"Seems like they took all of the good stuff back up," Marrill said, wrinkling her nose.

"This is...wow." Remy's eyes were huge as she took it all in. "I think I need to sit down."

"I know, right?" Marrill beamed. "Don't worry, you'll get used to it." She turned to Fin. "So what now?"

"Exploring?" he offered. "Mayhem? Fun?"

"Escaping from the evil death ship? Solving the mystery of the Iron Tide?" Remy suggested. "And then, I don't know, getting us *home*?"

Marrill seemed to deflate a bit. Fin instantly felt his shoulders sag at the thought of her leaving the Stream. "Right. All that."

"Well," Ardent said, swinging one leg over the railing. "I'm declaring this place Iron Ship–free...for now at least. Let's see what the locals know about this Iron Tide." He paused mid-dismount. "Iron Ship...Iron Tide...oh my. That's a bit of a coincidence. A bit too much of a coincidence..." He trailed off, shook his head, and leapt to the docks.

Marrill brightened. "I'm coming, too!" she chirped, chasing after him.

Remy popped out of her chair so fast it made Fin's head spin. "Oh no you don't. Not without me, anyway. No way you're getting lost again."

Suddenly, she stopped and whirled around. "And there was another one," she muttered. "Marrill, and..." Her eyes landed on Fin. "Umm..."

Fin's heart stopped. She was looking right at him. She *saw* him. He was sure she hadn't remembered him earlier. His pulse quickened. Could everyone from Marrill's world remember him?

"Fin," he offered. "I'm Fin. You…remember me?"

Remy shrugged. "Don't flatter yourself, kid. You don't make an impression. But northern Arizona's best babysitter does *not* lose a kid. There's Marrill plus one—that's all I need to know."

Fin couldn't contain his excitement. Close enough! "All right," he cried. "Let's go exploring!"

A moment later, they were over the railing and plunging into the crowd. The hodgepodge of dullwood walkways and drifting planks buzzed with life and bobbed with every motion of the tide. The docks were a floating city all their own, covered with stalls and huts constructed of whatever scrap was around, and swarming with all sorts of creatures, from tall gangly insects to bowlegged dworks. There were even a few barbarian plantimals, savage and green as they soaked in the sun.

Fin practically strutted as they wormed their way through the throng, thrilled to be even *partway* remembered. He nudged Marrill as he caught sight of a scaly orange head popping out of the crowd on a long, coiled neck. "Check it out! A giraffalisk!"

Ardent had seen it, too; he stopped and rubbed his beard. "Most peculiar," he mused. "The entire giraffalisk population died from a single nasty head cold years ago. Stuffy nose can be fatal when you breathe fire, I understand."

As they made their way toward the Wall, Fin noticed more and more things that seemed out of place. Here was a short, spiny creature sporting the sigil of the now-fallen Khesteresh Empire. There a dark shadow of a woman sat on a bucket, merrily plucking an ancient melody on an even ancienter stringspoon, as if both were brand-new. It was like the creatures here had fallen out of time.

Just then, Marrill jabbed him sharply in the ribs. "Is that . . . ?" Across a narrow gangplank was a squat dollop of a man squished into a chair that was way too small for him, sipping on a long straw as he stared out at the marshes. His bulk overflowed the armrests. But that seemed appropriate, since most of the features on his face overflowed his head.

Fin recognized those too-big features, that too-jutting jaw. "It's Pickled Pate!" he gasped.

The resemblance was unmistakable, but whoever had drawn Pate for those metal plates had been very, very kind. In person, he looked even lumpier. And it was like the word *patchy* had been invented to describe his hair.

It suddenly occurred to Fin that the "Pickled" part of the man's name might come less from a penchant for strong drink than from his strong resemblance to an overgrown pickle.

"Mr. Pate?" Marrill cried, running over to the man. Fin raced to catch up.

Pickled Pate looked up at them from his seat. "Ayup," he said. He licked his hand, then smoothed it over the few tufts of hair sprouting from his temples. "That'd be me." With a grunt, he tried to push himself up. But the chair, wedged as it was, didn't seem to want to budge from his behind.

After a few more heaves, Pate gave in and rocked back down onto the dock. "Pleased ta make ya howsits." He held out his hand. A thick web of spit still glistened between his outstretched fingers. "Who are ya ta be?"

Unfortunately, Fin had forgotten how quickly Marrill could think on her feet. She made a curtsying motion and fluttered backward, like it was all part of the same movement, leaving Fin between her and their new friend. "I'm Marrill. This is Fin. You should definitely meet him first."

Before Fin could do anything about it, Pate's slimy paw slapped against his palm. "Ah, pardon, young man. Didn't even recognize thar was two of ya." Fin gave him a halfhearted smile and slipped his hand away. The slime smelled like asparagus.

Fin glared at Marrill, who struggled valiantly to keep her grin in check. "So," Fin said, "you *are* Pickled Pate? As in 'The Colloquy of Pickled Pate'?"

"Blathersnabble!" Pate snapped. He pushed himself back, rocking the chair on two legs. "I ne'er been a fan of ka-lilly tea, and whoever told ye diff'rent's a filthy liar."

"No, no, my good man-thing," Ardent said, stepping forward with a swish of his robes. "*Colloquy*. What this . . . young man?" He cocked an eye in Fin's direction as if confirming.

"Young man! What this young man is saying is that you seem to be the main character in a rather aged story."

"Ah," Pate said, like that cleared it up. "And yer ta be?"

Ardent pull himself up straight. "I am the great wizard Ardent." He swept into a bow. "Perhaps you have heard of me?"

Pate struggled against his chair, but it stayed firmly glued to his posterior. He leaned forward, peering at Ardent. "Anope," he said. The wizard deflated slightly. Fin suppressed a giggle.

"We read your poem," Marrill added quickly. "We came here looking for the Iron Tide you talked about!"

Pate rubbed his nose vigorously as he considered the statement. "Anope twice. Ya must have the wrong Pickled Pate. Poemin's not really my style. An I ain't heard of no Iron Tide, I fear."

"But...you went to the place where the water bends, right?" Fin tried. "The Shattered Archipelago?"

Pate scratched at his chin and then scraped his nails clean on his teeth. Fin stifled a shudder. "Tha's how I got yere, sure's stuff."

"And then you saw it coming at creeping stride," Marrill continued. "The doom what fears you, the Iron Tide?"

Pate licked his palm, running it over his head again. "That's where ya lose me. Though I do like yer rhymin'."

Fin furrowed his brow. It did seem impossible that this could be the same person—after all, the metal plates were thousands of years old. But then, what were the odds of there being two Pickled Pates, at the same odd place, getting here the same odd way, and having the same oddly shaped nose?

Ardent leaned in, inspecting the swollen little man. "How long have you been here in…this place…?"

"The Grovel?" Pate offered, looking around the docks. "Or are ya meanin' Monerva proper?" He gestured up at the walled city.

"Monerva," Fin and Marrill breathed as one. *Like the Syphon of Monerva.*

Pate shrugged. "'Sbeen a bit. Long 'nough that I've had ta sell off mosta ma ship as scrap. But I still got a few good solid chunks left out there." He pointed to an arch of timber, nearly sunken in the marsh. "I'd say I've another few weeks afore I'm driftwood proper. But don' bother a feller too much. We's all trapped here together, ain't that right?"

"Oh dear," Ardent said. He twittered his fingers.

"Oh no," Marrill breathed.

Fin glanced up at the gargantuan city above them, its turning gears, its ever-falling debris. "Um," he said. Apparently no one else was going to ask. "*Is* that right?"

Pate slapped his knee, struggling to stand with the chair still wedged on his behind. He spread his arms wide. "A'course it's right. I reckon you folk are new arrivals, huh?"

They all nodded.

"Well, welcome to Monerva," he said. "Hope ya like it. Bein' as how ya can't never leave."

CHAPTER 11
A Reunion (About Time)

Little bubbles of dread floated up through Marrill's gut like fizz in a soda. "What does that mean, 'never leave'?" Remy asked beside her. "That doesn't mean, like, 'never leave,' right? That's, like, weird-person talk for 'have a pleasant stay,' right?"

"Nah, means you're here forever," Pate croaked. "Anyways, nice makin' yer acquaintance and what for, but if you don't mind, I *was* in the middle of some good water-staring." He jammed a finger at the marshes. Without another word, he popped his chair up and swiveled away from them on one rickety leg.

"Oh," Ardent said, "of course. How rude of us."

"Hold on." Remy planted her hands on her hips. "Just wait a second. We're here forever?" But no one answered. The only sounds were the groan of the sinking city and the bustle of the crowd.

Marrill gulped. Forever was an awfully long time.

Ardent reached over to Coll and squeezed the young captain's shoulder where the end of his knotted-rope tattoo peeked out above the collar of his shirt. "We'll figure it out, my friend."

The expression on Coll's face was startlingly severe. He sighed and mumbled something about heading back to the ship just in case.

"Oh, come on," Fin interjected, breaking the tension. "What does this yokel know?" Pate swiveled back around sharply. Fin pointed to a six-legged centipede of a man who'd just ambled past, tossing his long dreadlocks from side to side. "Can you believe that centipede guy just called you a yokel? Some people."

Pate frowned, muttering something about "more legs than brains."

Marrill shook her head. Sometimes she forgot how easily Fin could get away with stuff. Then again, with Remy hovering over her like a prison guard, it occurred to her that maybe being forgettable wasn't so bad after all.

"He may not have manners," Ardent declared, "but that manipede had a point. The Pickled Pate of legend clearly left Monerva, or there would be no legend of Pickled Pate. Whether our friend here is the same person or not, there is more afoot than he knows."

Pate grunted. "Ah, 'sfair enough. I don't know fer much. Ya *could* try further up the Wall, I reckon. There's smart folks and all up there, I hear. Even a wizard come in just a few weeks ago, and headed up that way."

Ardent clapped his hands. "Another wizard? Why didn't you just say so?" He turned to Marrill and Remy with a huge, satisfied smile. "This is excellent news. We wizards are seekers of knowledge and collectors of secrets. Even the least worthy among us—*cough*StagadortheBald*cough*— would know far more about this place, and I daresay the Iron Tide, than anyone down here."

He turned quickly back to Pickled Pate. "Sir, if you will point us the way upward, we will trouble you no more."

Pickled Pate looked at them suspiciously. Slowly, he pointed one finger toward the sky.

"Oh, for…" Ardent rubbed his forehead. "What I *meant* was, how do we get up the Wall from here?"

Pate clattered in his chair thoughtfully. "Sure, sure. That 'un's easy at least. Only 'un way up the Wall. Someone from up there has ta cast a line down fer ya."

"And how do we get someone to do that?"

Pate considered. "Reckon you go up there and ask."

Marrill scratched the top of her head in troubled confusion. "But how can we go up the Wall to find someone to help us if we have to find someone to help us before we can go up the Wall?"

Pate nodded in sympathy. "Reckon that would be whatcha call a dilemma."

Remy threw up her arms in frustration. "So we really *are* stuck here."

"Lizardwhiskers," said Ardent, ushering them away. "Let's take a closer look before we declare defeat. I'd wager there are thousands of ways up that Mr. Pate here has never even contemplated."

As they neared the Wall, Marrill felt even more like an ant at the base of a skyscraper. Only this skyscraper was more like a jungle gym. It was all sheer boards and stripped wood, the naked bones of the city above, stretching back to the gray stone of the Wall before them. As they watched, it sank eternally into the marshes below.

At the edge of the docks, Ardent studied the swirling water. "Fascinating. It looks like we've found the source of the whirlpool in the Shattered Archipelago. Something beneath this Wall is actually sucking in the Stream!"

"Super," Remy said drily. "The city's thirsty. Now how do we actually climb this thing?"

Fin slapped his hands together as he surveyed the bare

wood. "Let's see, rough surface, plenty of handholds, lots of ledges...yeah, I got this." He cracked his knuckles and nodded to Marrill. She raised an eyebrow.

Without warning, Fin took off. He leapt to the nearest board, then jumped again moments before it hit the waves. Marrill held her breath. His foot barely even landed before he bounced away again, up onto a crossbeam, then tossed himself to a nearby ledge and scrambled across it.

She could see the sweat on his brow as he shimmied up the frame where a window had once been, pounded up a flight of stripped-bare stairs, and leapt heroically over a massive gap. He just barely made it, wrapping his arms around the broken base of a column on the front of a once-majestic building.

Casually, Marrill reached out her hand. Fin took it, still panting, and stepped back onto the dock. For all that effort, he had barely kept pace with the sinking city.

"I repeat," Remy said. "So how do we climb this thing?"

Ardent adjusted his hat. "Hmm...it appears I'll simply have to find a way to contact this other wizard—"

Before he could finish, a loud *WHOMPWHOMP-WHOMP* sound rushed through the air. Something bright and gushy exploded against Ardent's shoulder, showering him in thick orange goo.

"Agh, slimed!" he shouted.

"Or she could find *you*," a voice called from above.

Globs of sludge dripped down Ardent's robe as his eyes grew wide in disbelief. "It can't be," he whispered.

A woman floated down through the air like a whirling dandelion seed on the breeze. She looked just a little older than Marrill's mom, but taller, her limbs long and elegant. Her skin was a deep amber, her dark eyes both serious and gentle over her high cheekbones. Black hair hung in braids down her back. The robe she wore had a high neck and a flowing hem, unlike Ardent's frumpy purple getup. But even so, it left no doubt (if the floating wasn't clue enough): She was a wizard.

Fin leaned toward Marrill. "Do we know her?" he asked under his breath.

With a jolt, Marrill realized that she did. "I think it's..."

"Annalessa," Ardent gasped.

The woman strode toward Ardent, a wide smile breaking across her face. When she reached him, she touched a finger to the goop dripping from his sleeve. It burst into a flock of bright-winged moths, scattering up into the sky.

"You're out of practice," she told him. "You're getting slow."

Ardent's voice came out nearly a whisper. "You're here." And then he grabbed her. The old wizard seemed to melt into her as he pulled her into a tight hug.

⊹⊹ ⊹ ⊹⊹

As they made their way back to the *Kraken*, Ardent explained everything that had happened in a gush, with Marrill, Fin, and even Remy chiming in along the way. From the quest for the Bintheyr Map to Everywhere, to the battle aboard the *Black Dragon*, to Serth's end in the Pirate Stream, right back through their recent encounter with the Iron Ship.

Annalessa stayed silent throughout it all, two lines furrowing the spot between her eyes as the group boarded the *Kraken*. Coll, perched atop the stair to the quarterdeck, stopped inspecting his tattoo and did a double take. Behind Annalessa's back, Ardent gave him a vigorous thumbs-up.

"Took you long enough," the Naysayer grouched, lumbering forward and depositing Karnelius in Marrill's arms. It wasn't like the ornery old beast to hand over Karny so easily.

"Everything okay?" Marrill asked, worry tightening her chest.

The Naysayer's only response was a grunted "Business meeting" as he swung a leg over the railing and rather awkwardly dropped to the floating docks.

Marrill caught Fin's eye. "Did he just say 'Business meeting'?" she mouthed. But he looked just as lost as she was. With a shrug, she lifted her cat to her shoulder and trotted to join the others.

"Serth's gone," Annalessa sighed, sinking onto a chair. "I can't believe it. I failed him."

Ardent waved a hand sharply. "No. I failed you both. I should have listened to you when you told me he'd resurfaced. I should have helped you track him down. I should have tried to save him."

A moment of darkness flitted over Annalessa's eyes as she pressed her lips together. As friendly as they were now, Marrill got the strong feeling that her last meeting with Ardent had not been a pleasant one. "Perhaps," she agreed. "But he was probably too far gone already, if all of this happened in the few months since we last spoke."

Ardent stopped cold. Marrill shifted uncomfortably. As far as she knew, Ardent had been looking for Annalessa for *way* longer than that.

"Months?" Ardent said. "Anna, it's been years!"

Annalessa's eyes flared with surprise. She clicked her fingernails against her teeth, pondering. "No," she said. "It's just been a few months since I told you about the rumors. If you'll recall, I asked you to come help me search for Serth...."

"Years," Ardent said softly. He crouched in front of Annalessa's chair and took her hands in his. "That's how long I've been searching for you. I've scoured half the Stream."

Annalessa seemed shocked by this, but then a smile lit her face. "You have?"

Normally Marrill would have enjoyed the touching moment. But she couldn't. Because something was clearly *very* wrong.

Why would Annalessa think months had passed when it had really been so much longer? Marrill's attention slid to where Pickled Pate sat, seven thousand years old but not looking a day over forty. And hadn't both Fin and Ardent remarked on the supposedly extinct creature ambling around the docks?

"Time is different here," Marrill mumbled, absently running a hand down Karny's back.

The wizards looked at her with amusement. "Beg your pardon?" Ardent said.

Now that she'd said it out loud, it totally made sense. "No, seriously! Time is different here. *That's* why Pickled Pate is still around, even though he should be thousands of years old. That's why Annalessa thinks months have passed when we know years have! This place is, like, out of time."

Everyone stared at her for a long moment. Marrill felt the heat of a blush creeping up her neck and onto her cheeks.

But then Annalessa smiled and let out a rich, deep laugh that made Marrill feel like all was right in the world. "Of course!" she said, popping up to her feet. "Oh, you clever, clever girl! How could I have missed it? The creatures that should be extinct, the people from kingdoms that fell before I was born...that explains it all."

Ardent chuckled. "Yes, I suppose it does."

Coll and Remy exchanged a meaningful glance. "Does it?" Coll asked.

"Quite. If you stop thinking that time moves the same everywhere," the old wizard explained. "Once you enter the whirlpool at the heart of the Shattered Archipelago, it seems, you're on Monerva time."

"Right," Marrill said, getting into it. "Like, for the rest of the Stream, Pickled Pate entered the whirlpool thousands of years ago and left right after. But the guy we met thinks he arrived just a few months ago, and he *still* hasn't left. The same for all the other folks here!"

Remy shook her head in confusion. "Wait…so…a day out on the Stream could be, like, a week here?"

"Perhaps," Annalessa said. "Or a year. Or a decade. Why, time might not even pass on the Stream *at all* while we're in here."

Marrill hugged Karnelius tighter. "And we know we *can* get out, because Pickled Pate does in the legend!"

Annalessa laughed. "Your apprentice is on a roll, old man." This time, the blush totally reached Marrill's cheeks. "Exactly so—if that's the Pickled Pate who sailed in according to legend, then one day, he will sail out again. *All* the sailors here will. And we, my dear, will be with them."

Marrill spun to her babysitter, beaming. "Remy, don't you get it?" From the look she got back, Remy clearly did *not*. "If time doesn't pass here, no one's missing us! We can stay in Monerva as long as we want!"

On the stairs, Coll let out a low growl of disapproval. Remy, oblivious, leaned forward, her voice urgent. "Wait. Seriously? As in, my parents might not even know I'm gone yet? As in, I don't have to freak out about them being worried?"

Ardent shrugged. "Freaking out is a personal decision. I have no idea how time here relates to time elsewhere. But sure. Why not?"

Marrill nodded enthusiastically. "And my parents won't be worried, either!"

"Oh yeah, mine either," Fin interjected. "Because I am also a crew member who has at least one parent, and you all know me and like me, incidentally. Quick question—what about the Iron Ship? I mean, it was *right* behind us when we went in the whirlpool. Doesn't that mean it could still be coming?"

As if to echo the point, a rope from the rigging snapped sharply in a sudden breeze. Light waves lapped in, rocking the docks and the *Kraken* with them. Karny struggled against Marrill's grip. When she set him down he bolted belowdecks. She crossed her arms and shivered, not just because the breeze carried a chill.

"I suppose so," Ardent said. "At any time, really. Why, for all we know, it's already here. Who's to say things happen in the same order here as they do outside?"

Coll coughed and gestured to the marsh around them. "I may be a little slow, but I'm pretty sure we'd have noticed if there were a floating death ship about."

Marrill smiled. At least the sailor still had his sense of humor.

Annalessa tented her fingers together. "Which brings us

to the reason we all came here, myself included. The Iron Tide."

"Oh, right." Marrill slumped back against the mast. She'd been so caught up in being able to stay here without worrying her parents that she'd forgotten why she'd returned in the first place. "Any idea what it might be?"

Annalessa shook her head. "Unfortunately, no. Only that it's mentioned in the Meressian Prophecy, in the very first verse." She took a deep breath and recited:

The Lost Sun of Dzannin is Found Again

And as in the beginning, so it will end.

The ship drowns in the bay.

The guides thought true betray.

The city that slides, the ships collide,

The storm will rise the Iron Tide!

Annalessa stopped there, but Marrill mentally added the last few lines, which she'd left off. *The Key to open the Gate. The Map to show the way. And when Map and Key come together with me, the Lost Sun dawns, the end is nigh!*

"Needless to say," Annalessa continued, "it's deeply troubling that the Iron Tide is so prominently mentioned in the same verse as the Lost Sun." She waved a hand toward the

Wall behind them. "And this would be the city that slides, I'm sure of that. Yet no one here seems to know a thing about the Iron Tide. And now...with this Iron Ship of yours and all this business about the wishy-washiness of time..." She let out a sigh. "I'm afraid more than ever that the Iron Tide may be less something that *is* and more something that *will be*."

"But all that other stuff already happened," Marrill protested. "We already stopped Serth from freeing the Lost Sun. And the Meressian ship sank in the bay of the Khaznot Quay...Rose betrayed us...the Iron Ship and the *Black Dragon* collided...."

Ardent's expression turned grave. "The Iron Ship sank, and yet that did little to stop it from chasing us a few hours ago. Things are not always as they appear, and words often have more than one meaning, young Marrill." He fiddled with the tip of his beard between two fingers. "Pickled Pate and all the others did come home raving of the Iron Tide; I assumed it was something in the past. But the Meressian Prophecy is, well, a prophecy. If no one here knows about it..."

"Then it *will* happen," Annalessa finished. "And it stands to reason the Iron Ship is likely involved, if not the cause."

"Shanks," Fin whispered.

Marrill agreed. The cold metal visage of the Master of the Iron Ship thrust its way into her mind. A being so powerful he had nearly beaten Ardent in a wizards' duel. And now he'd cheated death...if he'd even been alive to begin with. She couldn't imagine what lay behind that cruel, faceless mask. But she was certain anything the Master unleashed would be terrible beyond imagining.

Ardent nodded. "Shanks indeed." He spun around to face them, kicking aside the hem of his robe. "Regardless, I think we know our course of action. Step one, figure out what the Iron Tide is so we can move on to step two, which is figuring out how to stop it. And if that doesn't work, then it's on to Plan B."

Marrill wasn't sure she wanted to ask, but someone had to. "Which is?"

"Figuring out how *we* get out of Monerva without the Iron Tide getting out as well." He straightened, flipping the tip of his floppy purple cap over his shoulder. "But never fear! We now have *two* wizards on the job. And I suspect there are few dangers in the world that *two* wizards can't best. Right, Anna?"

Up until this point, Annalessa's face hadn't lost its eager smile. Now it fell completely flat. So flat, in fact, it gave Marrill the heebie-jeebies. "Let's hope so," Annalessa said. "For the sake of all of us, let's hope so."

CHAPTER 12
Things to Do While Wizards Save the World

Annalessa's apartment danced on long wooden bird-legs, forever hopping and skipping along the edge of one of the great turning gears that jutted out from the Wall. Halfway between the floating docks of the Grovel and the sparkling city above, it was just high enough to look out across the three and a half moons that now rose over the marsh.

Being in the apartment had to be the most amazing experience a kid could ever have, Fin thought. Which made it even more frustrating to be looking up at it from the deck of the *Kraken*.

The wizards had left everyone else behind while they headed up to Annalessa's dancing cabin, supposedly to "find a way to fight off the Master of the Iron Ship," and to "hunt down a solution to the mystery of the Iron Tide." Fin had spent enough time around Ardent to know that was wizard-talk for "stare at old books and rub your chin a lot" and "shout phrases like 'intratemporal contemporaneity'" as though they mean something.

In other words, boring stuff.

Coll apparently understood this, too, because he and Remy, the acting adults-by-designation, had quickly agreed that waiting on the ship was vastly preferable to watching old people read books and argue.

But Fin hadn't planned on sitting around doing nothing while the wizards saved the world. Not with the Wish Machine out there somewhere, and the connection between his mom and the weird circle-mountain-dragon symbol left unknown. *He'd* planned on sneaking off into the city the second no one was looking to hunt down answers. And being stuck on the *Kraken* made that plan way harder.

It was time, he decided, for a jailbreak.

He made his way over to where Marrill lounged in a hammock strung between two masts. Karny was curled in her lap, and her sketchbook was propped on her knees, the pages filled with details from the Wall stretching above them. Somehow, with only candlelight and the glow of the Stream to draw by, she'd managed to capture the chaos of it all. The workers pulling apart buildings, the gears spinning, all of it constantly sinking.

She was an amazing artist. But right now, the pencil lay limp in her hand. And from the way she stared at the Wall forlornly, he knew her thoughts were in the same place as his. He slipped closer, a grin stretching across his face.

"Sooo..." he said. "Who's up for tracking down a wish machine? Anyone, anyone? No one? Nobody at all?"

Marrill pushed her sketchbook aside. "Oooh, me!" she said. "I do! Choose me!" Excitement lit her eyes. But then she fell back with a sigh, pulling Karny onto her stomach. "Not that we *can*. We don't even know where to start looking."

Fin laughed. He was way ahead of her. "Sure we do. We'll just use a little something called, I don't know, the *Bintheyr Map to Everywhere*?"

Marrill twirled Karnelius's tail through her fingers. "I wish. Ardent will never let us borrow it. He's supersensitive about that whole 'capable of ending the world' thing."

Fin smirked, loving how well she'd set him up. "He totally won't *let* us borrow it," he agreed. He quickly checked around to make sure the coast was clear.

Remy and Coll sat together on the bow, her tongue caught between her teeth as Coll taught her basic sailing knots by the lantern light. Over on the gangplank, the

Naysayer seemed to have organized some kind of black-market salvage operation, and was greedily collecting a small mountain of junk from the marshes. Everyone was completely engrossed.

Fin nudged Karnelius aside and snagged Marrill by the arm, tugging her around to the other side of the mast. With a flourish, he shoved one hand deep into his thief's bag and pulled out a crystal star. With the other, he produced a tightly rolled piece of parchment. "Good thing I didn't ask."

"The Map!" Marrill squeaked. "The Key! You stole them!"

Fin bowed, trying to look humble even as his chest puffed with pride. "No need for the bravos and the thanks and all that tralada. I'm a thief; it's what I do."

She leaned around the mast, eyes darting toward the front of the ship. Worry pinched her forehead. "Fin!" she whispered harshly. "You can't just take stuff!"

"Sure I can!" Fin laughed. He tossed the Key up in the air between them, then whirled around to snag it behind his back.

Marrill gave him a strangely serious look. "That's not what I meant," she said. "I meant you *shouldn't* just take stuff. Like, it's wrong to take stuff that isn't yours. You know?"

Fin squinted at her. He didn't know. His whole life, he'd taken stuff that wasn't his. *Nothing* was his. How else was he supposed to get anything? Besides, it wasn't like he ever took stuff people really *needed*.

"Look," he told her. "Things only belong to you because

other people treat them like they belong to you. The Map doesn't *belong* to Ardent. He didn't have it until you showed up yesterday. And he didn't even know the Key still *existed*. Why does he get to say what happens with them now?"

Marrill screwed up her face. "I don't know...."

"Okay, fine," Fin said, stamping his feet on the deck. "Stealing is bad for some crazy reason. But we don't have to steal them. They're already stolen!" He jangled them in front of her face.

Marrill tried to look away, but her eyes kept drifting back. He pressed his advantage. "Look, don't you want to *do* something? I mean, this is important work! If we find the Wish Machine, we can *wish* the Iron Tide away! And wish the Iron Ship gone..." He leaned in, knowing what would convince her the most. "And you could wish for your mom to get better...."

Her eyes went wide, misting with tears. She swallowed thickly and then nodded. "Okay. Fine. I mean, since they're already stolen and all. And, I mean, we are kind of here on an awesome timeless adventure. It's not like my parents are expecting me home anytime soon."

She leaned forward. "But you have to promise we'll give them back right after."

"Oh, promise," Fin said, as though that had been his plan all along. Which wasn't *entirely* untrue.

He grabbed a lantern and crouched before she could change her mind. With a flick of his wrist, he unfurled the

Map. While Marrill poked her head around the mast again to make sure no one could see them, Fin slipped his fingers between the familiar rays of the crystal sun. Carefully, he touched the Key to the face of the Map.

"Okay, Map," he whispered. "Show us how to find the Wish Machine!"

Immediately, the paper burst to life. A surge of energy flowed through and around him, catching his senses on fire. He caught the sweet cherry scent of the color red, felt the taste of salt prickling along his skin. The world rushed at him, rolling like seasickness as images zoomed across the Map, blending together as they went.

Finally, the blur resolved, and he found himself looking at the Wall, a view from the water, all in dark ink. He recognized the *Kraken*, bobbing at the base of the city, the mountains to either side. The vastness of Monerva stretched high above.

The picture tilted, then zoomed up the Wall so quickly he felt his belly turn sour. It finally came to a stop, focusing in on the crooked tower on the very top. Dark smudges of ink fluttered all around it.

Fin examined the scene for a moment, then nodded. "Crazy, creepy, slightly dangerous. Yep, looks like the place *I'd* stash a wish machine."

Marrill put a finger to her nose in thought. "Totally. But how do we get all the way up there? Someone has to throw a line down, remember?"

He glanced up, searching for the answer. From above, the distant tinkling of wind chimes filtered down over the creak of the docks and the groan of the falling city. All about, the Stream was a firefly's belly, soft and yellow in the night. He watched the lines of the current carrying it in, though where the water went once it reached the Wall, he couldn't say.

"Too bad we don't have that grassberg anymore," Marrill muttered. "We could climb on, have Ropebone toss it into the air, and float all the way up."

Just like that, inspiration smashed into Fin. He flashed her a wily grin. "Ropebone could toss us, you say?"

Marrill shook her head. "Oh no. I see where you're going with this."

"Why have a line thrown down," he whispered, "when you can throw a line *up*?"

She held out her hands. "No way—we'll crash against the Wall and die."

"I've got my skysailing jacket," Fin offered. "I could just glide on down gently...."

She crossed her arms. "And what about me? Sure, you'll be fine. You're *always* fine. But where's my jacket, huh?" She stopped. "Wait a second," she said. "I think I've got an idea. Stay right here."

With that, she darted out onto the main deck and let loose a furious yawn. "Well," she said loudly, "I think I'll grab some sheets and blankets and turn in on the deck tonight. How cool to sleep under the Wall, huh, Remy?"

Remy looked up. "What? Yeah, sure, that's fine. Just stay on the ship, okay? I swear, Marrill, if you even *think* about putting a foot on those docks, I will skin you and wear you as a scarf. Got it?"

"I solemnly promise I will not set foot on the docks," Marrill said. Fin tried not to giggle too loudly. She was telling the truth. No way were they touching those docks. Now, the giant gears hundreds of feet above them—that was a different story.

"And that goes for your plus one, too!" Remy added. Fin felt himself blush as he caught hold of one of the ship's ropes. It was weird to have someone talking about him. Even if Remy didn't know *him*, exactly.

A few moments later, Marrill reappeared carting a carefully folded sheet. "Got it," she said. "Ready when you are."

"And away we go!" Fin grinned and handed her a rope. "We'll have to aim for one of the gears. Otherwise, we'll just sink right back to the marsh. But make sure you overshoot them, so we have room to glide down." He checked the strings in his jacket sleeves with his fingers. "Oh, and you'll have to give the command. Ropebone always forgets me."

Marrill cocked her head. "Aim for a gear, overshoot it. Got it. Ready, Ropebone?" she whispered. "Fling both of us when I say, and make it high!"

Fin felt the rope go tight in his hand. Overhead, the Ropebone Man squealed.

"Now!" she cried. With a jerk, they were lifted off their

feet. And then they were zipping through the air so fast Fin was pretty sure he'd left his stomach behind on the *Kraken*.

"What the—" Coll shouted.

Remy's voice grew distant as the docks fell away. "Marrill Aesterwest, I will hunt yoooooooooooo . . ."

The Wall zoomed toward them. The ropes fell away. They were up, arcing higher. They passed the gear where Annalessa's cabin danced; he caught sight of Ardent's purple cap bobbing furiously through the candlelit window.

Higher, higher.

Marble now dotted the wood of the Grovel. People dangled like puppets to pluck it off before the buildings dropped too far. Fin let out a laugh of triumph and waved as they rocketed past.

Higher, higher.

Gravity snatched at them. Another gear passed. They were slowing.

Starting to fall.

Fin fumbled with the strings of his skysails. Marrill's face twisted in terror beside him. She struggled to throw out her big silk sheet, puffing it up behind her as a giant parachute. Even so, they were hurtling toward the Wall at an unhealthy speed. At this rate they would hit it and plummet to their deaths.

This plan had gone terribly wrong.

"Aim for one of the gears!" he cried as he fumbled for the climbing knives tucked into the back of his belt. He pulled them free just as he clipped the corner of a roof and tumbled through a wide gap where a building had once stood.

Nothing but an expanse of smooth gray stone loomed. He'd completely misjudged; he was coming in too fast, and too high. He smacked against the Wall with enough force to knock the wind from his lungs. Still, he had the presence of mind to swing the knives, slamming them against the stone.

A shock of impact traveled up his arms, spreading through the rest of his limbs until his entire body vibrated from the force of it. Yet his blades barely even scratched the Wall's surface.

He slid downward, landing with a thump on a massive gear jutting out like a shelf below. A moment later, Marrill landed gracefully next to him. Her cheeks were flushed and her eyes bright with excitement as she pulled the makeshift parachute down behind her.

"That was *so* amazing! Can you believe—" She cut herself off. Frowning, she tilted her head, listening. "Do you—"

Fin nodded before she even finished. He heard it, too. At first he'd thought it was blood rushing through his ears, or maybe even the gear turning slowly beneath them. But the sound grew and grew until he realized that it wasn't in his head after all.

"What is that?" Marrill shouted. A rising wind washed down over them. It came with a *whumpwhump* sound, like an oncoming stampede. A stampede charging down the Wall, straight at them.

"Whatever it is, it's not a parade of puppies. Let's get out of here!" He pushed to his feet.

Marrill was already retreating across the wide surface of the gear.

Fin made the mistake of looking up as he chased after her. The lights of the city above them had vanished into darkness. The air beat with the sound of a hundred birds flapping. The darkness overhead *writhed*.

"Faster!" he cried. But it was too late. He could see them now.

They were blacker than black, flapping and crawling. Long, spindly fingers raked the air instead of wings. They were like shadow puppets cast from the hands of someone who couldn't decide whether to make a bat or a spider.

Fin threw his arms wide. They were coming too fast. All he could do was hope to hold them back so Marrill had time to escape.

He scrunched his eyes shut and braced as the swarm engulfed him.

CHAPTER 13
The Most Fun You'll Ever Have Dangling from a Snail

F
in!" Marrill cried as the creatures washed over him.
She reached for him. And then they were on her, too.
She was enveloped in darkness. A thousand hands
climbed across her body; ten thousand fingertips fluttered
against her skin. At the touch of each one, she felt her flesh
rippling like liquid.

Visions poured into her mind, memories complete with
taste and sound. At first they were her own—a picnic with

her parents, a tribal dance in the Brazilian Amazon. But then they were unfamiliar; then *she* was someone else.

Two-faced men in shimmersilk robes twirled with chittering beetle maidens, their shells inlaid with gems and gold. The smell of roasted butterbeast filled the air. It was a joyous day. For today, the Boundless Plains were united.

More memories came, memories she knew belonged to others. So many they overwhelmed her. They filled every thought, cut off everything about her.

The King and the Dawn Wizard walked together through the Dangling Garden, admiring the way the sunferns reflected up into the sky. The King had to admit, he hadn't expected the Wizard to be so small. All eyebrows and whiskers, like a kitten caught in the rain. Could he trust such a creature?

"Wishes are great things, O King," the Wizard chirped. "But for every wish made real, a thousand possibilities must be ended. Are you ready to end a world you've never seen before?"

The King breathed deep, the smooth scent of morning dew setting his nerves at ease. "Can you make it?" he asked again.

Marrill stumbled backward. The images, the *moments*, rushed over and past her like a waterfall. She felt her foot teetering on the edge of the gear.

The builder balanced on the edge of a girder, far in the air. One day, they said, this wall would be big enough to keep all of the Boundless Plains safe from the Pirate Stream.

His master held up a tube of odd, shiny glass. "The Stream water'll flow in through this stuff," she said. "So we'll be using a lot of it. Don't know how it works myself, but that wizard says it's better than dullwood."

The builder waited until she wasn't looking, then horked a glob of spit over the side, just to watch it fall.

Marrill reeled. The turning gear buckled beneath her. She clawed at the air, trying to regain her balance. The builder's nasty spit wasn't falling—she was!

"Help!" she yipped.

And then a long arm slung around her waist, and she was flying. Or rather, she realized belatedly, she was swinging. Out and away, like a weight on the end of a pendulum.

"Gotcha!" an unfamiliar voice said in her ear. It was low and mellow, with just a bit of an accent. "Hold on tight, now."

Marrill didn't need to be told twice. She grabbed on to anything she could reach. She felt buckles, and rough cloth, and something spongy, like rubber, as she threw her arms around her rescuer. "Wh-what were those things?" she stammered, her skin still crawling at the memory of the bat-like creatures sweeping over her, their legs dancing across her skin.

"Wiverwanes," her rescuer said as she stretched a rope of green jelly around Marrill's waist and cinched it tight. "Newcomer, you must be. Don't see too many of you up here." The woman reached up and tugged on the line above them that stretched impossibly high into the sky. Slowly, they started rising. "Normally," she continued, "they stay up in their tower, and only come out when folks scratch the Wall. Up and carry them away to the *other* side."

The way she said the phrase "*other* side," Marrill knew it wasn't good. "Thank you for saving me," she managed. Her voice came out strained and raspy. She swallowed and tried not to look down.

Out of the corner of her eye, she caught a glimpse of her rescuer's profile. The woman's skin was smooth and gray, but something about the arrangement of her features was off. It was the nose, Marrill realized. It seemed to jut out at an odd angle.

"Ah, happy to do it," her rescuer replied, turning toward her. "Wasn't much worth scrounging left on those buildings anyway."

Marrill blinked and tried not to stare. The woman had two faces, split by a deep cleft down the middle. Two noses pointed away from each other, two chins moved two mouths that met and became one in the middle. An eye looked out from each side, with a third in the center.

"Name's Slandy, by the way," she continued. "Good thing for you I was prospecting just above you when the

Wiverwanes came, eh? You're lucky they didn't take you. Didn't see anyone else there, so I guess they were just passing through."

Something about what Slandy said caused Marrill's thoughts to pile up on one another. She frowned, the flood of stolen memories clogging her head and making it hard to focus on what had really happened. Something about scratching the Wall. She hadn't scratched the Wall. But...

Her stomach dropped. "Fin!" she gasped. In the confusion and the falling and the excitement, she'd forgotten him.

"Pardon?" asked Slandy.

"My friend," she explained urgently. "He was on the gear with me."

Slandy shot her a dubious glance, but slung them back down anyway. When they reached the gear, there was no sign of him. Marrill's chest tightened.

"Lose something?" Fin casually leaned on a sinking portico as it dropped into view. Judging by the sweat on his brow, he'd been trying to climb the buildings after her. Which made Marrill feel even worse about leaving him behind.

She breathed a sigh of relief. "You're okay!"

He grinned. "Always."

"Sorry, kid," Slandy said, "didn't mean to take your friend away without telling you. Just didn't catch sight of you." She raised her chins to the sky. "But look at me jawing, when there's a party coming down the Wall tonight! The missus will be wondering where I got off to." She reached up to tug on her line, then paused. "Climb on if you're comin'."

Less than a minute later, Fin was strapped awkwardly next to Marrill, his face pressed so hard into Slandy's shirt he could scarcely speak. Their feet dangled free in the open air as the green line hauled them up and Slandy played tour guide.

"We call this the Chimes!" she shouted, as the tinkling they'd heard below grew to the deafening sound of church bells. All about, a hundred little gears stuck out from the Wall at random. They were strung like chandeliers with dangling crystals, all clattering and banging against each other. The ones that were turning dashed their crystals against the Wall as they moved, shattering them into a waterfall of tinkling glass. Marrill pressed her palms against her ears to drown out the noise.

"Oversleep, and the Chimes'll wake you before you sink too far," Slandy said once they'd passed the din. "Not that you'll have a lot of time left to do much about it. More'n likely you'll end up stuck in the Grovel with the rest of the driftwood anyway. Best rule of Monerva: Don't oversleep."

As they rose farther, the city grew more and more intact, and more and more inhabited. Pipes filled with Stream water weaved through the buildings, lighting them up with a warm, gentle glow. Marrill scarcely saw wood anymore, just polished stone and cold glass. Even here, though, cranes moved to dismantle the biggest and nicest pieces and carry them higher up the Wall.

"That's the Gallery of Lost Kingdoms," Slandy said, pointing at a big shell of a building that jutted out beside them. "A bit far down this season, but I'm sure they'll raise it back up soon enough."

Marrill couldn't help but shudder at the jagged black iron that ran across its roof. It reminded her all too much that the Master was still out there, sailing in across the tides of time.

"Faffilating," Fin murfled against their host's chest. Marrill patted his hand to let him know she heard him. Even if she couldn't quite *understand* him.

They threaded through hollow gears as they rose, passing gardens that hung like moss from silver trellises, and marble arches that reached outward to gather starlight. Glass fountains swiveled as they dropped, sending little curlicues of glowing Stream water dancing through the air.

"But how does it all work?" Marrill asked. A needle-pointed tower went by. Someone had balanced another building on its peak, and more and more buildings were jumbled on top of that. "I mean, everything's sinking! How does anyone, you know…not sink?"

"Get higher, you mean?" Slandy said. "Oop, one side." She swung them gently, just as what looked like a full restaurant, still serving dinner, came flying up past them, hauled by five separate cranes. "It's easy! You just grab what you can get, build it as high as you can go, then scrabble up on top of that pile before it all drops away again. You build your own way, by the sweat of your brow!"

Marrill thought for a moment. That didn't seem terribly possible, given the way they were currently traveling. "But...how do you get up in the first place?" she asked. "I mean, don't you have to have someone haul you up?"

They passed an open-air market where all the shops hung down from poles stuck into the city above them. Glass pathways snaked up and down through the air, connecting one to the next.

Slandy shrugged. "Well, sure. But that's because you bring up stuff for them. And then *they* get higher, and pull you along with them. And eventually *you* start pulling people up, and they start bringing *you* stuff. The higher you are, the higher you can get, and the more people you can pull up after you. And that's the way *everyone* gets to the top."

"But...the whole thing's sinking," Marrill pointed out again.

Slandy nodded thoughtfully. "All the more reason to haul up as much as you can!"

Marrill was sure this made sense, even if she didn't quite see how. "And...what about the people *all* the way down in the Grovel? Everything's gone by the time it gets to them."

"Well, they should have thought of that before they went and started at the bottom." Slandy swung them to one side again. In the space where they'd just been, a rising piano nearly collided with a falling flagpole. Before Marrill could respond, Slandy wrapped one big arm around them. "End of the line coming. Get ready!"

Just above them was a giant shell the size of a cement mixer. It moved like one, too, its contours spiraling in on themselves in brightly colored patterns that shifted and glowed. Squishy green ropes, just like the one that held them, sprang out from round holes up and down its sides and stretched off down the Wall.

"Atta girl," Slandy said, smacking the base of it as they came within reach. With one leg, she hauled them onto a makeshift scaffolding built across the creature's back. Deftly, the Monervan unlatched her belts, popping Fin and Marrill free. The squishy rope retracted from around her waist and shot back into the shell with a slurp.

Slandy pulled a lumpy piece of purple fruit from a bag at her waist. "Thanks, old girl," she said, tossing it into the air. A warm, gooey tongue licked past Marrill's cheek, leaving a trail of slime as it snagged the fruit. A dozen eyes flashed behind the mouth, before the entire head retreated into the shell.

She wiped away the slime on her cheek, and stared at the glistening goop. "Um, this isn't going to make me grow feathers, is it?" It wouldn't have been the first time that had happened after all.

Slandy laughed. "Nah. She's just an old levator snail,

harmless as she can be." She patted the big creature. "She'll keep us riding high, long as we're on her."

Marrill glanced around. While the city was sliding downward as fast as ever, *they* weren't. The snail was currently scaling the front of a house, climbing up the Wall at the exact same rate the building fell.

"Whoa," she breathed. Now that she knew what to look for, she could see hundreds more snails scattered across the top third of Monerva. Lines reached down from all of them, and workers like Slandy hung at the ends. They swarmed over the face of the city, stripping down the buildings by the light of lanterns. They were, Marrill thought, like a school of glow-in-the-dark piranhas stripping a cow to the bone. But she felt bad about making the comparison. She had swum with piranhas before, and they were *way* more discriminating than the Monervans.

She turned back to their own snail and bent to get a closer look. "Aren't you pretty?" she whispered. She'd always been a sucker for animals. "What's her name?"

Slandy shrugged. "Name? Don't think anyone's ever given one to a levator snail."

Marrill frowned. For all the work these creatures did, she couldn't believe they didn't get *named*. "Well, we're fixing that right now." She crouched, resting a hand against the shell and petting it lightly. "A name for a levator snail. Hmmm...Beatrix?" The creature didn't react. Marrill bit her lip, running names through her head.

Then it came to her. "Elle!" she declared in triumph. "Elle the levator snail! It's perfect!" The creature's big tongue came out and swiped up her cheek. Marrill took that as confirmation. "Elle it is!" She stood up. "Slandy, can I have a fruit?"

The Monervan looked back at her in amusement. "Sure, kid." She tossed one of the purple things to Marrill, who fed it to Elle with glee. "Seems like you've made a friend," their guide remarked. "She'll remember you for life, I'd wager. Levators are nothing if not loyal."

Slandy strode to the edge of the platform, leaping straight onto the roof of a sinking house. "Time to be off," she called over her shoulder. "Have to meet the missus; wouldn't want to be late for the party."

Marrill glanced at Fin, who seemed to have the same thought she did, because they both scrambled after her. "Wait," Marrill called. "Can we ask you a question?"

"Sure," Slandy responded. She didn't slow as she made her way across a series of interwoven glass beams, which stretched between the gap where an impressive tower must once have stood.

"Have you ever heard of the Syphon of Monerva?" Marrill asked.

Slandy paused halfway up a ladder, her right face giving them a strange look. Then she burst out laughing. Marrill's cheeks heated and she shifted, uncomfortable.

"A'course!" the Monervan said. "Where did you think you were?"

Fin and Marrill exchanged confused frowns. Right now, it looked like they were on a roof that was in the process of being dismantled. "Pardon?"

"Oh, well...hang on." Slandy glanced around, then leapt from her ladder onto the wide surface of a passing gear. She waved for them to follow. The gear rotated at a decent clip, and they had to walk to keep from being dashed against the Wall. With Slandy being over eight feet tall, what was a slow saunter for her was more like a gallop for Marrill.

"If you want to be technical-like, *this* is the Syphon of Monerva." Slandy stamped her foot against the gear. "Part of it, anyways. The Wall is part of the great machine, you know. Least the gears are. The actual wall part is rock. But I suppose what *you* want to know is where the wishes get made. And I'm afraid no one knows *that.*"

Marrill looked around, careful to keep her pace up. "This whole thing was the Wish Machine? Any idea how it works?"

"All I know is what anyone knows. Water gets sucked in. Gears turn. More water comes in, more gears turn. It was all pretty regular for a while, though it's been speeding up the last couple years, which is a bit hard on the folks what built atop 'em. Can't help but be a good thing, though, I reckon." Slandy shrugged. "Beyond that, you'd have to ask the Dawn Wizard; he's the one who built it."

Fin tugged Marrill's sleeve. "Hey, didn't Ardent say something about it taking a whole lot of Stream water to grant wishes?" he whispered. "That must be what's happening! The Syphon sucks in Stream water to turn it into wishes."

Marrill nodded eagerly. But her steps slowed as she was drawn back to the strange memory the Wiverwanes had given her. *The King and the Dawn Wizard walked together through the Dangling Garden. "Wishes are great things, O King," the Wizard chirped. "Are you ready to end a world you've never seen before?"*

"So, can we? Talk to the Dawn Wizard, I mean?" Marrill asked, sprinting to catch up.

Again, Slandy laughed. "Course not! He was Dzane, that one—a powerful and tricky bunch, they say, and the Dawn Wizard was the last of 'em. Hasn't been heard from since he made the place."

Marrill's heart raced. The Syphon had been built by one of the Dzane. The only beings, according to Ardent, who might be powerful enough to make a machine that could grant wishes. It was the last bit of confirmation she needed. The Wish Machine was real.

"And even if 'twere possible," Slandy continued, "I wouldn't recommend it. He's a trickster, that one. 'S why it's taken so long for the Salt Sand King to get his final wish." She reached out, wrapping a hand around a trellis that had slid within reach.

"Last question," Fin said, surging forward. "Has anyone else ever found the Syphon and made a wish? Is it possible?"

Slandy glanced around, clearly wondering where he'd come from. "Far as I know, no one's ever tried." She stepped off the gear and started to climb.

"Why not?" Fin called.

She looked back, eyeing them both for a long time. "Who wants to go fooling with Dzane magic? As the old saying goes, 'To get what you want, you must give what you have,' and who's to say the getting is worth the giving? Legend has it, our King was given three wishes, and three noble wishes he made. Two came true. Ever since, the Boundless Plains have been lost and burning, and Monerva's been cut off from the Stream."

She went back to climbing. "Wishes are tricky things is all I'm saying. And that's what happened when a good smart fella like the Salt Sand King used the Machine. He was the one what ordered it built in the first place. Who knows what would happen to you or me?"

She slung her leg over a railing. "Now let's party." And with that, the Monervan disappeared out of sight.

CHAPTER 14
That One Dream Where You're Falling

A thrill of excitement shot through Fin as he leapt onto the trellis. He held out a hand for Marrill. "Did you hear that?" he asked as she joined him.

"Yeah," she said, struggling to catch her breath. "Ominous."

Fin shook his head, laughing. "Everyone thinks everything's ominous. I think it's just confirmation we're on the right path."

She looked at him quizzically, so he explained as he climbed. "Now we know for sure that the Syphon exists and that it grants wishes. The Salt Sand King got his, right? Most of them at least. Who's to say about that last wish anyway? I bet he just wished to get out of here and never looked back."

On top of the trellis, they found themselves in the midst of a massive party, already in full swing. The timing couldn't have been more perfect. "Come on," he said. "This is something to celebrate. There's a real honest Wish Machine right here!"

Even though night had fallen across Monerva, the grand terrace was lit up as bright as daytime. Pipes filled with glowing Stream water weaved everywhere: through the glass underfoot, along the railings, even overhead, splitting into branches like the limbs of a tree.

Music swirled from every direction. Some of the instruments made the air heavy, almost solid, so that you had to wade through it, kicking aside chord progressions along the way. Others were more taste than sound, causing Fin's tongue to tingle. All around them, split-faced Monervans danced and laughed as the broad terrace dropped slowly down the Wall.

"Whoa," Marrill said, eyes wide as she took it in. "This is crazy. What do you think they're celebrating?"

Fin gave her a wink. "Let's find out." Before she could stop him, he bounded on top of a nearby table crowded with Monervans. He swiped a mug from the hand of a rather surprised-looking creature with glowing hair, then bounced away before the owner could do anything about it. With a shout, he held the mug up high. "A toast, everyone, all together now!" he bellowed. "Here's to . . ."

The Monervans around the table raised their glasses. "To the turn of the gears!"

"Here's to the turn of the gears!" Fin echoed, egging them on. *"Because..."*

"When the last gear turns, the King gets his final wish!" they cried, lifting their mugs even higher.

"And Monerva returns to the Stream, and the King reigns over all the lands!" said one particularly wobbly-looking man.

Fin knocked back whatever was in the mug, cringing at the sweetly bitter taste. The crowd around him cheered. He danced a little jig, just to show off a bit.

After a huge bow, he dropped back to the ground next to Marrill. She was laughing, her eyes bright, and it made him warm inside to know he'd been the cause of her happiness. "There you have it," he told her. "Gears turn, King gets his last wish, everyone gets back to the Stream."

A bit of worry crept back into her expression. "So that's how everyone returns to the Stream, huh? The Salt Sand King's final wish." She tapped her fingers against her mouth, thinking. All around, the Monervans wheeled into a raucous dance, singing.

The Salt Sand King made Wishes Three

Who knows what his wish will be?

One for an army that never falls

Two for strength to bring peace to all

Three for everyone to be free

Turn those gears, let wish three be!

Fin's belly growled. He glanced around and spotted a woman carting two bowls of green stew nearby. With a quick step, he dodged in front of her and swiped them. Then he ducked behind her and dodged back out again, sweeping the bowls behind his back. "He went thataway," he said, giving her his most innocent eyes. The woman growled and pushed her way through the crowd after the nonexistent thief.

Once she was out of sight, Fin presented a bowl to Marrill with a "Tralada!"

She sighed, but took it. "You shouldn't steal, you know."

"So you keep telling me," he replied with a grin. Then he took a deep sip of the soup. It exploded across his tongue with sharp flavors that made him gulp it even faster.

"You're not going to be able to do that anymore once you're memorable," Marrill told him as she took a cautious taste.

"Why not?" he asked.

She shrugged. "You just can't. When people remember you, they get opinions that are hard to change. You have to worry about what folks are thinking all the time."

Fin's expression turned serious. "No, you don't. You be yourself—if they don't like you for it, they're not worth your time." And then he grinned. "Case in point—you can remember me just fine, and you seem to think I'm all right."

She shook her head, but didn't argue. "I wish I could be like you sometimes. Doing whatever I want, going on great adventures. Sailing the Stream."

Fin took another deep gulp. He braced himself, unsure how to say the next bit. So he just spat it out. "You could, you know. Just stay on the Pirate Stream." He tried to make it sound like a joke, but he couldn't keep the earnestness out of his voice.

Next to them, several snail lines dropped down, snatched a segment of the terrace, and hauled it up into the sky. It did little to stop the party; the people on board continued with their revelry, even as the terrace swayed under their weight.

"If I don't get my wish," Marrill said, her voice cracking, "maybe I *will* stay here forever."

Fin didn't miss how troubled she sounded. Deep down inside, he knew that would never happen. Sure, they had to stop the Iron Tide and save the Stream from . . . whatever. If everything went as planned, they'd even get their wishes.

And then she'd go home to her real family, just as she had before.

But at least he'd be memorable. He'd make lots of friends then. And until that point, well, relying on himself was the first thing he'd learned to do in life. That's what the Quay taught a kid. Relying on others just left you hungry and alone.

It was a tricky balance—still hoping and yet holding on to reality. Hope too much, and the setbacks would be crippling. Don't hope enough, and he'd have never gone searching. Because if there was anything that meeting Marrill had taught him, it was the limitless possibility of being seen and remembered. The joy of it, but also the pain. The knowing that even if someone remembered you, you still couldn't count on them being there. They would still leave.

He reached out and gripped Marrill's hand. "Don't worry," he told her, even though the words hurt to say. "We'll get it done. We'll find the Wish Machine and get your mom better. And then you can go home."

She smiled up at him. The moonlight caught the edges of her tears, making them shimmer. "Thanks, Fin." She leaned her head on his shoulder. "You're the best friend ever."

Something squeezed tight in Fin's chest. These were the moments he'd missed the most after she'd left. The shared ones. When you could look at another person and know what they were thinking. And know that with a glance they could share what you were thinking.

Beside him Marrill yawned. He felt his own eyelids growing heavy. He stretched, pulling away. "It's late," he said. "We should sleep for a bit. We'll hitch a ride up the Wall in the morning. Then we'll find that Wish Machine and wish the Iron Ship right into rust."

She glanced around. "I didn't happen to see any hotels on the way up."

He grinned and pressed a hand to his chest. "Luckily, you happen to be with the Stream's foremost expert on scavenging for snacks and dark corners to nap in," he pronounced. That expertise came, he thought, with never having a place to call your own.

++ + ++

Fin crept into the tall tower, silent as the wind. The shadows wobbled around him. Outside, the lights of the Khaznot Quay burned bright, all the way down to the bay. In the middle of the room, the forgettable girl waited. Over his head, a huge bell clanged to life.

BONG!

"Remember me?" the girl asked.

BONG!

The symbol on her bracelet burst into flames.

BONG!

Also he wasn't wearing any pants.

BONG!

Fin woke up to the clanging of bells all around him. He jumped to his feet, instinctively looking for guards.

Instead, he found himself teetering on the edge of a massive drop, looking down at the ship-strewn marsh. The sun smacked bright in his eyes. Reflected, he realized, from the hundreds of crystals hanging all around him. The same crystals that now clanged with noise.

"Marrill!" he shouted, lunging toward her sleeping body. "Get up! We're in the Chimes!"

"MmmIdonwannagotoschool," she mumbled, "gunnasleep-furfivemoreminutes...."

He shook her vigorously. "Marrill, come on," he said. If Slandy was right, it was get up now or fall all the way back to the Grovel. He couldn't believe how far the city had dropped while they'd been asleep! "We've got to start up the Wall before it's too late!"

She let out a big sniffly snort and rolled over, right to the edge. Her eyes fluttered open, then went wide. "Bwaa!" she shouted, scooting away. "All right, all right, I'm awake!"

"About time," Fin grumbled. He hauled her to her feet. Together, they leaned out, searching for a way up.

Climbing was totally out of the question. The city was falling too fast. A nearby gear—barely a cog, really—had been level with his feet when he woke up. Now it was almost even with his head.

But then, there was another cog just beside it, and another beside it, and another, and another, each jutting half out of the Wall. Like stepping-stones in a river, they led across the face of the falling city, over to a much larger gear. One of the few they'd seen, he realized, that *wasn't* turning. If they could reach it, they could get a moment to think.

He grabbed the little cog next to him. It was just small enough to wrap his hand around. Unfortunately, unlike their destination, it *was* turning, disappearing into the Wall on one end and reappearing out of the other. He pulled his hand away quickly before it could get crushed.

Fin took in a deep breath. They fell farther; the cog was now even higher above them. The moment was passing.

He made up his mind quickly.

"Okay," he told Marrill, "I'll grab this one and swing you to the one beside it. If we move fast, there should be just enough time for you to grab it, swing me, then let go before your fingers get smashed. Then repeat. Swing, grab, go, swing, grab, go. Got it?"

Marrill shook her head furiously. "No," she said. "Just...no."

Fin glanced up at the gear. They'd almost passed it; it was now or never. And he didn't see another way. "It'll be fine. Just, you know, do what I do."

With that, he leapt up and grabbed the gear. In the same motion, he swung his body out of the alcove, kicking against the face of the falling buildings.

"Come on!" he shouted to Marrill. "I'll swing you, you grab that next one!" He reached for her with his free hand. "Trust me!"

"You're crazy!" she yelled back. For a second, he thought she wouldn't do it. The gear turned in his grip. Time was running out.

"This is a terrible idea!" she cried. But she jumped for

him anyway. Her hand hit his. He pulled her out, swinging her past him as hard as he could.

Marrill's feet skipped across the buildings. Her weight yanked against his arm. The turning gear yanked the other arm the other way. Fin twisted around as she swung, pulled in two directions. "Yuuurk!" he cried.

"Got it!" Marrill shouted triumphantly. Fin let out a cry of relief. Back now to the Wall, he planted his feet for a brief second, gripped Marrill's hand tight, and kicked off toward her, letting go of the gear at the same time.

"Agh, what have you been eating?" Marrill warbled as she caught his weight. His feet skimmed along windowsills, bounced across buttresses as he swung. He launched himself up, as high as he could, and caught the next gear. Then it was his turn to be a human rope-swing again.

Four swings later, they made it. Marrill landed safely on the big gear. Fin scrabbled up behind her. He rubbed the pain out of his shoulders. "This must be what Ropebone feels like," he muttered.

"Totally," Marrill said. "I feel strangely sorry for taffy."

But there was no real time for rest. The gear may have been still, but the city all around was falling. And according to the Map, the way to the Wish Machine was still somewhere far, far above them. In the creepy tower of the creepy Wiverwanes, all the way on top of the Wall.

"What do you think?" Fin asked. "Hope to flag down

another Slandy? I mean, we have to go up, natch, but how...no clue."

Marrill didn't seem to hear. She just stared up at the city, lost in thought. "Hello?" Fin tried again. "Got an idea?"

"Huh?" she said. "Oh, right. I was just thinking we have to go up. Natch."

"That's what *I* said."

Marrill smiled at him. "Sorry. Just got...distracted."

Fin's cheeks burned. Of course, it was perfectly reasonable. They had just teased death, like, seven times. The Chimes still clanged noisily below them. And they were stuck on a gear, way up in the middle of a falling city, in a place where time had no meaning. Of course she was distracted.

Still, he couldn't help feeling the sting of being ignored. Even if it was silly. Even if it was Marrill. *Especially* if it was Marrill.

He pushed it away and peered up at the Wall. Overhead, beyond the turning gears and the hanging markets, past the workers hauling up buildings just so the higher-ups could dance on them before they slid back down again, past the snails hauling up workers just so they could haul up buildings again, the heavy smoke clouds from beyond the Wall mixed with the dark gray of rain clouds. Clouds that seemed to have formed out of nowhere in the clear blue sky.

"We better get moving," Fin said. "It's looking dangerously like Iron Ship weather out here...."

"Waves," Marrill said.

"Pardon?"

She pointed down. "Waves!" Far below them, the Grovel was a splotch of ugly brown surfing the golden swells of the Stream. Swells that seemed to grow as they rolled through the marshes, covering and uncovering the skeletons of once-great ships. Even from up here, Fin could see the flotilla of docks practically bouncing with each one.

"It's the Iron Ship coming," Marrill gasped. "It has to be!"

Just then, the Stream billowed like a sheet being tossed in the air. Huge white-tipped breakers came rolling in. And a wall of water raced after them.

Fin gulped. It was taller than the tallest mast of the tallest ship. It was taller than the lowest of the gears. So tall, he realized, that its crest was dead ahead of them.

For a moment, everything went very still.

Even the Chimes seemed to calm.

As if the wind

had been

sucked

a   w   a   y   .

And then it all hit at once.

"TIIIIIIIIIIIIIIIIIIDAAAAAAAAAAAAAL
WAAAAAAAAAAAAAAAAAAAAVE!!!!!"

ShoutS and ScreamS
from above
ShoutS   all around and   *ScreamS*
below them
ShoutS and ScreamS

All around   s   l   s
               n   i   n
               a   n   a
               i   e   p
               l   s   p
                              e
                              d

workers up to safety.

"Climb !" Marrill screamed.

Fin threw himself at the Wall.
He leapt for a ledge,
yanked himself up into a doorway,
shimmied like mad
up a
long
glass
pipe
full of
Stream
water.

Marrill scrabbled
just inches behind.
Even with the city sliding,
they were making some
headway.

Fin dared a glance over his shoulder.

And immediately regretted it.

The whole of the Grovel, the entire floating network of docks, was buoyed up as the wave struck it. Everywhere, people held on for dear life. Ships that had been toy-tiny moments ago now grew to full size and surfed straight at them.

He tugged himself over someone's front stoop and struggled up a battered trellis. Against his better judgment, he dared another look back. And found himself locking eyes with a terrified girl, clinging to the foremast of a pirate ship.

In the space of a single heartbeat, the girl's eyes skipped from Fin down to Marrill. Raw fear warped into confusion. Confusion warped into fury.

"*Marigold Mae Aesterwest!*" Remy screamed. "You are *so* dead!"

CHAPTER 15
And the Waves Came Crashing

All the Chimes rang at once as the wave broke against the Wall. Marrill shrieked, but her voice was lost in the noise. She didn't know what to be more scared of: the sprays of pure magic splashing all around her? The looming threat of the Iron Ship, no doubt riding in just moments away? Or her very, very angry babysitter, who was nearly within striking distance?

Then the wave was sucked away, drained by whatever was under the Wall, and the *Kraken* dropped down with it.

Raw magic hung in the air like Remy's angry yell; the hairs danced on Marrill's skin. Her leg itched where a tiny droplet had sloshed onto it, but fortunately it wasn't enough to make her kneecap sprout whiskers.

But it was too soon to breathe a sigh of relief. There were more waves coming, each one larger than the first.

"Keep climbing, Marrill!" Fin's shout tangled with the clatter of the Chimes. She'd dropped almost a dozen feet in the span of a few thoughts. Quickly, she pulled herself up onto a motionless gear... and felt it rumble beneath her.

"Wha? Whoa!" she yelped as the gear began to turn. She threw out her arms to keep her balance. The buildings slid past even faster than before. All across the Wall, gears *everywhere* started turning.

The sound of the Chimes beat against her skull, causing her teeth to vibrate. She could practically feel the crush of air as the next wave approached. It reminded her of the time in Kenya when she and her parents had stood on a massive rock as a stampede of wildebeests coursed past them. Only, she didn't think the *wave* would part around her.

She struggled to keep her balance as the gear spun beneath her. Soon she was running in place, facing the great wall of water as it swept straight toward her. A familiar mast and crow's nest rose up its face.

"Marrill!" Remy screamed through the sound of a thousand alarm clocks going off at once. She stood in the center of the *Kraken*'s forecastle, hands cupped around her mouth. "Come on! Jump! I'll...probably not be quite as mad at you!"

The rigging squealed as Ropebone Man threw lines to anyone on the Wall who needed help, plucking them free of danger and dropping them onto the cluttered deck. "Welcome aboard, ya freeloaders," the Naysayer bellowed. "Keep yer hands to yerself, and pay what you can. *Everything* you can. Throw it on the pile. Direct your complaints to the cheerleader."

Marrill braced herself. She knew she should jump. If not on this wave, then the next. Ropebone Man would catch her and she'd be safe.

But then, she'd also be back in the Grovel. Back at the bottom of the Wall. Helplessly far away from the tower at the top, and the Wish Machine hidden there.

Helplessly far away from saving her mom.

There had to be another way. She searched around desperately. A few workers dangled on their snail lines nearby, snagging debris before the next wave hit. But the closest one was several yards to her right and a dozen yards below.

She thought about the time she'd stood on top of the cliff with her mom, the water terrifyingly far away. As her mom had told her then, sometimes you just had to jump. And if she wanted the chance to have more adventures with her mother in the future, that's what she'd have to do now.

With a deep breath, Marrill threw herself off the gear. And was free-falling.

"Oh, heck no!" she heard Remy shout as the *Kraken* crested the incoming wave.

Below, a very shocked-looking Monervan glanced up, saw Marrill plummeting toward him, and began tugging desperately on his line.

He wasn't fast enough. Marrill smacked straight into him, scrabbling for purchase. "Yo, bwah, ho, no!" the split-faced man protested.

The wave struck the Wall with a thundering crash. The force of it set the Chimes clanging in a deafening cacophony. She clung to the snail line tightly as she and the Monervan spun wildly through the air.

"Up, up!" her new host shouted. Over the clang of the Chimes, she heard a loud, wild scream. A second later, Fin dropped toward them, his skysails billowing. He wheeled once through the air around her. She stretched out her hand as he came past, and he grabbed it.

"Not another one!" the Monervan shrieked. The snail line yanked them up into the sky. Fin scrambled for purchase, his foot smacking right into the man's stomach. "Oof!" he cried.

"Sorry," Marrill told him. But inside, she was cheering. She'd done it! They'd made it!

"Nice moves." Fin laughed. The Monervan grumbled.

Moments later, they scrabbled free onto the scaffolding of a giant levator snail.

All around them was chaos. They were up high now,

higher even than the party had been the night before. Way down below, the docks rose and fell with each wave like a car on a roller coaster. Above, cranes hauled large terraces filled with Monervans to safety.

"This way," Marrill said, leaping onto a staircase and darting up it.

She'd almost reached the top when a familiar voice shouted, "Marrill Aesterwest, don't you dare move a muscle!"

"Trouble incoming," Fin warned, pointing to where a nearby levator snail hauled in a line. On the end of it was an extremely perturbed Monervan, an agitated sailor, and a very, *very* unhappy babysitter.

"Get me over there," Remy demanded. *"Now!"*

"I'm fine!" Marrill called to Remy, trying to act like everything was normal. She continued up the staircase, her legs burning and breaths coming in gasps.

But Remy didn't give in so easily. She scrabbled up a ladder, bringing her level with Marrill. "Oh no you don't!" she cried.

Marrill hadn't made it this high only to fall back down the Wall again. As the top of the staircase slid past the bottom of a massive vertical gear, she jumped. She managed to snag a hand around the edge of one of its giant teeth as it swept upward. For a moment, she was afraid she'd misjudged—the angle was too steep and her grip was slipping. Her stomach dropped as her feet kicked at the empty air.

"Hold on!" someone shouted. From the corner of her eye, she saw a small figure leap onto the gear above her. He scrambled over the teeth, not once hesitating as he climbed his way down to her.

Marrill's arms shook with effort. Just when she couldn't hold on any longer, she felt hands around her wrists. She looked up to find a kid not much older than her, floppy black hair falling in his face.

"If you're going to keep threatening to fall, we're going to have to get you your own skysails," he grunted, heaving her up to safety on top of the wide tooth.

Marrill took a moment to catch her breath as the gear spun them higher. "Thanks," she wheezed. "That was a pretty big risk you took to save me."

The kid looked at her strangely, meeting her eyes for a moment. She blinked; she was staring straight at Fin. How had she not realized that before?

She let her head fall against his shoulder, hoping he wouldn't notice her embarrassed blush. "Thanks for saving my life, Fin."

After a brief pause, Fin chuckled, though it sounded a bit forced. "Of course. What are friends for?"

"Incoming!" Remy swung in next to them on yet another snail line. She landed with a grunt on the tooth above theirs and immediately popped her head over the edge. "Marrill," she said, eyes scanning over her charge. "Marrill plus one," she added with satisfaction, nodding at Fin. Apparently, the craziness of Monerva was no match for a determined Remy.

A second later, Coll scrambled onto the vertical gear

next to her, looking furious. "What were you thinking?" he bellowed. "What were *both of you* thinking? I had to leave the Naysayer in charge of the *Kraken*!"

Remy glared at him. "No kid gets lost on my watch," she growled.

Coll crossed his arms, glowering, but said nothing more. They rode the rest of the way up in strained silence, like an angry family on a Ferris wheel. But that didn't stop Marrill from enjoying the ride; she'd always loved Ferris wheels.

When they reached the top of the gear, they stepped off onto a crooked balcony. The facade of the building attached to it was cracked, the entire structure split in two. One side slipped down the Wall at a slightly faster rate than the other. It seemed that the damage from the waves had reached all the way up here.

Workers in harnesses were already scrambling to dismantle several beautiful stained-glass windows. More and more joined with each passing moment, so that the air was alive with the sound of sawing and hammering and prying and shouting.

Remy's hand clapped on Marrill's shoulder. "You're mine, kid." Marrill tried an innocent smile, but the babysitter wasn't buying it.

"We should get back to the *Kraken*," Coll told them, eyes on the horizon. Dark clouds now filled the sky, boiling black. Just looking at them made Marrill uneasy. But thankfully, there was no sign of red lightning. No sign of the Iron Ship.

Yet.

"So you think the waves might be from that Iron Master dude?" Remy asked.

Coll rolled his shoulders, wincing slightly. He rubbed at the rope tattoo stretched across the base of his neck. "Could be. Hard to say how long until he makes it through, though."

"What about Ardent and Annalessa?" Marrill asked. "Are they okay? Have they figured out anything about the Iron Tide?"

Coll nodded. "They came back to the ship last night, said they'd found a promising lead. Got some supplies and took off this morning. We told them you were sleeping, which you *will* be paying me back for someday. They told us not to go anywhere and to stay out of trouble." He eyed Remy and Marrill pointedly.

Sheepishly, Marrill glanced at the ground, running her toe along a crack in the balcony. Normally, she wasn't someone who broke rules. Well, at least not the important ones anyway. But she'd never felt so close to something so important before.

"Let's go," Coll said. He jabbed his chin sharply down toward the Grovel. From this far up, the *Kraken* was a distant dot, riding the rising tide.

"No," Marrill said, straightening her back. "I'm not going back to the *Kraken*. I'm going to the top. I'm finding the Syphon, and I'm going to wish my mom well." If the tables were turned, she knew her mother would move heaven and earth to help her. Marrill resolved to do the same.

Beside her, someone cleared his throat and Marrill glanced at him. Her cheeks flamed. "I mean *we're* going up to the top," she corrected. "Fin and me. The two of us. We're both going. Me. With Fin."

Coll crossed his arms. "No way, nohow."

Remy nodded. "Exactly. You march yourself back down this vertical wall to that magical pirate ship and go to your room, this instant."

Before Marrill could argue, though, Fin stepped toward Coll. "Marrill's right. The Monervans told us last night that the Salt Sand King—the guy who made this place—had to get his last wish granted to put Monerva back on the Stream. If you can think of another way out of here, you let me know." His gaze flicked toward the tattoo wrapped across Coll's neck.

Coll's eyes widened and then his face collapsed into a frown. For the first time, Marrill realized that the captain's tattoo was getting tighter. And he was really, really uncomfortable with staying here. "What's it to you, kid?" he rasped. He turned to Marrill. "You can't just wish your problems away, you know."

Marrill bit her lip. But she stood tall and met his eyes. "What if I can? What if we *all* can?" She stepped toward him and dropped her voice. "There has to be something you'd wish for. Right?"

Coll stared at her for a long moment. Then his gaze flitted back toward the horizon as he considered the question. "Okay," he said at last.

"What?" Remy squeaked.

Coll ignored her. "Where do we go?"

"The Wiverwanes' Tower," Fin told him, "on top of the Wall. Now, how we get *there*..."

Marrill sighed. That was the question, indeed. They couldn't reach the top of the *city*, much less the Wall. Even the levator snails could only get them so high.

Then her eyes landed on an entire building being hauled up from below. She smiled as it slowed to pass. According to Slandy, the choicest bits of building material were always taken to the highest of Monerva. That looked pretty choice to her.

"All aboard!" she cried, leaping for its open door with a laugh. But the sound died in her throat as she stumbled inside and looked around. Long rows of empty shelves greeted her. On the floor, a dust-covered bottle of detergent stared up with the eyes of a cartoon bear.

Her chest constricted painfully. Something was very, very wrong.

The others followed behind, crowding in after her. "Uh," Remy said. "This looks..." She wandered deeper into the building, speechless.

"Familiar," Marrill finished weakly.

"Wow, this place has definitely seen better days," Fin remarked. He stood by a massive plate glass window covered in grime. "I haven't seen anything like this before. Doesn't look Monervan at all."

Marrill had a sense of déjà vu so intense it left her breathless and off balance. "That's because it's not," she whispered. Her heart raced and her head spun. She pressed her back against the wall and slid to the floor.

"Marrill, you okay?" Coll asked as he crouched next to her.

"This building…" She swallowed. "This store—it's from my world." Her voice trembled. "From the parking lot that touches the Pirate Stream."

"Roseberg's. I used to shop here as a kid," Remy added. "Before it closed." She craned her neck. "How is it"—she waved her hands around—"here?"

Marrill shook her head. She had no idea how a convenience store from the middle of the Arizona desert could end up as part of a timeless city on the Pirate Stream.

Coll sighed and rubbed the base of his throat. "Seems like most of this city floated in on the tide. Half the buildings on the Wall are made from ship parts jammed into place. That balcony we were just on was a crow's nest plated in marble. And I'd wager a lot of the nicest things here were once some poor sailor's cargo."

Remy tugged on her ponytail. "So?"

"So," he said, "if that whirlpool can swallow ships from all across time, who's to say it can't suck in parts of a whole other world?"

Marrill pondered the idea with a sinking stomach. "I think he might be right. We were in the Roseberg's parking lot when the wave washed us onto the Stream." She remembered the wild current that swirled all around them. The way the car-creature had struggled and dived to escape it. "It must have taken the store along with it."

"Okay," Remy said, glancing from Marrill to Coll, her expression alarmed. "But what does that mean?"

Marrill thought for a long, long moment, her sense of unease growing into something more. Coll stood and pushed away from the Wall. "It means the Stream's touching your world. Which we already knew." He clapped a hand on Remy's shoulder. "It'll be okay," he reassured her. The babysitter let out a long breath and gave him a tentative smile.

"I wish I believed that," Marrill mumbled.

"Hey, speaking of wishes," came a voice beside her. Marrill, startled, turned to find Fin holding out a hand to her. She hadn't realized he'd been standing so close. He helped her to her feet. "Aren't we looking for a machine that can grant those?" Marrill nodded. "And isn't it supposed to be at the top of this Wall?" She nodded again.

Fin tugged her toward the door and threw it open with a flourish. "Looks like we're here!"

CHAPTER 16
Emberfall

"W elcome to the Emberfall!" Monervans cried,
greeting them as they piled out of the store.
Fin blinked and took the place in.

They weren't at the top of the Wall exactly. But they
were close. The cranes had maneuvered Roseberg's into place
amidst a series of balconies and terraces, all teeming with
folks still partying from the night before. Nearby, a dozen
workmen were busy jacking up several tall, rickety spires so
they could slide the new structure underneath them.

"So that's how they do it," Fin mused. "They lift the top buildings and add in beneath them, so the real tip-tops never fall." He had to admit it was pretty clever.

"Do they not realize that adding so much weight up here is probably making the city sink even faster," Remy pointed out. "I mean, shouldn't they be reinforcing the foundation instead?" They all stared at her. "What?" she said. "I did a project on engineering for extra credit last year."

"So now that we're here," Coll cut in, "how do we get up there?" He pointed past all the balconies and terraces, past the tips of the spindly spires that reached up toward the top of the Wall, past the wide band of smooth stone that marked that top, to the crooked tower that looked down on it all. The Tower of the Wiverwanes.

No staircases or ladders led up to it. There was nothing at all to bridge the gap between the highest spire of the city and the top of the Wall. Fin's fingertips tingled—there was nothing like a good climb to get the heart pumping. But what was there to climb?

Remy shivered. "*That's* where we're going? It looks…pretty creepy."

Coll shrugged. "I've seen creepier."

Even as he said the words, a flash of orange light burst over the top of the Wall, casting the Tower in dark shadow. Bright sparks showered down, pouring over the partygoers, who shrieked merrily. Fin saw now why they called this place the Emberfall.

"I take that back," Coll said.

Fin laughed. As far as he was concerned, this was just another challenge between them and the Wish Machine. They'd come this far—nothing would stop them. "Only thing to do is keep on going," he called to the rest of the crew. "Onward!"

As he plunged into the crowd, he heard Coll grumble, "Who's that kid?"

He pushed forward, not waiting—not wanting—to hear the answer. Instead, Fin did what he did best: got lost in the shuffle. He slipped between legs and darted behind backs, enjoying the bustle of it all.

He appreciated a good mob. It was a lovely thing really; so alive and full of people, and you could be a part of it just by existing, no matter who knew you. In fact, the less anyone knew you, he felt, the more a part of it you became.

He reached a great staircase and bounded up it, two steps at a time. As he neared the top, he felt a rumble under his feet, growing in intensity. All at once his stomach lifted into his throat as the entire city dropped several feet. From the terraces below, partygoers shrieked, as much in delight as in fear. Another wave had hit. Only the people up here thought it was fun to ride the chaos of it. Which, if he was honest, it was.

He pushed onward, upward. Whereas the rest of Monerva was a mishmash of found and repurposed materials, the uppermost spires were constructed from slabs of unblemished stone. At their peak, a glass staircase twisted its way up to a high, circular platform. As they climbed it, Fin could see through it to the city falling away with each crash of the waves below.

"I think I don't like heights," Remy said weakly. But she didn't turn back. Probably because Coll was behind her and kept nudging her forward.

As Fin crested the last step, three burly Monervans closed together, blocking the way. Nine eyes glared at him. "Ay, refugees," one of them barked. "No admittance."

Coll stepped around Fin. One hand scratched at his tattoo. And then, in a flash, one of the guards tumbled down the stairs past them. Fin dodged out of the way. In the second before he glanced back up, the other two somehow ended up piled on top of the first.

Coll looked at them sternly. "Violence is never the answer," he said. "The gentlemen all tripped."

"Remind me to stay on Coll's good side," Marrill mumbled. Fin was about to agree, when he caught sight of what the guards had been blocking. Then everything else vanished from his mind.

Perched in the middle of the wide marble platform, a triangle of jagged black iron jutted into the air. There was no question where it had come from. No mistaking the cruel edges, or the ruddy line where the water once struck it. It was salvage. The bowsprit of a ship.

The Iron Ship.

"This is bad," Coll muttered. "This is very, very bad."

Marrill shook her head. "That's not what I think it is, right? I mean, it can't be, can it? The Iron Ship was *behind* us."

Fin's heart dropped. He got it now. "Ardent called this one," he said. "Who's to say things happen in the same order here as they do outside? Remember? 'For all we know, the Iron Ship's already here'?"

Beside him Marrill pressed her palm to her forehead. "Continuity is not guaranteed," she groaned. "Just like the obelisk said."

Coll massaged the base of his neck. "Let's keep moving." He gestured to a ladder leading up the side of the prow. "Might as well see..." He paused, clearly struggling with the rest of the phrase. "What's up," he said at last, lips fighting back a grin. Remy smacked him on the arm.

The joke, as lame as it was, made Fin smile. And the smile made him feel strong again. Like whatever awaited them, they could handle it. He bounded up the cold metal rungs of the rickety ladder toward a circle of glass balanced on the bowsprit.

Coll and Marrill followed behind, while Remy flat refused to let go of the ladder and climb up. Fin could understand her hesitation. There were no railings of any sort, and the circle tilted slightly to one side, so that he had to lean in the opposite direction to keep from slipping right off. Every now and then, a falling ember landed on his skin, stinging him for just a second before going out. But all he could do was wriggle and hope his hair didn't catch fire.

From overhead came the sound of arguing. "I'm clearly the highest! Have you *seen* this pedestal?" shouted one voice.

"Pedestal, pah! My canopy towers over your pedestal!" snapped another.

Fin looked up. At the very top of each pillar, a Moner-van perched. One balanced on a strange collection of junk: books, bottles—anything really. Another, a tiny little man, swayed on a plaster pedestal nearly as tall as the column itself. The third, a tall woman who dwarfed the others, had a very dirty-looking rag flapping from a tiny pole over her seat.

But as high as they all were, the Wiverwanes' Tower was still out of reach.

"Canopy?" scoffed the little man. He teetered on his pedestal dangerously. "*Canopy?* That's barely a flag!"

"Um, excuse us?" Marrill called up. "We're trying to get up to the Wiverwanes' Tower?"

The tall woman with the flag crossed her arms. "Tell you what, Necarib, we'll put it to a vote. Anyone who has a canopy gets a say. Wait, it's just me? In that case, it's a canopy if I *say* it is!"

"Hey, high-ups?" Remy tried, climbing a little higher on her ladder. "A moment of your time?"

"Only solid, stable structures count, Talaba!" shouted the woman balanced on her junk pile. "A canopy is not a solid, stable structure!"

Coll waved his arms. "Where'd you get this bowsprit? Hey! Hello?"

"Oh, and that trash heap of yours is?" Talaba scoffed back.

Marrill threw up her hands. "Hold on, hold on. Are you seriously all bickering about who is higher than who?"

The Monervan on the pillar peered down at her. "Of course. How else would we know who's in charge?"

Marrill frowned. "But what does height have to do with that?"

The junk lady crossed her arms. "It matters because the highest is the *Highest*," she said as though it were obvious. "That's what makes them in *charge*."

"Which would be me, by the way," interjected the little man on his pedestal. "I'm the Highest. You may bow. It's fine."

The woman with her flag gasped. "Are you kidding? This is *not* settled, you little..."

"How can that be all you care about?" Marrill demanded, her hands clenched in fists.

The flag woman snorted. "Young lady, you will refrain from speaking up to *us*. *We* will talk down to you. *We* are the Highest of the High. Just look how far up we are!"

"But the city's in trouble down there," Fin protested. "Don't you care about your people?"

The little Monervan man teetered on his pedestal. "*Of course* we care about those lower than us. We're not heartless. But you have to see the big picture."

"Big picture?" Fin asked. "What big picture?"

The little man tilted forward, talking to Marrill as if *she* had asked the question. "We serve a valuable purpose.

We carry on the Salt Sand King's decree, that the great city of Monerva should never fall." He lifted his chins proudly. "That it should always rise up, up from the mire. That whatever may happen below, we, the Monervan people, should seek to be highest in all things!"

The junk lady clutched a hand to her chest. Beneath her canopy, the tall Monervan wiped away a tear. "Oh, it is our charge," she muttered. "Our solemn duty to be highest in all things."

"Seriously?" Remy shouted. "My mom says the same thing. She doesn't mean it literally!"

"Ahem," said the Monervan from her junk pile. "This conversation is beneath us. *As are you.* Clamber on back down, lowlings. Your highers have loftier matters to discuss. Like which one of us is highest." They immediately fell back to arguing.

"Wait!" Marrill protested. "We need some answers!"

The Monervans all scoffed as one. "We will let you know when we're interested in hearing more from you," the junk lady informed them. And from that moment on, they stopped responding to anyone other than themselves.

Fin shook his head knowingly. Now Marrill was getting a taste of what it was *really* like to be him. To be ignored.

"Give it up, kid," Coll told her. "They won't listen to us, because we're lower than them. And there's nowhere else to climb. We can't get to their level."

Fin looked around. He was right. They were at the peak

of the city. Even as new material was hauled up, it was added *below* them. There was nothing at all nearby, and no room to stack anything if there had been.

They needed a way to get higher. Fin licked his thumb and held it out to the smoky air. Warm currents flowed around it. Updrafts, billowing over from the other side of the Wall. Drafts he could ride.

"I know!" Marrill announced. "We'll stack on each other's shoulders. Like a cheerleading pyramid."

Remy was already shaking her head. "I wouldn't know, because I'm not a cheerleader. But that sounds like a *very* bad idea."

"Well, what else is there?" Marrill asked.

Fin puffed his chest. "I can fly up," he proposed.

Marrill glanced at him and blinked several times, a small frown pinching the skin between her eyes. Then she shook her head. "They won't remember you long enough to have a conversat—"

"Let's get this over with," Coll interrupted her. He helped the shaking Remy up from the ladder, then cupped his hands for her to climb onto. Remy turned so pale she was nearly see-through, but she stepped onto them nonetheless.

Fin snorted. It was like they thought he was useless. Well, he didn't need them. He was used to doing things himself.

He pulled the strings on his skysails and jumped off onto a rush of warm, rising air. Just as he'd predicted, it caught him and lifted him. He gave a whoop of triumph as he rose.

It was nowhere near enough to get him up to the Wiver-wanes' Tower, but it was plenty to put him on same level as the Monervans.

He wheeled around, dodging between the pillars. "Okay," he said. "Now that we're all equally high, let's talk about how we get up to the top of this Wall."

The three Monervans eyed one another, then began tit-tering. "What's so funny?" Fin asked. He lifted his arms, circling to make another pass through the pillars...and had to bank sharply around Marrill, who'd just climbed on top of Remy, who stood on top of Coll.

"Where did that prow come from?" Marrill demanded. Fin huffed in frustration as he glided back around. She had completely stolen his conversation. Did she not even see him?

"Oh, that?" the little Monervan said. "It was a gift to us. From the man in iron."

Fin's frustration melted. Fear shot through him. Marrill gasped and wobbled on Remy's shoulders. The Master of the Iron Ship had already come.

Fin struggled to steady himself, to keep his arms from shaking. And when he heard what came next, he nearly dropped out of the sky.

"Oh yes," said the tall woman under the canopy. "That was *years* ago. Right before he set off to find the Syphon of Monerva. I'm sure he'll get his wish any moment now."

CHAPTER 17
Honestly, That Could Have Gone Better

A sick feeling shot through Marrill, worse than Remy and Coll wobbling beneath her feet. It was true. Back on the Stream, the Iron Ship had entered the whirlpool after them. But in Monerva, it had come out *years* before the *Kraken* arrived.

Continuity cannot be guaranteed.

The Master of the Iron Ship was here, now. And he'd gone to the Wish Machine.

"He must have found the Syphon and kicked it into high gear," the tall lady, Talaba, added from under her rag canopy. "It *really* started pulling in the Stream water after he showed up. And then the gears *really* started turning. Which has been quite exciting, as you can imagine. Lots of fresh building material coming in on the tide."

The little man on his pedestal nodded enthusiastically. "Look at this great new stuff!" He pointed down to where several cranes struggled to lift an entire warehouse. "There hasn't been a haul like this since the time of the Salt Sand King himself, when the Syphon sucked in some poor little backwater world and ripped it to pieces."

"The Shattered Archipelago," Marrill whispered. Once again, Ardent had been right. It *had* been a world like hers, drawn onto the Stream and torn apart by its raw magic. Drawn in, she now knew, by the Syphon of Monerva.

A world *like hers*.

"Marrill?" Fin said, circling around her. "Are you okay?"

Everything seemed to spin. Her eyes unfocused, sliding up the smooth surface of the Wall to the gnarled tower at its top, to the plumes of smoke and orange fire rising up from whatever lay on the other side.

First, there'd been the flash flood back in Arizona, and the mysterious message on the stop sign. Then Roseberg's. Now this warehouse.

The Stream will touch your world again. But if it's close

enough for you to stumble upon, something has gone terribly, terribly wrong.

"Oh no," she whispered. "Oh, oh no."

Remy clamped a hand on Marrill's leg. "What? What 'oh no'?"

Marrill clutched her hands to her chest. A tear formed in her eye. "It's our world this time, Remy," she said. "The Stream is leaking into our world. Arizona, Boston—all of it!"

"That's it," Remy ordered. "Put us down, Coll. Team meeting!"

Coll grunted. "With pleasure," he said as he lowered them to the ground. Fin landed on the platform next to them.

"Explain," Remy said. "Now."

Marrill swallowed, trying to keep her voice from trembling. "It's the Syphon," she said. "The Master of the Iron Ship is already here. He did something to make the Syphon suck in Stream water faster, and now it's going so strong it's sucking our world onto the Pirate Stream. The magic will tear it apart, just like it did to the world that became the Shattered Archipelago!"

Remy stumbled, grabbing onto Coll's arm to steady herself. "Okay, now I'm really sorry I asked."

Fin touched down next to them. "I hate to step on your tails when they're already drooping, but is anyone else worried about what the Master might be wishing *for*?"

Marrill dropped her head into her hands. Things just kept getting worse. "The Iron Tide," she muttered.

"That's my guess," Fin agreed.

"Okay." Remy clapped her hands. "New plan. First, we stop the Wish Machine from pulling our world onto the Stream. Second, we stop the iron dude from making his evil wish. Third, we get the Salt Sand King's wish granted so everyone can leave, fourth we all go home and never look back. Everyone on board?"

Marrill nodded. A weak smile played across her lips. Remy was right. They had to find a way. "So how do we *do* any of this?"

"I vote we use the Map to figure out the quickest way up to the Wiverwanes' Tower," Fin suggested. "We find the Syphon ourselves, and put this all to rest before it gets any worse."

Coll laughed, but there was no humor in it. "And just hope the evil wizard ghost-captain is fine with that? Listen, kid, I don't know you, but you don't look like a wizard to me. I know I'm not. We wouldn't last two seconds against the Master. We need to find Ardent and Annalessa before we do anything else. They're the only ones who can stand up to him."

Marrill nodded. She'd been thinking the same thing: They needed to call in the big guns for this one. "Coll's right. We've got to get Ardent. He'll be able to stop the Syphon in time."

"That's great and all, but we don't exactly know where Ardent and Annalessa are," Remy interjected. "They went off this morning to follow some lead on the Iron Tide and they didn't say where."

"Then we'll just use the Map to Everywhere to find them," Marrill said, holding out her hand toward Fin.

Fin clutched at his thief's bag, taking a step back. "No need to be hasty, bloods," he protested. "Let's think through all the options here."

"Our only option is to stop the Syphon from powering up all the way," Marrill said firmly. "And we need Ardent and Annalessa to do that."

"No, we don't." Fin pointed toward the Wiverwanes' Tower. "Look, we're almost there!" He pulled the Map from his jacket. "We just need to use the Map to figure out how to get up the rest of the way."

Marrill shook her head. Frustration bloomed hot in her chest. This had to be the third time today they'd fought over how to do things. "Look, we can't do this on our own. There's too much at stake." She reached for the Map, but he danced backward, holding it out of reach.

"We can't stop now," he urged. He glanced toward Remy and Coll. "Right?"

"I vote we do whatever gets us out of Monerva fastest," Coll suggested, his voice raspier than usual.

Marrill couldn't believe Fin was being so difficult. "Fin, this is my *world* we're talking about. My *home*." Her voice cracked as she took a trembling breath. "This isn't just about the Iron Tide anymore. We have to stop the Wish Machine before my world ends up like the Shattered Archipelago."

"And if we get to the Wish Machine, we can fix all of that," he argued. "We can *wish* everything back into place."

"What if we fail? What if the Master's already there?

We can't risk it." She started to move around him, but he grabbed her hand.

"We can," he said. "We stopped an evil wizard. We sank the Master of the Iron Ship. We can do this. Together."

Marrill searched his eyes, her throat tight. All she knew was that she'd been sent back to the Stream to save her world. That's exactly what she planned to do. No matter what it took.

With a sour taste in her mouth, she nodded. "You're right. We'll use the Map to find a way up to the Tower."

The lopsided grin Fin gave her made her heart squeeze tight, but she forced a smile. She watched as he flicked open the Map, the move more grandiose than necessary. But that was Fin, ever the showman.

He pulled the Key from his thief's bag and knelt. Holding it just above the surface of the Map, he began, "Show us how—"

Marrill lunged for the sun-shaped crystal. Her hand fell on top of his, tugging it between them. "Show us how to find Ardent," she quickly spouted.

"What are you doing?" Fin yelped. He tried wrenching the Key away from her, but she held tight.

"I'm saving my home," she told him through clenched teeth. "I'm doing what's *right*."

"So am I," Fin argued. He pushed the Key down to touch the Map. "How do we get to the Tower?" Ink swirled up to the surface, bubbling and shifting.

"No, to Ardent!" Marrill corrected. The images on the Map fell away, then re-formed in a jumbled mass. She pulled one way. Fin pulled back. He slammed his free hand on top of hers, pushing the Key down again. She did the same, her hand covering his.

They both opened their mouths at the same time, speaking over each other.

Marrill saying, "We have to find a way to stop the Syphon!"	Fin saying, "We have to figure out how to get to the Syphon!"

The Map buckled beneath their hands. Marrill's blood roared in her ears. They stared at each other, their breaths coming fast, their fingers still tangled around the Key.

It was like he was a stranger to her. Like they had never been best friends. Had never cared about what was best for the other.

The sound of squealing hinges rose up through the air. "Uh, guys," Remy said.

Marrill ignored her. "How could you?" she whispered to Fin. A familiar scent coated her tongue, like the moment before lightning strikes.

"Seriously, guys?" Remy said again, this time more urgent.

Fin's eyes went wide. "Me? How could y—"

And then Marrill was tossed backward. There was the loud bang of a giant door slamming, and a searing flash of light. Her head smacked into the base of one of the glass pedestals.

She blinked to clear the pain. Coll and Remy had ducked down, covering themselves. Fin lay across from her, practically on the edge of the platform. The Key spun in loose circles beside him. The Map lay curled and blank on the ground.

"What just happened?" Remy asked.

Marrill swallowed, hard. The sound of the door, the searing light—she recognized that from the deck of the *Black Dragon*, when she and Fin had faced the evil Oracle, Serth. When he'd assembled the Map to Everywhere into a massive Gate and used the Key to open it, so the Lost Sun of Dzannin, the star of destruction, could shine its deadly light out to destroy the Pirate Stream.

Dread pooled in her stomach. Somehow, she and Fin had opened that Gate again.

Slowly, she turned around. A thin line sliced straight through the Wall behind them. In the middle of it, a gear wobbled unsteadily, one of its teeth sheared clean off.

Fin pushed to his feet, holding out a hand to help Marrill. As they stood, the crack widened, pieces of the Wall falling away. "Shanks," he whispered.

There was quiet, the bustle of Monerva falling silent for once. And then a voice screamed:

"They broke the Wall!"

Everything dissolved into chaos. The three Monervans,

who just moments before had been arguing over who was the highest, leapt from their spires and pushed their way down the ladder in a jumble.

"You're the highest," the first said, pointing to the second. "You deal with it!"

"Me?" the second said. "You've still got that fabulous canopy!"

"They're coming!" the third shouted, pointing. A dark smudge drifted from the Tower at the top of the Wall. Like smoke, but heavier. More substantial.

The edges of the cloud writhed. The air filled with the sound of beating wings.

Marrill's heart tripped over itself, hammering against her chest. The darkness coalesced and crashed against the Wall, rushing down it like a melted shadow. Directly toward them.

There was no time to run and no place to hide. Below, the Monervans flattened themselves to the ground. But the Wiverwanes weren't coming for them.

They were coming for Marrill and Fin. For the two who'd broken the Wall. Fin scooped up the Key. Marrill lunged for the Map, crumpling it into her pocket. And then she was swallowed by dark bodies.

The tips of handless fingers danced across her skin, causing it to ripple. Memories seeped into her, through her.

The King ran his hands across his prize, a raggedy length of black cloth, all covered in frayed ends of fabric from bottom to top, as if it had been worn to threads by wind and rain and vast expanses of time.

The Dawn Wizard eased closer. One of his eyes, the King realized, was noticeably larger than the other. "The cloak you won from me, my lord, is far more than mere cloth. It is memories made real. The memories of the Dzane, my brothers and sisters, who went before and are no more. It's very precious to me, and me only. But a wager's a wager, I expect. So I come here looking for another wager, hoping to make myself whole again."

The King shook his head. "No more wagers. But I can offer a trade. I need your help."

The Dawn Wizard smiled and bowed. His teeth were black, with just a touch of light blue around the edges. "What could a humble Dawn Wizard like me do to satisfy you, O King? You've united all the lands of the Boundless Plains, and here I can scarcely keep from gambling away my own clothes!"

Marrill struggled to fight them, to stay conscious. But it was too much. She was dimly aware of her feet leaving the ground—of a sensation of weightlessness. And then she was lost in someone else's memories.

CHAPTER 18
The City of Burning Ladders

The Wiverwanes encircled them, blocking out the light. Before Fin's eyes, Marrill was lost in the swirling darkness.

"Hey!" Remy shouted, "Get your...hands...fingers... whatever—just let her go!" She lunged into the mass of writhing creatures. Coll grabbed after her. In a moment, they, too, vanished.

Fin dove into the fray, struggling to pull them free. He slipped through the Wiverwanes easily; apparently they didn't notice him any more than anyone else did. "Marrill!" he called. "Coll! Remy!" But no one answered. He pushed harder, swatting the creatures away from his face just in time to see Marrill being lifted into the air.

Fin grabbed her hand, but she didn't react. Her eyes stared blankly. Her lips moved softly, but no sound came out.

Without hesitation, Fin threw his arms around Marrill's waist, holding on for dear life as the Wiverwanes carried them both up and away.

It wouldn't have been the first time, or even the second, that Fin had hitched a ride out of a scrape. But it was definitely the first time he'd flown away on an unconscious girl being carried by a flock of hand-creatures. He just hoped everyone involved was stronger than they appeared.

The spires of the Highest fell away. Seconds later, the Wiverwanes swooped and spiraled as they broke over the top of the Wall. Fin clutched Marrill tighter as the Tower of the Wiverwanes came into view. It was dark and sinister, twisted and crooked, filled with holes like a dovecote or a hive of wasps.

And it was totally within reach. All he would have to do was let go. It was an easy enough drop; he probably wouldn't even need to use his skysails. He could be there in seconds— right at the entrance to the Syphon, the way to the Wish Machine. The very place the Map had sent them.

Everything he'd ever wanted was within reach. So close it made him physically ache.

If he let go now, he could be *memorable*.

His fingers twitched as he imagined it. Ardent greeting him with a cheerful "Fin, my boy!" when he came on deck. Coll clapping him on the back, telling stories about their latest adventure. The Ropebone Man would swing him aboard whenever he ran up a dock, and the pirats would never, ever set sail without him.

But that would mean abandoning the others to deal with the Wiverwanes, and whatever lay across the Wall, alone.

What was it Slandy had said?

To get what you want, you must give what you have.

His gut twisted. Could he give up Marrill to become memorable?

Fin closed his eyes. What terrified him the most in that moment was that he was so unsure of the answer.

And when he opened his eyes again, the opportunity had passed. The Wiverwanes had crossed over the Wall. Regret and relief mixed together inside him.

His first glimpse of the other side, however, gave the edge to regret. The falling embers and the plumes of smoke should have been a clue. Because as far as Fin could see, the plain below was on fire.

The flames stretched to the horizon and beyond. They raged through low, flat scrubland. They raged through sheer canyons of blackened glass that scoured the earth, as if a giant Karnelius had raked his claws across it. They raged over rolling hills and across stony wasteland, devouring trees and bushes and endless seas of grass, flowing and changing like the Stream itself.

Here, the flames burst into showers of sparks like white-caps of waves. There, they guttered and smoldered like the outflowing tide. All across the scorched land, the fire eternal burned everything it could touch, ever hungry for more.

It burned, in fact, right up to the base of the Wall, licking at the squat structures crouched there. Devouring them hungrily.

The city below wasn't nearly as big as Monerva, nor as beautiful. Instead of marble spires and gleaming terraces, half-built stairs and ragged scaffolds thrust up from a mass of dark buildings hunkered at its base. From the air, Fin couldn't tell one building from the next; they were all just a single long, fused lump.

"At least we're not down there, eh?" he asked Marrill.

Before the words had even left his mouth, the swarm of Wiverwanes dipped, moving stomach-flippingly fast. Their fingerlike wings fluttered, letting go.

Marrill and Fin were falling. They plunged into the smoke. Not since his earliest days at the Khaznot Quay had Fin found himself unexpectedly tumbling through the air. But a kid only had to plummet toward certain death once to hone his reaction time.

Quick as lightning, he wrapped his legs around Marrill's

waist, flung out his arms, and pulled at the strings in the sleeves of his coat. His skysails fluttered, just barely catching against the wind before the two of them collided with the pitched spire of the tallest building.

It was enough to knock the air from Fin's lungs, but not enough to break bones. Together, he and Marrill slid down the slick surface toward the raging fire below.

Smoke choked him. Flames licked at the edge of the roof, waiting for them. The heat of it washed over Fin, causing sweat to drip down his cheeks.

There was no way to slow or halt their slide. All he could do was hold on to Marrill and hope. He squeezed his eyes closed, waiting for the end.

And then the angle of the roof lessened, the speed of their slide slowed, and they tumbled, fairly unceremoniously, off the side and onto a patch of smoldering ground.

Fin threw his arms over his face, bracing for the inferno. When it didn't come, he cracked open an eye. Just moments before, this entire area had been engulfed in flames. Now, it was as though the fire had somehow passed it over, leaving nothing but smoke and a pulsing heat.

Beside him Marrill sat up with a stretch and a yawn. "Careful, those pipes are flammable," she muttered.

"Marrill!" He crawled toward her. "You okay?"

She stared at him blankly for a moment, as though still lost in the trance that had overtaken her. She shook her head, frowning in confusion. "Yeah. I mean, I think so."

Fin stood, offering a hand to help her up. She reached for it, then hesitated. Suddenly, she snatched her hand away and pushed to her feet. "This is your fault!"

"*My* fault?" Fin took an involuntary step back. His surprise at her accusation turned quickly to indignation. "How is this *my* fault?"

"You opened the Gate!" she spat. "You almost let out the Lost Sun of Dzannin!"

Fin couldn't believe what he was hearing. "What? That was your fault! You're the one who tried to yank the Key from me while I was using it."

Marrill lifted her chin. "I wouldn't have had to if you'd just listened to reason and used it right."

Fin's cheeks burned. "Are you ribbing me? I was *trying* to get us to the Wish Machine. You know, where we both want to go?"

Marrill's eyes narrowed. "And where *I'll* be totally helpless if we don't have some magical backup, while *you* just waltz in undetected and get *your* wish."

Fin clenched his hands into fists against the anger boiling in him. "I could sneak in and make *all* of our wishes," he pointed out.

"*My* world is on the line, Fin," Marrill snapped. "I can't just *hope* you're somehow able to bluff your way past the Master of the Iron Ship and wish for me. We don't even know how the stupid machine works!"

Fin wanted to spin on his heel and leave. Let Marrill

forget him. He'd be better off without her anyway. Not have to explain himself. Not have to justify his actions, or change his plans. He could do what he wanted, go where he wanted, make whatever wishes *he* wanted.

He couldn't believe how quickly having a friend turned into a burden.

But where was he going to go? All around, the ground was burnt and smoking, right up to the dusty buildings themselves. He didn't even know where he was. Which was also Marrill's fault. "I should have just let the Wiverwanes take you on your own," he grumbled.

Her eyes went wide, two bright spots of red blazing on her cheeks. She opened her mouth, then paused, forehead crinkling. "Wait. Last time the Wiverwanes totally ignored you. Why *did* they take you this time?"

Fin shuffled his feet and shrugged. "Nothing. I... er...hitched a ride on your legs."

"So you *chose* to come here?" She seemed surprised.

"It's not like I had a ton of time to think through the consequences."

A smile twitched Marrill's lips and then she let out a giggle. "Let's face it, that's not really your strong suit anyway."

Fin was still trying to decide whether to take that as a compliment when an alarmed yelp came from above, along with a shouted "Watch out!"

He looked up just as Coll came sliding down the steeply pitched roof, Remy not far behind. Fin didn't have time to dodge out of the way. The captain crashed into the clearing, taking both Fin and Marrill down with him.

Remy landed on top of the heap a second later with an "Oof!" For a moment, it was just a jumble of legs and arms as the four of them untangled themselves. And then Remy was free enough to scramble toward Marrill, grabbing her into a hug. "Marigold Mae, don't you *ever* get abducted by strange hand thingies again! No way am I going to try to explain that one to your parents."

At the mention of her parents, Marrill bit her lip, eyes on the ground. "Sorry," she mumbled.

Remy spun and, spotting Fin, pressed a hand to her chest, letting out what sounded suspiciously like a relieved breath. "Same goes for you, mister!"

Heat infused Fin's cheeks. Whether it was from the smoldering remains of the fire, being scolded, or just flat out being remembered, he wasn't sure. And he wasn't sure he cared. Because she'd remembered him. Or at least that there *was* a him. Again!

"Uh, sorry," he said after clearing his throat. Then he frowned. "I guess the Wiverwanes held you responsible for breaking the Wall, too, huh?"

Coll jerked a thumb toward Remy. "Nope. As soon as Marrill got airborne, this one grabbed my knife and attacked the Wall with it until they came back for us."

Remy tapped a finger against her temple, leaving a smudge of ash behind. "Arizona's best babysitter, remember?

No one's getting dragged over a massive magical wall without me while I'm in charge." She then glanced around. "So . . . this place is rather . . . um . . . sooty."

Fin had to admit, there wasn't much to look at. They seemed to have landed in the dead end of a back alley, surrounded by the remains of charred huts.

"This would be the City of Burning Ladders," a voice buzzed. "And you are not welcome here."

CHAPTER 19
A New Ally (Flames Take His Name)

In the space of a moment, the air around Marrill went from shouldn't-have-worn-long-sleeves warm to opening-the-oven-on-an-Arizona-summer-afternoon hot. Her eyes stung from lingering wisps of smoke. At any moment, it seemed like flames might burst to life again, and then they'd *really* be toast.

Unfortunately, a rather monstrous beetle seemed to be blocking their only exit.

Marrill let out an audible gulp. Remy laid a hand on each of her charges' shoulders, pushing them behind her.

Coll stepped forward, drawing himself up straight. But even at his fullest height, the beetle-like creature towered over him by several feet. Its sleek black shell came together in an angular sort of beak, just below a single red compound eye. The edges of its razor-sharp wing casings clicked together.

"You are wanted," the beetle buzzed ominously. "And on the Burning Plain, being wanted is a dangerous thing."

"Wanted for what?" Coll demanded.

The beetle's wings clicked again. "I would not know. I know only that a wizard's want is deeper than most, and flames will continue washing over the city until it is extinguished. And so that one's want has become our want, too, further fueling the fire's desire."

Remy leaned back. "Did that make any sense at all to you guys?" she whispered out of the corner of her mouth.

Marrill shook her head. "Not one bit."

"Hold on," Coll said, relaxing out of his fighter's stance. "Did you say 'wizard'?"

"Indeed," the beetle clicked.

"Tall guy? Old? Kinda distracted sometimes?"

"Maybe?" the beetle clicked. "I can't tell any of you apart, if I'm honest."

"You need to take us to him," Coll ordered.

The beetle considered the young sailor for a long moment. Sweat dribbled down the back of Marrill's neck, causing her damp shirt to stick to her back. "No," the beetle finally said. "We do not *need*. The fire *needs*. It burns where it can. *We* are water, and we flow where we flow."

With that, the beetle headed calmly down the alley. Glowing embers, scattered along the ground, dimmed as he passed. But in their little clearing, flames had sprung up to lick at the melted structures around them. It wouldn't be long until the entire area blazed anew.

"That sounds like something my yoga teacher would say," Remy muttered.

"Um, does that mean he's taking us to Ardent?" Marrill asked.

Coll rolled his shoulders. "I guess we'll find out," he said, leading the way after the creature.

At the end of the alley, Marrill got her first real view of things on this side of the Wall. It was not, she had to admit, terribly impressive. Scorched structures slumped against the base of the Wall like marshmallows burned over a campfire, smashed together, then dropped into a lump on the ground. Charred ladders sprouted up here and there like forgotten hairs on an old man's scalp.

Most everything smoldered, at least the parts of the city not actively burning. And yet scores of the beetle-like creatures continued to scuttle about, as though the fire were nothing. "How does anything survive?"

Coll paused, knocking a fist against one of the buildings. "Seems to be made out of dullwood."

"And dullwood doesn't burn?" she asked.

He lifted a shoulder. "Burning is interesting. Dullwood's not."

They headed through open, fire-scarred streets, past so many identical lumps of buildings that Marrill couldn't tell if they were making progress or going around in circles. Finally, the city didn't so much end as melt, the ground dropping into canyons of black rock.

At the lip of one canyon, two figures stood surveying the distance. The one on the left wore a purple robe, his white beard trailing behind him from the wind blowing up from the fires. The other was a bit shorter, her long hair flowing down her back. They were holding hands.

Marrill grinned.

She felt an enormous sense of relief at having found the two wizards. As much fun as she'd had exploring Monerva, the stakes were too high now. She needed them to save her world.

As their bedraggled crew made their way over, streaks of fire burned up the canyons, crashing against the sides in great waves, as bright as Stream water and just as deadly.

"Awesome," Remy griped as they carefully made their way across the slick rock. "I just got used to being terrified of water and heights. Why not add fire to the list, too?"

Coll shouted a greeting as they neared. Ardent turned. His expression morphed from surprise to delight to concern. "Well, isn't this unexpected!" he cried. "What are you doing here?"

Coll started to explain, but Marrill interrupted him. "It

was an accident," she said. The last thing she wanted was for Ardent to learn that not only had Fin stolen the Map, but also that they'd nearly unleashed the Lost Sun of Dzannin and destroyed the Pirate Stream. "We were trying to get to the Tower on top of the Wall and...let's just say it didn't go well."

"Why would you think the Wish Machine was in the Wiverwanes' Tower?" Ardent asked. He looked at her intently.

Marrill gulped. "Um...because..." There was no way she could admit the truth. She looked to Fin for help but he took a large step backward. She shot him a glare before turning back to Ardent. "It just, uh...we just guessed?" She chuckled nervously.

Thankfully, Annalessa nodded. "The highest point in a city obsessed with height; not a bad deduction."

Marrill slowly let out her breath in relief. "It's wrong, I'm afraid," the wizard added. "But still quite logical."

Marrill sucked the breath right back in. Fin piped up next to her, giving voice to what she was already thinking. "Wait, what do you mean it's wrong? The Wish Machine *is* there. We're sure of *that*."

The skin around Ardent's eyes crinkled as he laughed. "Oh, Marrill, where do you run into these characters? No, my mysteriously unremarkable lad, there's no Wish Machine in the Wiverwanes' Tower. Annalessa and I stopped by there on our own trip over the Wall, so I'm quite certain the place is empty."

"Also, we will not be invited back," Annalessa added.

Ardent coughed. "Yes, well, the less said about that the better," he mumbled.

A numbness stole over Marrill. She couldn't believe it. The Map had been...wrong? Her heart dropped. The Map *had* acted strangely in the past. Betrayed them once, even. She swallowed, thinking about how she and Remy had planned to use it to find their way home. If it was totally unreliable, then what?

"No," Ardent continued. "Nothing in that tower but empty space, a weird smell, and a cloud of old memories."

Memories. At the word, Marrill felt oddly faint. The memories the Wiverwanes had shown her flooded back, overwhelming her....

The Dawn Wizard stood high atop the barrier Wall, in a tower full of holes and rookeries. On one side, the last of what had once been the Endless City slid slowly into a dank and fetid marsh, bounded by glowing waters that led to nowhere. On the other, the kingdom burned, consumed by the raging fire.

"You are the price I pay," he said to the frayed ends of his cloak. No wind buffeted him, no breeze set the thousand fingers to moving. But move they did. They stretched and twitched, shuffled and squirmed. Then, as one, they took to the air.

"I must leave now," he said. "And someday, this Wall must fall. Until then, watch over it, and keep the fire at bay."

Dark shapes spiraled out in a cloud around him. Living memories that would never forget, that would guard the Wall eternally and without fail. They flapped and floated, and circled and whirled. For the first time, the Wiverwanes took flight.

"Marrill?" Ardent laid a hand gently on her shoulder.

She shook her head, clearing away the traces of the memory. She wondered how many others they'd given her, how many more she'd suppressed.

Right now, though, she had bigger issues.

"It's nothing," she told him. "Look, the Master of the Iron Ship is already here." Quickly, she explained what they'd learned from the Highest: that the Master had actually appeared in Monerva years earlier, and was powering up the Syphon of Monerva.

"It's pulling my world onto the Pirate Stream!" A familiar pain twisted in her gut at the thought. "That's how I was able to come back."

Ardent squeezed her shoulder. "It will be okay, Marrill."

Sniffling, she let out a watery smile. It was good to have a powerful wizard like Ardent on your side.

"That *is* terrible news, however," Annalessa said. "If the Master has, in fact, been increasing the intake of Stream water to power this Syphon of Monerva, and it is, in fact, reaching your world, then the Syphon has consumed a truly massive amount of magic. It must be nearly ready to grant his wish. And with that much power, he really could wish for just about anything. There's no telling how much time we have left."

Ardent held up a hand. "It isn't all bad news. We traversed

the Wall for a reason. Whatever the Master may have told the Monervans, the Salt Sand King is real, and alive."

At the mention of the name, the beetle who'd brought them let out a hissing buzz and flicked his fingers in the air, but said nothing more.

Marrill looked at the dusty ground. "So...what does that mean?"

Ardent clasped his hands behind his back in his classic lecture stance. "Well, according to our research, the Salt Sand King appears to be responsible for building this Syphon of Monerva in the first place...with the help of the Dawn Wizard, of course. Assuming we cannot find the Dawn Wizard, and that is a safe assumption given the nature of the Dzane, one can conclude that the Salt Sand King is likely the only person, or thing, who knows where to find it or how to *stop* said machine. Not to mention the fact that he doubtless does not want to see someone else use it instead of him."

There was a moment of silence while everyone tried to work through the logic. "It means we may have an ally in the King," Annalessa translated.

Ardent grinned, but his voice was steady and stark. "Quite so."

"I hate to interrupt," said someone beside her. Marrill jumped. It was Fin. For some reason, she hadn't noticed him standing there earlier. "Perhaps we should have this discussion somewhere less...flamey?"

He pointed behind them. On the plain, the fire-tides had grown in strength. They broke against the lip of the canyon, sparks filling the air like sea spray. It reminded Marrill of the time her parents took her out to the beaches of Vieques in Puerto Rico, to watch the glowing plankton light up the waves at night. Only, plankton wouldn't burn you.

"Perhaps we should go," Ardent suggested.

"I just said that," Fin noted.

Annalessa turned to the beetle, who was standing quietly off to the side. "Kind beetle—I don't believe I caught your name?"

"I am called Rysacg," the beetle answered. The name started with a buzz, then a click and a pop, and ended with a sudden stop, not to mention a few sounds Marrill was pretty sure her mouth didn't make. They all looked at one another nervously. Next to Marrill, Remy quietly popped her lips together, trying to imitate it.

"Yes," Annalessa continued. "Well, let's stick with 'sir,' then. Kind sir, we have a need to converse with the Salt Sand King. How would we go about finding him?"

Rysacg again hiss-buzzed at the mention of the King. "The Salt Sand King, flames take his name, lives in the barren lands that way." He held out a claw-tipped hand, pointing toward the boundless expanse of flat scrubland. Marrill squinted. All she could see was fire, smoke, and more fire. "But be warned: You clearly want much," the beetle added.

"I can feel it. The fire can feel it, too. You must suppress your desires if you wish to make it across the plain. As to what you will find out there, I cannot say."

"Weirdo," Remy mumbled under her breath.

Rysacg pivoted toward her. "Through unthinking desire, the Salt Sand King—flames take his name—set the plain alight. He trapped us behind the Wall. He split the people of the plains apart, even as he brought them together. We have learned to fear desire, and we have learned to hate the Salt Sand King. Flames take his name."

Ardent clapped his hands. "Well, on that ominous note, I guess we should be off." He headed toward the tip of the plateau, where a steep set of steps had been carved into the black rock of the canyon.

"Anything if it means finding a way back onto the Stream," Coll murmured, following after. He rubbed at his tattoo. It was wound several times around his throat now. "I need out of this place."

The words had barely left his mouth when another wave of fire crashed over the lip of the canyon behind them. Hot air blasted them, hotter than Marrill had ever felt. She threw her arm over her face, but there was no escaping it.

Glowing embers spotted the wind. "Memory-of-Rain," Rysacg buzzed. "It's coming."

Marrill didn't even have time to ask. A wall of flames raced up the valley toward them. The fire was a hungry tongue, licking the sides of the canyon as if it were licking frosting from a giant bowl. Up one side, down the other, blazing in oranges and reds and blues.

Marrill turned to retreat toward the city, but the fire reached the lip of the canyon and exploded upward, blocking the way. It swept in from two sides now, chewing at anything it could find as it came.

Annalessa lunged forward and threw her arms wide. A wall of snow and ice billowed from her sleeves, only to disappear in a hiss of steam as it struck the conflagration before them. It did nothing to stem the tide.

She glanced over her shoulder. Her eyes were pinched with worry. "These flames burn with the old magic of the Dzane," she called to Ardent. "Only Dzane magic will put it out."

Ardent began searching through the pockets of his robe. He pulled out four corkscrews, half a dozen rocks, and a measuring set. "No, no, no," he said, tossing it all aside. The flames licked at the debris, growing closer.

As Marrill watched, her anxiety grew. It seemed that with every thought, every beat of her heart, the strength of the fire increased. And then she remembered something Rysacg had said.

She spun toward the beetle, who stood calmly behind them. "What did you mean about the fire feeling our want?"

"The fire is drawn to need and want," Rysacg said simply. "Only those who can suppress their desires can escape it."

Marrill swallowed. Her mouth tasted like ash. "So, if we just don't *want* stuff, the fire can't burn us?"

"No," he said. "It's still a fire. It's very hot."

"Then what do we do when it catches us?" Fin asked, stepping forward.

The beetle chittered. "If you suppress all desires and focus on wanting for nothing, you can roll into a ball and your shell will be enough to protect you."

"But we don't *have* shells!" Remy cried.

Rysacg looked at each of them in turn. "Oh," he said. "Then you should probably run."

CHAPTER 20
Firefleers Fleeing the Fire Fleetly

"Aha!" Ardent finally cried. "Yes, you'll do nicely." He held out two bronze bowls. Fin looked at them dubiously. He wasn't really sure how they were supposed to help.

"Stand back," Ardent warned. He tossed the bowls high in the air, sending a swirl of sand and sparks chasing after them. When they clattered back to the ground, they'd been completely transformed.

They'd grown. And now had feet. Chicken feet, to be precise.

"They look like ostrich legs," Marrill pointed out.

"I'm calling them Ardent's Magnificent Firefleers," Ardent announced proudly. He'd fused two pieces of glass together to form makeshift wind goggles. "AMFFs for short," he added.

"That's a terrible name," Coll interjected.

Ardent shrugged. "I made 'em, I get to name 'em. If you don't like it, make your own magical transport creature."

"Fine," Coll grunted. He turned to face the crew. "Split up to even the load on the firefleers."

"AMFFs," Ardent coughed, but Coll didn't pay him any attention.

"Marrill, you and Rrric...sack"—he shook his head—"you and our beetle friend are with Ardent. Remy and I are with Annalessa. Now let's get out of here before we're all toast." The firefleers were already dancing, ready to run as everyone started climbing aboard.

"Hey, wait!" Fin called, waving his arms. "What about me?"

Ardent leaned over the rim of the bowl, giving him a once-over. Fin waited for Marrill to say something—remind Ardent who he was like she normally did. When she didn't, an all-too-familiar tightness squeezed his chest.

It almost seemed like she'd finally forgotten him.

"Hmm," the wizard finally said. "Very well, climb on up.

I suppose you do look a bit too flammable to be out here on your own."

"Gee, thanks," Fin muttered as he clambered aboard. The firefleer took off running before he could get all the way in, sending him tumbling into the bowl. He fell back next to the beetle, who didn't even seem to notice him.

Not even bugs cared about him, Fin thought with a sinking heart. He watched the way Marrill knelt next to Ardent as the 'fleers raced along the ridgeline. The way the wizard shifted to the side, giving her room. As though she belonged there.

The same old ache bloomed in his gut. The one where he wished more than anything that he could be normal. That he didn't have to constantly fear Marrill would forget him one day, the way everyone else in his life always did. That he could just find a place where he finally belonged. He wanted it so badly it hurt.

At the very moment the feeling hit him, a geyser of fire erupted beside them, showering them with sparks. The firefleer danced awkwardly, struggling to avoid the burning spray.

"We must leave the plateau fast," Rysacg buzzed. "The blood flows ever hot here, hot with need and want. Now it boils. The flametide will be on us at any moment."

"But we're surrounded by fire," Marrill cried. "How do we get past it?"

Fin closed his eyes. It was all about want, the beetle said.

And the flame had exploded right when he was wanting something the most. It gave him an idea.

"I want a home," he mumbled. "I want to find my mother," he added, this time louder. The tips of nearby flames bent in his direction.

"What are you doing?" Marrill hissed at him.

Fin pushed to his knees, clinging to the rim of the bowl. "It's all about want," he explained. "That's what draws the fire. And if it comes closer to us, that means it moves away from them." He jabbed a thumb at Annalessa's firefleer. "I want a tricornered hat to wear on the *Kraken*!" he shouted at the flames. "And a new pack of lockpicking gum, preferably cantelberry-burst flavored, which would be really nice and refreshing right about now!"

It was working. The flames arched toward them, pulling away from the edge of the canyon just enough to create a narrow path for the other firefleer to escape. Annalessa laughed in triumph and snapped the reins, driving through the gap.

Over the crackle of the blaze, he heard Remy shouting, "I want to pass my calculus exam! Even better, I want to never have to take an exam again for the rest of my life!"

The fire shifted. Like a cat after a string, it leapt after Annalessa's crew, leaving an opening for them to follow.

And the race was on. They darted through the canyons, one on one side, the other on the opposite, each crew shouting out wishes and wants. The fire sliced up one ridge-line, then rushed down the middle and up the other, drawn back and forth by the competing desires.

"I want shoes that never get wet!" Fin hollered.

"Oooh, I've been desperate for a full set of *Stapleton's Theories on Best Practices for Juniperia Distillation*, including apocrypha, in original mint condition," Ardent chortled. "With mint-flavored conditioning!" he added.

"I want a new box of coloring pencils, with lead that never breaks!" Marrill yelled.

"How about a new pair of double-sided decision dice?" Annalessa chimed in, laughing.

"A new ship's wheel made of bronze," Coll said, finally joining in.

Remy grinned. "A car that doesn't have teeth!"

They went on and on, their requests growing more and more absurd, until finally they were clear of the City of Burning Ladders, clear of the glass rock canyons, clear of the flametide, and out on the plain proper. Fires still raged all around—if anything, more so—but in the wide open, there was space to maneuver. Fin slumped back against the curve of the bowl and pushed his sweat-soaked bangs from his forehead.

"So, how's that for some good old-fashioned Pirate Stream adventure?" he called to Marrill. She still knelt next to Ardent, her hair flying out in the wind behind her.

"Hmmm?" she asked, seeming distracted. She glanced at him a moment and then frowned, her eyes shifting toward the beetle. "You didn't say anything—when we were all shouting wishes. Why not? Isn't there anything you want?"

"Everything wants something here," Rysacg buzzed. "My people want to climb the Wall. The buildings want to be rebuilt. The grass wants to grow. The fire wants to eat."

"That's how I made the AMFFs!" Ardent announced proudly. "Ordinarily, I would never bring an object to life like this; too much responsibility, you know. But I realized straight off that everything here already *wanted* to escape the fire. I just had to give it legs!"

Rysacg clicked his wing casings, and Fin noticed there weren't any actual wings underneath. "Just so. Even now the land wants to regrow, to heal. But wanting can be dangerous. It can burn too hot, turn destructive. It will feed off whatever fuel it can find until there is nothing left but want itself."

The beetle reached out a claw toward the far distance. "And see, the fire is dying. Soon it will have consumed all there is to consume, and burn itself out. The grass will grow quickly, and everything else, not much slower. The plain will be bursting with life again in a few hours. And a few hours after that, the fire will come back, too."

Fin squinted at the blackened desert. The lone and level sands seemed to stretch out forever. Then he blinked. What had been nothing but an empty expanse a moment ago now seemed to be taking on shape, turning into something else entirely. He pushed to his knees, leaning out over the rim of the bowl.

"Whoa," he breathed. "Are you seeing this?" Around them, sand bunched itself into mounds, dunes, and valleys. They, in turn, coalesced into firmer shapes, with sharper, unnatural angles. It was like the whole desert was a sand castle being sculpted by invisible hands before him.

As the landscape took shape, the very nature of it changed, softening into earth, hardening into stone, smoothing into brick and clay. All of a sudden, grass sprouted from the dirt, even as rocks tumbled upward to form the broken walls of old buildings.

"Even now the city rebuilds itself," Rysacg continued. "Wanting to return to its former glory. But the wanting will bring the fire once more, and the fire will bring destruction."

Marrill had turned and tucked herself against the curve of the bowl, knees drawn up to her chest as she listened. "So how can the fire come back?" she asked. "Shouldn't it just...burn out?"

The beetle clicked his claws in a noise Fin had come to recognize as the equivalent of shaking his head. "The fire burns. Sometimes more, sometimes less. Sometimes it hides—embers still glow in the dirt; stones stay hot enough to catch anything that touches them. Sometimes, fire can even keep burning inside something, like an old log, or a tree or a wall, and you never know it until it comes out. Then it does, and all is ablaze once again."

"Such is the way of wanting."

"So how does the Salt Sand King survive out here?" Fin asked. "Does he have a shell like you?"

Rysacg hesitated. "That is not a question anyone has thought to ask."

Marrill scrunched up her nose. "But aren't you curious?"

"No," the beetle said evenly. "It is not anything I've wanted to know." The firefleers raced onward, flames leaping and bounding playfully in their wake.

They hadn't traveled much farther when Rysacg clicked his wings. "There," he said, pointing.

The firefleers slowed to a trudge. Before them, a wide clearing opened in the grassland. All along its edges, the remains of sailing ships were littered. It reminded Fin of the marshes of Monerva. Only here, there was no water, just pure desert.

Despite the sails that still flapped limply in the wind, Fin got the feeling these ships were very, very old. Older by far than even the ship-bones in the Monervan marshes. And yet, their style was all too familiar. The same style he'd seen on the Map, when he'd used it to look for his mother, and again with the forgettable girl's ship in Belolow. Then there was the mark each ship bore on her side: the sign of a dragon under a mountain-filled circle. Fin hopped down to get a better look.

"Hey, I recognize that symbol," Marrill said, leaning over the rim of the bowl. "It was on the stop sign in my world, and on the obelisk at the Shattered Archipelago."

Rysacg gave an angry buzz. "Unsurprising. It is the sigil of the Salt Sand King, flames take his name."

Fin froze. The ships that had carried the forgettable girl and his mother had come from this very fleet, he was sure of it. The fleet of the Salt Sand King. He swallowed, his throat thick with confusion as he tried, and failed, to make sense of the connection.

"This place was once a bay," Coll declared as he jumped from his firefleer. He helped Remy and Annalessa down, then went to explore one of the ships more closely. "The Stream must have run all the way back here, before the Wall cut it off. Look, you can still see the salt clinging to the old hulls," he said, running his hand across one, then wiping the white powder against his pant leg.

Marrill walked right past Fin to join Coll. She craned her neck, staring up into the rigging. "Why haven't they burned?" She turned, looking over her shoulder at Rysacg, who stood a ways back next to the firefleers. "Don't the fires reach this far?"

"There is nowhere and nothing on the plain beyond the fire's reach." The beetle clicked his empty wings. "Why it chooses to leave these ships be, I do not know."

Coll scratched at his neck. "Well, they're streamrunners, all right. Which means they're made of dullwood. Dullwood's too boring to want. Or to burn. Tidespirals, I'm bored just talking about it."

Fin followed as they wound their way past the ring of old ships. Beyond, a small clearing opened up, and in its

center sat a little hut, seemingly hand molded out of red clay. Whatever else this place might have been, it certainly wasn't where one would expect to find a king.

That didn't seem to give Ardent pause. "Shall we?" he asked. He strode across the barren clearing and rapped his knuckles against a crooked strip of wood that presumably served as the door. "Hullo?" he called.

A long beat of silence followed. Everyone listened for movement from inside the hut. Ardent cleared his throat. "Anyone home?" he asked, louder.

He'd just raised his hand to knock again when the door banged open. "Yunh?" a voice squawked. The sound set Fin's teeth on edge. But it was the sight that made him want to take a step back.

A pitiful creature hovered in the doorway. He was hunched and hunkered, swaddled head to toe in rags, even over his crooked little beak. The wrapping almost completely covered his face, so that only his eyes were visible through a narrow gap. From where Fin stood, they looked like dull pinpricks of embers that had long since turned to ash.

Fin's stomach churned with an odd mix of horror and pity, and he could see from the expressions on the rest of the crew that he wasn't alone. Ardent, however, seemed unfazed. He swept into a bow.

"Greetings, sir. I am the great wizard Ardent. Perhaps you have heard of me?" Even bent down, Ardent towered over the creature, and he looked at him expectantly.

"I see Ardent's opinion of himself hasn't changed," Annalessa chuckled under her breath. Fin could have sworn that a tinge of pink flushed the tips of Ardent's ears as he straightened.

"Yunh?" the creature squawked. Fin couldn't tell whether the thing was just hard of hearing or simply couldn't make any other sound.

"I said, I am the great wizard Ardent!" Ardent tried again, almost shouting. "And we are here to speak with the Salt Sand King!"

"Yunh?"

Ardent blew out a frustrated breath and cupped his hands around his mouth. "Do you know where we can find the Salt Sand King?!"

Fin braced himself for another shrill "Yunh?" but it didn't come. Instead there was a moment of silence followed by what might once have been considered laughter. Now it sounded more like the choking gasp of a dying fire.

"I know of him," the creature croaked. He lifted one bandaged hand, the fingers wrapped up together almost like a claw, and bent into a bow, mocking Ardent. "Because I *am* the Salt Sand King." He lifted his head. "Perhaps you have heard of *me*, yunh?"

CHAPTER 21
The King of Salt and Sand

Marrill wasn't sure she'd heard right. This little feeble creature wrapped in rags was the Salt Sand King? The King who'd united the Boundless Plains? Who'd built the Wall and first used the Wish Machine?

She had to admit, she'd expected someone grander. Pity stabbed at her—how far the poor creature had fallen. After the Dawn Wizard tricked him, the angry beetles must have forced him into exile on the Burning Plain and left him out here to fend for himself. If the bandages were any indication, it hadn't been an easy existence. She didn't even want to think about how many times he'd been burned, or what injuries those bandages might conceal.

For a moment she wondered what the proper etiquette was in a situation like this. Did one bow to a king? Curtsy? She glanced around, hoping to take cues from the others, but they all seemed to just be staring.

Except for Ardent, of course. "Most noble host, thank you for taking the time to speak with us," he said. "We've come searching for information and with the hope of some assistance."

The Salt Sand King said nothing but "Yunh!" in a tone that sounded more like fingernails down a chalkboard than speech. Marrill clenched her teeth, trying not to cringe.

"We're hoping for your help against a most dangerous foe. A powerful being of unknown origin, who seeks to unleash a great evil onto the Pirate Stream." Ardent held his hand up to the brim of his hat. "He's about this tall, has a very fine beard, wears a suit of armor."

"I'm familiar, yunh?" the Salt Sand King said. "He came for the Syphon of Monerva."

Marrill gasped. "Did you tell him?"

The Salt Sand King spun, fixing her with his gaze. "Yunh," he grunted. "And why wouldn't I?"

Ardent stepped forward. "We'd like the same informa—"

"Can't help you," the Salt Sand King spat before Ardent could finish.

Annalessa stepped forward and placed a hand on Ardent's sleeve. "Let me try," she murmured.

Turning to address the Salt Sand King, she said, "Most honorable King, it's very important to us to find this Syphon and stop—"

The Salt Sand King cut her off. "You're a wizard, yunh?"

She smiled and nodded. "I am."

"I spoke wrongly. I meant to say I *won't* help you, yunh?" he hissed. "I don't work with wizards. Tricksters, the lot of you."

It was all too much for Marrill. "But the Master of the Iron Ship is a wizard," she pointed out. "Isn't he?"

The Salt Sand King shrugged. "And I don't trust him either, yunh? But someone had to go to the Syphon and grant my wish. Now I don't need to work with wizards anymore. So I won't."

Frustration bubbled through her. She didn't understand why he didn't get it, why he wouldn't help. "But we have to stop him, he's bad!" She stomped her foot. "He's going to cause the Iron Tide and destroy the Pirate Stream."

The Salt Sand King fixed her with eyes that glowed a flickering shade of red. She swallowed, forcing herself to hold her ground. "And how do you know about this Iron Tide?" he asked, taking a step toward her.

Sweat trickled down the back of Marrill's neck. The air in the clearing was so hot it almost felt physical, like a weight in her lungs. "Because it already happened."

The Salt Sand King tilted his head to the side. "It has? The Stream has been destroyed and I missed it, yunh?"

Marrill glanced at the others. None of them looked eager to intervene. "I mean, the Tide hasn't happened *yet* but it does. We know it will. Because people have talked about it in the past." She waved her hand in the air, trying to explain. "Which is also...the future."

Her shoulders slumped. Even *she* realized how ridiculous it all sounded. "Just please." Her voice cracked and she bit her lip, trying to stem the sting of tears already clawing its way up the back of her throat. "Everything I love is at stake here. I *have* to stop the Syphon."

The Salt Sand King moved closer, his voice dropping low like the hiss of steam. "I know what it is to lose all that you love. Even more, I know how it feels to be responsible for that loss—to have it all fall on your shoulders."

Relief flooded Marrill's system. She let out a long breath. He understood! "So you'll help us?"

Behind the rags wrapping his face, the Salt Sand King's eyes pulsed, the coals of a dying fire. His clawlike hands reached for hers. She forced herself not to cringe or pull away as his grip closed around her fingers.

He was hot, more than hot. His touch was almost burning. "I know what it is to want. I know what it is to lose. But even more than that, I know what it is to be tricked."

He spoke as though his words were meant only for her. "I can feel the way your want calls to the fire." His entire body seemed to glow with orange light. He dropped her hand, stumbling back. "All of you—all your desires burn fiercely enough to consume you. To blind you. To deceive you."

He spun, his attention falling to Fin. "And you, boy, what is it that you want?"

Fin's eyes went wide, as though he was surprised to have been noticed. "Um...I...uh...like she said. I want to stop the Syphon."

The Salt Sand King threw his head back, cackling like the popping of dried wood on a fire. "You cannot lie to your King; you realize this, yunh?"

When Fin only blinked in response, the Salt Sand King laughed louder. "What is it you do not understand? That I am your King? Or that what you just said was a lie?" He held.is rag-wrapped arms wide. "Because both are true. Yunh?"

"I..." Fin glanced at Marrill but then darted his eyes away. "Er...wasn't lying." His cheeks seemed to darken, and it took a moment for Marrill to understand.

She gasped. He'd lied. About wanting to stop the Syphon. Even though they both knew that was the only way to save her world. "Fin?"

But the Salt Sand King wasn't finished. He stalked toward Fin. "You don't want to stop the Syphon, because you know using it is the only way for you to be remembered." He poked his clawed hand at Fin's chest. "Because you don't understand the gift that you have. How important your skills can be. What I had to give up for you to have the power to slip in and out of memory."

Marrill's heart stopped. Fin's mouth dropped open. She could see his lips trembling, his fingers quivering.

"I know who you are," the Salt Sand King hissed. "I know *what* you are. Yunh?"

But before the Salt Sand King could say anything more, Ardent strode between the two. "Enough of this nonsense," he said with a swipe of his hand. "You will tell us how to find the Syphon of Monerva."

A shiver passed down Marrill's spine at the sharpness of Ardent's voice. Whatever the King had been saying vanished in the wake of it. "Remind me to never tick him off," Remy breathed beside her.

The Salt Sand King cackled. "Directions, yunh? That's what you're asking for? You poor, poor wizard. You don't even know how lost you truly are, do you?" He cocked his head toward Marrill. "Never trust a wizard, and now you know why," he chortled. "The Dawn Wizard buried the Syphon deep, he did. And only two folks know the trick to getting in or out." He paused. "Well, three folks now that I've shared that tidbit with that ironclad gent."

"You helped *him*, but you won't help *us*?" Ardent practically growled the question.

"Perhaps I already have helped you as well. Yunh?" the Salt Sand King countered. "Everything in pairs, you see?

You and he! The Dawn Wizard and me! And two doors, land and sea!"

"Enough!" Ardent shouted. Marrill cringed at the force of the word. "Stop playing games."

The Salt Sand King hopped from one foot to the other. "But a game it has become, yunh? The pieces are set, the moves already arranged. And you"—he threw his arm toward the wizard—"have already lost!"

For a moment, nothing happened. And then a strange sucking noise seemed to pierce the air, almost like a giant inhaling. Not even like inhaling. Like a giant coughing, but in reverse. Smoke leaked from the gaps in the Salt Sand King's bandages.

And suddenly Marrill knew exactly what would happen next. She lunged toward Ardent, snagging his sleeve and yanking him to the side. "Fire can hide!" she shouted.

They made it only two steps before the Salt Sand King exploded into flames.

Ardent pulled Marrill behind his robes as heat blasted over them. "Run!" he shouted, shoving her toward the ring of ships circling the clearing.

Marrill didn't need to be told twice. She sprinted hard, not caring that every breath seared her throat. Ahead, a patch of ground blazed to life, causing her to skid and pivot.

But there was fire there, too. It wavered and flickered and paced beside her, like a thing alive—a creature stalking her. And then it wasn't *like* a creature—it *was* a creature: an enormous burning tiger, its coat orange fire and black smoke, its eyes burning with green flame.

A scream clawed up Marrill's throat. Her muscles tensed, ready to run. But if this creature was anything like the real tigers she'd studied while her family lived in India, she knew running would be the worst move possible.

Instead she dropped her eyes and hunched her shoulders. "It's okay," she murmured, slowly backing away. The creature padded a slow arc around her, catching more of the plain ablaze with every step.

"Marrill!" a voice called from somewhere behind her. "What are you doing? Run!" The fire tiger crouched. Every flick of its tail sent sparks flying.

Then it pounced. Marrill dropped to the ground and rolled, throwing her hands over her face. The creature bounded past her, the heat of it singeing the hair from her arms.

As she lay there catching her breath, a thin, wispy trail of smoke rose up from the ground beside her. Carefully, she pushed onto her hands and knees, crawling slowly backward. The smoke came thicker, wormlike. Snakelike.

She patted at the ground, searching for a weapon but finding hunks of charred wood instead. They would have to do. She grabbed one in each hand.

With a sudden burst, the trail of smoke resolved into a

serpent. Two sparks glowed for eyes. Burning orange fangs seared the air. Headed straight at her. She flung one of the pieces of charcoal at the creature and ran.

"This way!" a voice called. Through the smoke, she saw a boy crouched against the hull of one of the ships, waving for her.

She veered toward him, leaping over a flaming alligator and dodging through a flock of burning bats. Behind her the fire chased, licking and snapping at her heels almost playfully, driving her onward. She reached the ship and the boy pushed her toward a ladder. "Go!" he shouted.

She shoved the other piece of charcoal in her pocket and climbed. On the deck, she was relieved to find the rest of the *Kraken* crew, all slightly singed but none seriously burned. Even their beetle guide and the two firefleers were there, bronze bowls clattering as they huddled together.

Overhead, the old sails flapped and snapped, while around them fire crackled through the grasslands. Serpents of smoke twisted through the air. Green flame eyes moved through the brush. But for some reason, they left the ship alone.

"What now?" She coughed as she wiped her blackened hands against her shirt. No one seemed to have an answer. "You're sure you can't just magic away the fire?" she asked the two wizards.

They both shook their heads.

"This fire was given life by the Dawn Wizard," Ardent said. "One of the greatest of the Dzane. And as you know, what the Dzane have made, only the power of the Dzane can destroy."

Tears of frustration and fear pricked Marrill's eyes. She turned away. Behind her, Rysacg stood by the firefleers, his demeanor as calm and steady as ever. "I don't suppose you have any ideas?" she asked him.

"You could try not wanting," he suggested.

Marrill could only snort in response. Not wanting was impossible. Especially now, when there was so much at stake. She needed to save her world and save her mom and get home safely with Remy. She wanted to stay on the Stream and keep having adventures, and she wanted it to be possible to have all of that at the same time.

It all burned so hot inside her that it felt like she'd swallowed the fire of the plain herself. "Everything wants," she growled at the beetle, stomping her foot. Her outburst startled one of the firefleers, causing it to back swiftly away from her and cower.

Marrill felt a stab of guilt. "I'm sorry, little one," she cooed, holding out a hand. Her heart hurt to see it so scared. As upset as she was, the firefleer was basically just an animal, with no idea what was going on. She wished it could just fly away, taking them all with it.

A thought occurred to her. "Hey, Ardent," she called. "Could you give the firefleers wings?"

"Of course," the wizard said, nodding. "But not useful

ones," he added, before her hopes could rise. "If you'll recall, I made a promise to the wind when you last left the Stream that I would not call on it again; I can't ask it to support my creations now." Under his breath, he mumbled, "You'd think the villainous vapor would be willing to renegotiate at some point, but no."

Another gust of wind scorched up from the plain, rattling the rigging and bathing the ship in smoke. Marrill choked, her eyes stinging and lungs burning.

They needed a way out, fast.

The firefleer nudged her gently. She stroked its leg, wishing it really *did* have wings. Working ones, anyway. Overhead, the ship's sails flapped and snapped.

Suddenly, those thoughts came together in Marrill's head. *Firefleer. Wings. Sail. Hot air. Flying.* Marrill's mind raced back to a memory of being young. Going on a balloon ride with her mom out over Coney Island in New York.

Hot air lifted the balloon! She nearly wept with joy. "Ardent!" she yelled. The beleaguered wizard was stroking his now soot-covered beard, debating the merits of manual magical manipulation with Annalessa. "Can you attach that sail to the firefleers?" she asked, pointing.

The wizard looked at her quizzically. "Well, yes, certainly, but I don't know how we're going to sail an AMFF...."

Coll stepped forward. "*I'll* handle the sailing," he said confidently. He leaned over to Marrill. "What am I sailing again?"

"You'll see," Marrill told him. Quickly, she explained to Ardent just what she wanted. With a zip and a magic snip, the sails came loose, and he fashioned them into balloons and attached them with ropes to the two firefleers.

"Hot-air balloons?" Remy clapped. "Marrill Aesterwest, you little genius. Okay, math homework is forgiven. This once."

A few moments later, Marrill gently coaxed the two firefleers out onto the ship's old bowsprit—one for Rysacg and one for the rest of them. She cupped her hands around her mouth. "I want a great big glass of ice water! I want an A on my geometry homework! I want a vacation to the CrystalShadow Wastes about now!"

The others chimed in, shouting their desires. Even Rysacg managed an "I'd like to go home now, please." The fire roared beneath them, hot air and smoke filling the balloons.

Rysacg's took off first, lifting slowly, then drifting higher. He waved a clawed hand in their direction. "I want you to have the best of luck!" he shouted. The flames surged. Marrill had to strain to keep a grip on their own 'fleer as the rest of the crew piled on board.

She jumped in after them. "I want to find that Syphon!" she yelled, stoking the fire. "I want to save my world and my mom!" Heat blasted her in the face. She felt the jolt of their balloon taking off.

She let out a wild whoop of success, but it caught in her

throat at Remy's panicked cry of "Plus One!" The babysitter lunged over the rim of the bowl, almost tipping the thing. Coll grabbed her, hauling her back in. She struggled against his grip. "We can't leave him!" she said, pointing.

Marrill looked back, mind scrambling. Sure enough, they'd left someone behind. "Come on!" she called to him. "Hurry!"

But the boy didn't move. He just stood there, an intense look of regret on his face, watching as the balloon lifted higher and higher. Panic and confusion washed over Marrill. She didn't understand—why wasn't he coming?

"What are you doing?" she cried.

"It's okay, Marrill!" he shouted from below. "I have to stay! Just go and stop the Syphon, all right?"

There was a moment as they rose, just a moment, when she could have jumped. When she could have stayed behind. When it wasn't too late to save him.

But then the moment was gone.

"Fin." The word formed on her lips, but she couldn't say for the life of her what meaning it might have held.

As the balloon climbed higher, she thought she heard the dry crackle of the fire laughing. And she couldn't for the life of her remember why she would even think about jumping.

CHAPTER 22
A Piece on the Game Board

Fin watched them go, guilt tangling in his gut. After all the times he'd complained about nearly being left, he was the one who had decided to do the leaving. He could still hear Remy's voice in his head shouting for "Plus One!" The fact that she remembered him enough to care made him smile. But it wasn't enough to ease the pain of what he hadn't heard.

And that was Marrill, shouting his name. Sure, she'd yelled for him to hurry. She'd been concerned for him.

But she hadn't remembered him. Not really. She'd forgotten him for real. Despite her promises. He couldn't help the anger that surged in him. Even if he knew it wasn't her fault. It was just the way of things. The way of who he was.

His heart twisted thinking about it. That was why he'd had to stay behind. Because the one thing he wanted more than anything else, more than anything the Wish Machine could give him, was to understand. And that was what the Salt Sand King had promised him.

He dropped from the ship to the ground. The fire burned hot before him, rising high like a tidal wave. But Fin wasn't scared, not anymore.

A voice came from the crackling flames. **"I knew you would stay."**

"You said you know who I am." Fin swallowed, his throat thick with smoke. "*What* I am."

"You are my piece on the game board," the fire snapped. **"I am your King. You are mine to command."**

Fin's back stiffened. He was relatively confident he didn't have a boss, let alone a king. And he was absolutely certain that if he did, it wasn't a talking fireball. "I'm no one's to command."

"And yet you carry my sigil," the fire hissed.

Fin's fingers twitched—he wanted to pull the bracelet out of his pocket and take a closer look at the symbol—but he kept his hands clenched into fists.

"You poor lost soldier." The fire flickered, dimming, and for a moment Fin thought he caught a glimpse of the rag-wrapped creature trapped in the flames. "So lost that you fail to see what you have."

Fin lifted his chin. "I'm not lost," he spat.

Burning grass snapped and wood popped with laughter. "Are you not? Look around. You stand in the middle of a desert, in the midst of flames. Left behind. Lost to everyone but me."

The fire did have a point, Fin realized. But then he shook his head. Fire couldn't have a point because fire was a thing. Things didn't have thoughts.

Of course, fire wasn't supposed to talk, either, and this one seemed to be doing plenty of that.

"Stop playing games and tell me who I am," Fin ordered.

"But is this not all a game? Do we not move around the board, eliminating others to get what we desire?"

"Do you ever say anything that's not in the form of a question?" Fin shot back.

A whip of fire cracked toward him, popping inches from his face. Fin stumbled back, holding a hand up to his cheek.

"I can read your desires," the flame cackled. "They flicker across your face and flush beneath your skin like the crinkling pages of a burning book. But understand this:

Your destiny is not to be remembered. Your destiny is to serve me."

Fin felt his patience snap. He was tired of people making promises and then breaking them. The Salt Sand King promised to tell him who he was. Marrill promised to remember him. His mom promised to come back for him. "Forget it," he growled, turning on his heel.

A blazing wall sprang up before him, circling him in an instant. The heat of it drenched him in sweat. He struggled to draw breath against the searing smoke.

"I AM THE FLAME THAT FOREVER BURNS THE FIELDS!" shrieked the sound of hissing steam and crackling wood. **"I AM THE TONGUE THAT DRINKS ETERNAL! I WILL HAVE MY RIGHT AND DESTINY TO RULE OVER ALL THAT EXISTS!"**

The flames simmered down with a hissing fizzle. **"Apologies. Being a fire has made me a bit...overdramatic."**

"I was going to say 'hot-tempered,'" Fin offered, unable to resist.

If he heard the pun, the Salt Sand King ignored it, which Fin thought was probably for the best. The flames collapsed to burning embers, coating the ground all around him. From the midst of them, the bent form of the Salt Sand King rose, tattered rags glowing red. He pinned Fin with his gaze. **"Three things the Dawn Wizard** promised me: first, to hone my will into a weapon."

The King held his arms out wide and lifted them slowly. At his command, flames leapt from the ground, soaring pillars that roared into the sky. For a moment it felt like the world had only ever been nothing but fire. Fin threw his arms over his face against the intensity of it.

"Second," the Salt Sand King continued, "to give me an army of soldiers who can't be beaten and spies that can't be seen." He dropped his arms and the flames fell back to the ground, twisting and flickering as they resolved into the shapes of men and women. All of them with the same symbol burning in their chests: a dragon under a mountain-filled circle.

"You are a spy in this army. MY army." The king stepped toward him. "Come at last to fulfill your duty."

"Pretty sure not," Fin said. "I'm a thief, actually. A master thief, now that you mention it." He puffed his chest with pride.

"Thief and spy, spy and thief." The Salt Sand King shrugged. "It's all the same—you move unseen and unseeable save only to me."

Fin hated how much sense that made. A spy and a thief had the same skills, didn't they? He swallowed, trying to fit this piece of new information in his brain. So he was a soldier? In an army he'd never known existed? Did that mean his mother was a soldier as well? That the forgettable girl was one of the Salt Sand King's spies?

"I have a mission for you," the Salt Sand King continued.

Fin was already shaking his head. He wasn't so sure taking orders from a crazed ball of fire was a smart idea. "Uh, no thank—"

"You'll like this one, I think. Because I need you to come to the Syphon with me. And when we do, I will help you make your wish." The offer was made in a hiss of steam.

Fin's pulse jumped, but he tried to keep his hope in check. He knew better than to trust this creature. "But you said you wouldn't help us."

The fire cackled. **"I said I wouldn't help the wizards, and indeed I won't."**

"And I would again point out that the Master of the Iron Ship is a wizard," Fin said.

"Exactly why I need you," the fire replied. **"I helped the Master because I had no other choice. Someone had to power the Syphon. Someone had to wish. THAT is the price the Dawn Wizard set for me. I made my final wish—but it will not be fulfilled until I grant the wish of another."**

Fin smacked his hand against his forehead. "'To get

what you want, you must give what you have.' It was talking about your final wish!"

"**Such an easy price,**" the Salt Sand King sputtered. "**And yet here I've been, trapped for all this time, with no one but bitter beetles for company. They hate the Machine too much to use it and hate me too much to wish for anything other than my demise. When the Master came to me, it seemed like my only chance to put things right. But now I have another option. You are different. You, I understand.**"

"I'm listening," Fin said.

"**The Master of the Iron Ship has set everything in motion. Even now the Syphon gathers power, faster than even I thought possible. Now we must stop him from using it, and prevent whatever destruction he seeks to unleash. You will be my spy. You will wait and watch. And when it is time for a wish to be made, we will ensure that you are the one to make that wish.**"

The Salt Sand King strode closer. "**Just imagine. Once my lands are united again, we will find my army. Your people. Where you belong.**"

A bright spark of hope lit in Fin's chest. He swept a hand through his sweat-soaked hair, thinking over the Salt Sand King's offer. It was everything Fin had ever wanted. He'd be reunited with his mother. He'd have a place to belong.

And if he got to make a wish, he'd be remembered by everyone.

A cold fist of doubt squeezed around the hope. What about Marrill? He bit the inside of his cheek, torn. If he helped the Salt Sand King, it could mean the end of Marrill's world. At the same time, though, it would mean stopping the Master of the Iron Ship from using the Syphon.

It could mean preventing the Iron Tide, and wasn't that the whole reason she'd come back to the Pirate Stream in the first place? Really, if he thought about it that way, he'd be helping her by going with the Salt Sand King.

Everyone would win!

One question lodged in Fin's mind. "So...what *is* your third wish, anyway?"

The rag-wrapped figure dropped back to the embers. A flame blazed where he'd stood. **"Simple. That no world shall EVER be beyond my reach."**

The flame flickered and twisted, resolving itself into a dragon bellowing smoke to the sky.

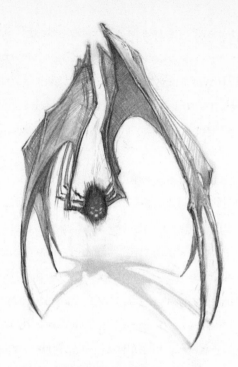

CHAPTER 23
The Tower of the Wiverwanes

As Marrill stared down at the expanse of the Burning Plain, a wave of anger crashed through her. She couldn't believe the Salt Sand King had refused to help them! He'd even seemed to understand how desperate the situation was, and what the consequences would be. He just didn't care.

She ground her teeth. "There has to be another way," she growled under her breath.

"Another way to get Plus One back?" Remy asked, brightening.

Marrill frowned. "Plus One?" She shook her head. "No, to stop the Syphon."

The babysitter's face fell. "Oh. Right. That." She let out a long sigh.

"It'll be okay," Coll said, sliding down in the bowl next to Remy. "He seemed a capable sort. Resourceful. He found us after all, didn't he? I'm sure he'll be fine. Whoever he is."

Marrill clutched at the rim of the bowl. "Everything in pairs," she mumbled to herself, thinking back through what the Salt Sand King had told them. She turned to face the others. "What do you think he meant by 'everything in pairs—two doors, land and sea'? Think that actually means two physical doors to the Syphon?"

Coll shrugged. "If you're willing to trust a giant insane ball of fire, that's how I'd interpret it."

"And maybe he meant there's one on each side of the Wall," she continued. "That would make sense, right? One on the land side, one on the sea side?"

"Seems reasonable," Annalessa offered.

Marrill chewed on her lip. "So, the Salt Sand King said only three people know the trick to finding the Syphon, right?"

"Correct," Annalessa said. "One being the Master of the Iron Ship. Presumably the other two would be himself and the Dawn Wizard."

"Well, the Master's out—no way is he helping us," Marrill grumbled. "Can we find the Dawn Wizard?"

Ardent tugged on one of the ropes leading up to the balloon, letting out a puff of hot air to level them off. "I fear not. Like all the Dzane, he died long ago, or at least that's the conclusion most everyone who knows anything has come to."

"Well, everyone except Marravellio," offered Annalessa.

Ardent waved a hand. "Marravellio is a senile old gossip who likes drama. I said anyone who knows anything, which rules him out."

Remy pushed herself up straighter. "Don't you guys have, like, a magical map or something that can show you everywhere?"

"Excellent point, sailor!" Ardent said. As he patted at his robes, his forehead furrowed. "I could have sworn I put it here...."

Marrill quietly slipped her hand into her pocket, hoping she could get the Map out without having to admit taking it in the first place. But as her fingers closed on the parchment, she realized it didn't matter. The Key was gone. And the Map was no good without it.

Her stomach churned. She was going to have to confess. She took a deep breath. "I've got the Map," she whispered. "But it won't work...because I lost the Key."

Ardent's eyes widened with surprise. "What? But I had both of them, I'm certain—"

"We took them," Marrill said quickly. "We thought it would be okay...."

"Who's 'we'?" Coll demanded.

Marrill opened her mouth to respond but suddenly didn't have an answer. "Uh...me and...um..." She could have sworn there was someone else with her. She pressed her fingers against her temples, trying to focus. Stealing the Map just didn't seem like something she'd do on her own.

"You and Plus One?" Remy offered.

Marrill snapped her fingers. "Yes, exactly. Me and Plus One," she said, relieved to have figured it out.

"You *stole* them from me?" Ardent pressed. He sounded very, very unhappy. More than that, he sounded disappointed.

A flush crept up Marrill's neck. Tears pricked her eyes as she dropped her head.

"Now's not the time for that, Ardent," Annalessa shushed. Her voice softened as she knelt in front of Marrill. "Now, Marrill, what did you do with them?"

"We used it to try to find the Syphon," she mumbled. "We asked where the Syphon was, and it showed us the Wiverwanes' Tower. That's why we were climbing up there. But you said the Wish Machine wasn't there..."

"No, definitely not," Annalessa said firmly.

"Well, what about the Key itself? Where did you last see it?" Ardent pressed.

She swallowed. "We used it at the top of the Wall— that's when we accidentally opened the Gate. And then—"

"Opened the Gate?!" Ardent interrupted.

Marrill cringed. "It happened by accident?"

"How?"

"I don't know," she confessed, her voice barely audible. "I was struggling with someone and . . . it just happened."

Ardent practically vibrated with unspent energy. If they had been back on the deck of the *Kraken,* he'd probably have been pacing furiously. But up here in their little bowl, there was nowhere for him to go. "Well, this changes things, doesn't it?"

Marrill hated the disappointment that dripped from the words. Biting her lip to keep from crying, she slumped back against the curve of the bowl. A deep ache spread through her chest. Everything had become so overwhelmingly complicated and difficult all of a sudden.

For the first time, failure didn't just seem like a big possibility, but inevitable. Everything she cared about was on the line and she'd screwed up. The Map had steered them wrong. She'd lost the Key, and now they'd never find the Syphon. It would continue sucking in water until it pulled her entire world onto the Pirate Stream, and everything she'd ever known would be ripped to pieces. And then the Master would make his wish and unleash the Iron Tide.

Marrill would never be able to save her mother, much less her world. Even the Stream—her safe haven, and her friends' home—would be lost to the Iron Tide.

She'd disappointed everyone, in the end.

Tears blurred her eyes. She swiped at them with the hem

of her shirt, recoiling at the stench of smoke. She took a cautious whiff of her hair. Everything smelled like fire, including her skin.

"I hate to point this out to a wise and powerful wizard," Remy said, breaking the silence. "But aren't we going the wrong way?"

Marrill snapped her head up, glancing over the rim of the bowl. Sure enough, the Wall was slowly growing more distant.

"Hmmm…" Ardent looked from the balloon overhead to the rapidly receding fire below. Drawing a deep breath, he raised an arm and said, "Okay, wind, I know we've had our disagreements, and I know that last time I said it was the last time, but I'm *seriously* serious this time: I'll only ask of you this *last* thing—to be taken back to the Wall."

For a moment, there was nothing. "Afraid you're still on wind's bad side," Coll muttered. Ardent scowled and dropped his arm.

"Perhaps I should give it a try?" Annalessa offered.

But before she could, a great howl grew in the distance, intensifying as it approached. Marrill felt the touch of a breeze rustling through her ponytail. Then the tips of her hair lifted, and strands drifted around her face. The balloon slowly reversed course and began coasting back toward the Wall.

Ardent smiled, pleased with himself. "See, I knew—"

He didn't have time to finish. A wall of wind hit them with such force it sucked the air out of Marrill's lungs. The bronze bowl jerked first one way and then the other, throwing them into one another. Above them, the tattered sailcloth looked as though it had been punched.

The balloon screamed across the Burning Plain toward the Wall. The wind whipped at them, snatching words from their mouths the moment they tried to speak.

In seconds, the Wall loomed ahead of them. The balloon jerked up. Marrill's stomach dropped down to her toes as they slingshotted into the sky.

It was like they were a toy caught in a puppy's mouth as he tore around the yard, flinging them from side to side. And this puppy looked nowhere near done playing with them.

The crew tumbled over one another in a pile of arms and legs, elbows and knees flying. The bowl was perpendicular to the ground, so close to the Wall that the poor 'fleer was practically running up as they crested the top. The Tower of the Wiverwanes filled Marrill's vision.

She thought again about what the Salt Sand King had said: Only three people knew how to find the Syphon. The Master and the Salt Sand King would never help them, which only left the Dawn Wizard. But as far as anyone knew, he'd been gone for ages.

But not his memories, she realized. *Not the memories of the Dzane.* Those lived on in the Wiverwanes.

"Of course," she whispered. Remy looked at her strangely as she clutched the rim of the bowl, hair flying out behind her.

"The Map *didn't* steer us wrong; we asked the wrong question!" Marrill had to shout to be heard over the roaring wind. "We asked *how* to find the Syphon. Not where. And the Map showed us!" She pointed at the Wiverwanes' Tower, now rapidly approaching.

In a heartbeat, they'd be past it. Flung out across the marshes, and who knew how far beyond that.

Too far to make it back in time to stop the Syphon—that much was for sure.

She threw a leg over the rim. "What are you doing?" Remy screeched, reaching for her. But she was too late.

Marrill had already let go. Suddenly, she was falling. It was both horrifying and thrilling at the same time.

The top of the Tower grew closer and closer and closer.

All too quickly, it became clear she'd jumped from too high. Her momentum was carrying her too fast. She was falling far too hard.

The impact would kill her. The realization sent her heart into overdrive.

"Do this for *me*, wind!" she heard Annalessa cry.

A silken cushion of air rose up around Marrill, cradling her. Slowing her. She struck the peaked roof with her shoulder. She scrabbled, raking her hands across the slate tiles as she slid down the slope.

And then she was airborne again. The air grasped her tighter this time and she landed on the top of the Wall with a teeth-rattling "Oof."

For a moment, she could only sit, stunned, gasping. She wasn't dead.

She searched the sky for the balloon. Far, far in the distance, she caught sight of it, slowly drifting downward while a dark storm brewed beyond.

"Thank you," she whispered to the air, knowing it was persnickety enough that it could have ignored Annalessa's order if it had wished. The wind picked the words up from her lips, sent a breeze through her hair, and then was off, leaving Marrill alone to face the Wiverwanes.

She stood, her legs still rubbery from fear. A brief wave of vertigo hit when she took in the view. To one side of the Wall, the Burning Plain extended clear to the horizon. And on the other...

A chill stole over her skin. Waves pounded the base of the Wall, sending the gears into overdrive. She was so high up that the ships and docks looked like matchsticks, flung about in the tide. She knew that Ropebone Man and the pirats were more than capable of handling storms worse than this, but even so, she hated to think of Karnelius being trapped on board. "At least he has the Naysayer," she reminded herself. Ornery or no, the two creatures would take care of each other.

And then she caught sight of something that caused her heart to drop. "What in the...?" Several of the cranes along the top of the city struggled to lift a parking garage, complete with cars. Not far below that was a Ferris wheel from the old abandoned amusement park down the road from her house. There were saguaro cacti, blinking stoplights, a roll of rusted chain-link fencing. More and more of her world was being pulled onto the Stream.

"Oh no," she breathed. Heart pounding, she skimmed the gears, looking for one that hadn't started spinning yet. She couldn't find one. The Syphon was nearly at full power.

She could already be too late.

She ignored the dizziness the thought caused and raced across the top of the Wall to the Tower. There was no door. Cautiously, she hauled herself through one of the thousands of holes that pocked its surface, and dropped inside. She found herself in a large open chamber. The air had the quality of twilight—a soft haze that made everything look like a movie filmed long ago. It reminded Marrill of the massive dovecotes she'd explored during her family's tour of medieval French châteaus a few years back.

The walls were rounded, made of stacked stone that curved inward as they neared the peak. Marrill's eyes trailed up them and she sucked in her breath.

The top of the Tower was a mass of writhing darkness. Its surface roiled like the underside of a thunderhead.

The Wiverwanes.

She took a trembling breath, trying to figure out what her next move should be. Could she just ask how to get to the Syphon? What would they do to her if she did?

But then a soft sound tugged at her ear, a whispering sort of clicking that seemed out of place. She searched around until she found a small dark shape hunched in the shadows at her feet. It shifted as she moved closer.

Crouching, she could just make out the hazy outline, like two hands glued back-to-back. A lone Wiverwane. "Hey there, little fellow," she said softly. "Why aren't you with the rest of your…" She searched for the right word. "Pack? Crew?"

Flutter, she realized.

The Wiverwane inched forward, quivering slightly. Marrill could see immediately what the problem was. One of its fingers was bent unnaturally, the edges of its hand-wing tattered. She sucked in a breath. The creature was injured.

She'd rescued enough animals in her life to know that a creature in pain could be dangerous. She didn't even want to think about how that translated into a world like the Pirate Stream. The Wiverwanes were a complete unknown. The smart thing would be to leave it alone.

But she couldn't do that.

Besides, she'd come to the Wiverwanes for help, hadn't she?

She held out her hand, moving slowly so as not to startle it, letting the Wiverwane come to her. "It's okay," she cooed.

Cautiously, the creature extended one limb toward her palm. At its touch, her skin rippled. The memory came slowly, haltingly, like an Internet video buffering.

A shadow fell across the stone floor of the Wiverwanes' Tower, darker than any shadow had a right to be. It fell from a man clad in black robes adorned with white stars. He reached up, trembling white fingers delicately plucking a Wiverwane free from the cloud swirling over him.

He ignored the way the creature jerked against his freezing touch as he dangled it in front of his face. A black, wet tear carved down his pale skin. He choked on a sob. "Girl with wings. I knew you would come."

Marrill stumbled backward, physically wrenching herself from the memory. She tasted bile. Her heart thundered in her ears. "Serth," she whispered.

He was alive. And he was here, in Monerva.

Not only that, he'd known she would come here, to this Tower, now. He'd been speaking to her directly. He'd known she would get that memory.

But how could that be possible? Serth was dead! Swallowed by the Pirate Stream.

But then, the Master of the Iron Ship had been too. And she knew he was alive and in Monerva.

Her eyes fluttered closed. Serth was also searching for the Wish Machine; she didn't have any evidence of that, but she didn't have any doubt, either.

Annalessa had said that the Syphon had already consumed a truly massive amount of magic. Perhaps even enough that it could grant any wish at all.

An awful feeling crawled up the back of Marrill's throat. She didn't want to think about what Serth planned to wish for.

CHAPTER 24
Everything Wants

"**T**his way," urged the Salt Sand King.

Fire raced across the dry plain with Fin fast after it. At times it blazed, choking the air with great puffs of smoke. Other times it smoldered waiting for him, only bursting to life when he came near. It was a pride of lions, running alongside him through the high grass. It was a flood of scorpions, snapping at his feet if he fell behind.

As he drew closer, a mound seemed to raise itself from the grassy earth. Stones rolled upward to build the walls of an enormous building. Towers shoved into the air like spears.

"Ah, the Palace of Water and Land," said a whoosh of rising heat. "Once this was all mine. See how it strives for its former glory. How many times have I burned it down in my madness?"

Fin pushed onward. When he reached the outer walls, archways snapped themselves together out of the dirt to mark the entrance hall. Bricks fell into place ahead of him, walling away the dappled sunlight.

Fin stepped inside, feeling the air grow cooler. He sucked it in, appreciating the way it dulled the burning in his lungs.

"Wait," the fire growled behind him. Fin turned. The flames had stopped just outside the newly formed doorway. "Take a lamp from the wall," the King commanded.

Fin looked around. He hadn't seen any lamps. There was a hook, though, where one might have hung. As he watched, dust swirled around it, turning into rust, which slowly formed into a little steel cage. Glass melted from its rim, down the sides, until it was exactly what the King had said: a tiny lantern, perfect for hanging on his belt. He grabbed it.

"What now?" he asked. As he turned back to the Salt Sand King, a great bloom of fire rushed straight at him. Fin let out a shout. But there was no need; the fire flickered and

dwindled, dying down into a tiny, floating spark. The spark landed inside the lantern, where it grew to a candle flame.

"Onward, my new friend," the King's voice sputtered from the tiny flicker. Fin glanced out the door. The Burning Plain was scorched black, but empty. No signs of the fire remained.

He made his way through the palace, following the King's directions from the lamp. Left and then right, right again and straight ahead. Sunlight filtered in through ragged holes in the stone walls as he went. Holes that narrowed and became windows, trailing a draping of glass across their surfaces.

They passed through huge archways and long halls, through galleries and grand open plazas. "This was my feast hall, where the butterbeast roasted day and night," said the candle in a room where long tables rose up, rebuilt from ash and splinters. "Ah, the celebration here, when I united the Boundless Plains and put an end to the Eleven-and-Thirty-Six Century War."

Fin ducked through a door and into a gallery with sweeping arched ceilings. "No one believed such a feat was possible." The flame flared brighter for a moment. "Joyous processions filled the streets, moving in time with the beat of the drum and the wail of the pipe. The entire kingdom danced for days and days."

"Sounds like some party," Fin remarked. He paused at

an intersection of corridors. The flame guttered to the right and Fin plunged into a series of smaller rooms. As he darted from one to the next, tables reassembled themselves from cinders. Game boards stacked on top of them, and playing pieces arranged themselves in carved wooden bowls.

"Here, I won the Dawn Wizard's cloak in a game of biffletacks. Yet another feat no one believed possible. He invented the game, you know."

"So you literally beat a Dzane at his own game?" Fin asked.

The flame flickered in a laugh. "It's hard to say if I played fair. But a wager is a wager. And I offered the cloak back to him, of course. For a price."

Fin snorted. "*Cheating* a Dzane. Now you're sounding a bit brainbroke." He didn't know much about the Dawn Wizard, but he didn't seem like the kind of guy you wanted to stiff.

The flame almost seemed to dance in the lantern. "It was a reasonable price. Only three wishes."

"So he built the Syphon of Monerva to grant them," Fin said. It made sense now. *The Legacy of the Salt Sand King.*

"Indeed. Ah, the baths," the King sighed as they passed a ring of empty stone pools around a dry fountain. "How long since I've had a good soaking."

After what seemed like forever, they reached a massive atrium with many passages branching off of it. Grass carpeted the floor, so thick it was practically a meadow. Around them, stones rolled up and inward, each falling into place to make a great domed roof.

"My private garden," said the Salt Sand King in his lantern. "We're close now. We shouldn't tarry here, though. The grass is already growing thick."

Fin stepped out onto the soft carpet of green. "What's wrong with the grass? It's nice, what without a fire to burn it and all."

But as he watched, the grass grew fast and even faster. Tough yellow shoots shot up between the gentle green ones, sprouting all over the garden. As they reached waist height, they coiled and burst into brilliant flowers, soaking the air in rich scents: lavender, honeydew, peppermint, and warm chocolate cake. Fin's belly growled with hunger.

For a second, he set aside the craziness of this journey. The Shattered Archipelago, Monerva, the City of Burning Ladders, Marrill forgetting him, all of it. Instead he simply enjoyed being here. He let out a little laugh of surprise when one of the flowers opened up to release a bumbling little bee. It floated across to pollinate another one. Other buds opened, springing loose grasshoppers that bounded through the fresh green leaves.

"Don't be fooled," the King whispered in his lamp. "Everything here has been forged by the same magic that forged me. Move on, before things get worse."

"Sure, sure," Fin told him. "Where to?"

"**Look up and follow my blade,**" the candle said.

Fin looked up. A cloud of dust shuffled across the newly formed ceiling, revealing a faded, ancient mural. As he watched, color flooded back into it.

A central figure stood in the middle with sword raised, a proud knight or a conquering king. He wasn't Monervan, or beetle; the man had deep olive skin, dark hair, rounded features like Fin's own. These really could have been his people.

All around the painted king, every sort of creature imaginable looked on with awe or envy. Beneath his feet, scrawled across the image of a flapping banner, were two words:

Fin studied the image. The king in the mural seemed so much grander. So much larger and fuller and . . . alive. Nothing at all like the bent creature Fin had met in the clearing. "So that was you?"

The lamp grew warm against his side. "**Follow my blade and keep moving,**" the flame warned. "**Quickly now.**"

As the Salt Sand King spoke, a sprig of grass so tough and dry and brown it was almost a branch pushed up before them. A large bud bulged out from its tip, then blossomed, revealing a yellow-skinned lizard.

It glanced around for only a second before leaping from its perch and devouring the nearest bug, then the next and the next, gulping them down as fast as it could, like it was starving. Meanwhile, other bugs buzzed frantically from flowers that bloomed heavily on the stalks that grew desperately across the room.

Before his eyes, the garden turned rapidly into a thicket. From grass to bugs to lizards, growing, buzzing, devouring out of control. What had started as pretty was now a bit scary. Even the scent in the air had grown sickly sweet and overpowering. It was like nothing here could ever be enough or get enough.

"What did I tell you?" the candle sparked at his side. "Do you think I'm the only thing on this plain that burns? Go. Now!"

The words broke Fin out of his stupor. He glanced back up to the mural, following the point of the blade to a passage at the far end of the room. "On it," he said. He shoved aside a thick tangle of grass, pushing forward.

Just then, he heard a hiss. Then a crackle. Then a *fwoosh*. It was the sound of a fire lighting.

"Too late," the King sighed from his candle.

In the center of the room, a red flame bounced from

stalk to stalk, catching each as it went. Fin stumbled backward, fear welling up inside him. The Burning Plain had relit itself. And he was standing in a tinderbox.

He raced for the passage, barely clearing its archway before the flames burst into a full-blown fire behind him. A wave of heat washed over him. The sickly-sweet perfume turned burnt and curdled in his lungs. As he tore forward, he glanced back to see flames leapfrogging after him.

"Do something!" he screamed as the passage plunged abruptly downward, growing steeper with each step.

"Like what?" the candle hissed. As they descended, the air ahead grew cooler, like they were dropping down into a cellar. But even as the walls dampened with moisture, Fin's feet continued to crunch over brittle dry grass.

"I don't know," he shouted, turning one corner and then another. No matter where he went, the heat still licked at his heels. "Isn't fire, like, yours?"

"Well, it won't hurt ME either way," the King remarked.

"Thanks," Fin shot back. "That's very reassuring." He sucked in great gulps of air, arms pumping in a full-on sprint. Ahead, the hallway opened up into a larger chamber.

"Almost there," the King called. "But watch out for the backdraft!"

Backdraft? Fin wondered.

Just then the air sucked past him with such force it almost carried him with it.

He twisted to look.

The orange flames guttered away from him. For just a second, a long second, he thought they might be dying.

And then the fireball exploded down the hallway.

Fin shrieked and dove forward. At the end of the chamber, a door loomed ahead of him. There was nowhere else to go. As he crashed into it, he whipped around, throwing his arms up over his face as if that could shield him from the flame.

But the heat didn't burn him. If anything, it grew a little bit milder, turning from stuck-in-an-oven painful to just super-hot-day uncomfortable.

"Well done, well done!" the lantern crackled. *"We made it after all!"*

Fin opened his eyes. In front of him, a wall of flame shimmered. He stood in what looked like a small antechamber, just at the end of the hallway. Ornate carvings decorated the walls on all sides, but he couldn't tell what they were, because every inch of them was covered in thick white and blue crystals from ceiling to floor.

He reached out a cautious hand and touched one. It was cool and dry, and a thin white sheen of dust came off on his fingertip. He sniffed it, then pressed it to his tongue. Salt. The crystals were salt.

Fin looked down to see his own footprints behind him, traced in the same sort of salt. Where the salt ended, the wall of fire loomed. That, he realized, was what kept the fire at bay. Just as it must have done on the ships around the Salt Sand King's clearing.

Something moved at the edge of the flaming wall. Fin peered closer. In the glowing orange curtain, he could make out the outline of the lizard, dancing as one with the blaze.

It leapt at him.

Fin cringed and tossed a spray of salt at the creature. It struck the flame-lizard with a fizzle, and it guttered and died. An air current whisked the remains up, swirling them around the room as errant sparks. A second later, it all winked out of existence entirely.

"Poor lizard?" Fin said. It didn't stop him from shoving a handful of salt into his thief's bag.

"Thus why you had to carry me," said the Salt Sand King. "It was the Dawn Wizard who did this, just as he enacted a price to keep me—no, US—from our destiny. But now, thanks to you, my loyal soldier, the Syphon is within reach!"

"No problem," Fin lied. Only he wasn't sure who he was lying to—the King or himself.

CHAPTER 25
DOWN…Down…down…

The injured Wiverwane flapped frantically in front of Marrill, struggling to keep aloft. The leg Serth had been clutching hung limp and the skin there was withered from frostbite. Serth had injured the creature beyond repair.

As much as she didn't want to be plunged into another memory, the poor thing was about to plummet to the ground. She shot out her arm, offering it a place to land. It clambered awkwardly onto her shoulder. She waited for the onslaught of memory, but it didn't come. Instead the Wiverwane stretched out one of its legs to tap gently against the bare skin of her neck. Where it touched, her flesh rippled.

The memory was brief and thankfully one of her own. A snapshot of her family laughing at one of her father's particularly terrible jokes, bringing with it a surge of warmth and love that drove away Serth's lingering chill. Marrill smiled. "Thank you," she whispered to the creature.

The Wiverwane had no face and no expression, but it hunkered against her shoulder, the way a dog might lean against its master's leg. It took care to touch only her shirt, and Marrill realized with relief that so long as it didn't come into direct contact with her skin, it wouldn't transfer any memories.

"Can you help me?" she asked it. "I need to find the Syphon of Monerva, and I'm hoping you can show me how to get there."

The creature hesitated. Marrill held her breath, waiting. If it couldn't or wouldn't help, she wasn't sure what she'd do. "You're my last hope," she whispered to it.

Slowly, it stretched out its leg and tapped the side of her neck.

She was completely unprepared for the visions that filled her mind.

The Dawn Wizard glanced over his shoulder, surveying the docks to ensure he was not being followed or watched. And then he slipped through an unassuming door and headed to the farthest reaches of the palace's sprawling catacombs, where the heart of his creation awaited.

Wishes were double-edged swords. The old creature knew that from long experience. He was Dzane; his brothers had lit stars in the heaven as testaments to their glory. Now those stars burned on, their makers all but forgotten.

The little creature stopped at the entrance to the chamber. His long blue fingers drummed against an empty crystal orb. The key was to look at things from both sides, he thought. The in and the out. The cost and the gain. Land and water, salt and sand.

Already the room was beginning to sink under the weight of the city, as the Dawn Wizard had intended. And it would continue to do so for eternity.

Burying the Syphon along with it.

Marrill sucked in a gasp as the Wiverwane retreated, the memory nothing more than a ripple across her skin. "The Syphon's buried under Monerva!" She scrambled to her feet. "I've got to find a way down there!"

She started toward the narrow hole she'd climbed through to get into the Tower. Then she hesitated. The Wiverwane still crouched on her shoulder. "Don't you want to go back to your friends?" she asked, nodding at the roiling cloud amassed on the ceiling inside the Tower.

The creature tucked into itself and clutched at her sleeve. "So I guess we're in this together, then?" she asked.

With a touch of its appendage, she felt a wave of half-formed memories, all of them reassuring.

Marrill blew out a long breath. "Okay, then. Let's do this thing." She pushed her way outside and eased along the top of the Wall.

Thankfully, it looked like the Highest of Monerva were back at it, and Talaba, the tall woman with her canopy, had enlarged it in a bid to take the crown. It flapped beneath where Marrill stood. "Hold on," she warned the Wiverwane.

And then she jumped.

Marrill would have thought she'd be used to the sensation of plummeting through the air by now, but she totally wasn't. She landed against the canopy with an "Oomf!" and the sound of fabric tearing. It gave way, and she tumbled down to the small glass platform, coming to rest against one of the pillars.

"My canopy!" Talaba wailed. "My only shot at being highest, and you ruined it!"

"Oh, give it a rest," Necarib scolded.

"Sorry!" Marrill cried. She started down the iron ladder, then the twisty glass stairs between the spires. At this rate, even with the city sinking as fast as ever it would take hours—if not an entire day!—to get all the way to the Grovel.

She needed a shortcut. She sprinted across a glass bridge, jumped onto a sinking staircase, and found her way onto a lush garden overhang. She stared down, about to give up, when the swirl of a familiar shell came into view.

"Hey, Elle!" she called. "How about a lift?"

A thick green snail tail sprang from Elle's shell and whipped toward her. The tip of it slipped over Marrill's shoulder before wrapping securely around her waist.

"To the bottom, Elle!" she cried.

Ever since they'd visited Kawarau Bridge in New Zealand when Marrill was younger, she'd wanted to bungee-jump. But her parents always said she wasn't old enough. Now she finally had her chance. She threw her arms in the air, squealing and whooping as the city flew past.

"W
      H
        E
          E
            E
            E
            E
            E
            E
            !
            !
            !"

she cried as she dropped
down
down
down
down.

In the distance she could see a large wave gaining steam, plowing toward the Wall. As it reached the edge of the Grovel, it lifted docks and any remaining seaworthy ships, including the *Kraken*.

"Ropebone Man!" she cried as the ship surfed up toward her. "Incoming!"

A line shot from the rigging, zipping straight for her. The transition was seamless. Elle let her go, tossing her through the air like a trapeze performer. She was airborne for several long, gut-wrenching moments. Then Ropebone had her.

"Thanks, Elle!" she shouted, hoping the snail could hear, as Ropebone Man lowered her carefully to the deck. The green snail tail waved at her before retracting back up the Wall.

The moment her feet touched solid-ish ground, she felt the tap of the Wiverwane's leg against her neck. A series of memories flooded through her, all of them with one dominant emotion: relief. "I'd think you'd be used to wild rides like that!" She giggled as the creature retreated back under her collar.

"Thanks, Ropebone Man!" Marrill said, giving the rope a tug.

She'd barely been on board for half a second when a small door leading below deck burst open, and a ball of orange fur came bounding out. His claws scrabbled against the wooden deck as he charged toward her. He leapt and she caught him midair.

"Hey, you!" Marrill cried, burying her face in Karny's fur, letting the rumble of his purr warm her heart. He bonked his head against her cheek, shifting his legs so he could snuggle even closer.

She closed her eyes, and for a moment it felt like being home.

She felt a stab of sorrow at the thought of her house in Arizona. When had she started thinking of it as *home*, and not just a place where they were living until her mom got better? Hopefully, she'd be waiting there when her parents got home, and they'd never even realize she'd been missing. Hopefully, she would have a world left to be waiting in.

Speaking of home...Marrill glanced around the deck of the *Kraken*. Almost every available surface was loaded down with junk. And most of it looked uncomfortably familiar. A collection of portable electronics sat next to a pile of sporting equipment and a heap of holiday decorations. With each wave, it all shifted and rolled in a great clattering cacophony.

The Naysayer shuffled between the mounds, all four of his arms full of junk. He looked her way, and his sour face brightened. "Where'd you get off to?" he asked.

Marrill smiled back. "I went up the Wall looking for the Syphon—"

"Not you," the Naysayer grunted dismissively. He shifted his piles until he'd freed a hand to reach for Karny. When Marrill twisted away, he settled for giving the cat a scratch under his chin. "Doesn't like the waves, y'know," he told her.

"Where is everyone?" she asked.

The Naysayer shrugged. "Gallivanting, I assume. Wasn't invited. Wouldn't have gone if I had been. Mannerless cretins."

Marrill bit her lip and searched the sky. She thought she caught a gleam in the distance, an errant ray of light reflecting off the bronze bowl of the firefleer. She was pretty sure the balloon was headed back toward Monerva. Still the air must have been really angry at Ardent to have blown him so far off course.

She wondered if she should wait for them before going to look for the Syphon. On the one hand, having two wizards by her side would definitely increase her odds of success. On the other hand, they still seemed a long way off.

She shook her head. "So, what is all this stuff?" she asked the Naysayer.

He looked her up and down. "Mine. And don't go thinking I won't notice if any of it's missing. Some of it's been washing in with the tide. Some of it I salvaged from the deep. Turns out when ya let a city slide into the sea for who knows how many years, a lot of stuff gets taken down with it. Catacombs are full of interestin' stuff."

Marrill froze. "Did you say 'catacombs'?"

That's when Karny tensed in her arms, and before she could do anything to stop him, he pounced toward her shoulder. The Wiverwane flailed, scrambling up the side of Marrill's head.

Her skin rippled. Memories assaulted her, hitting in bright flashes. Serth standing in front of a font of golden water, lifting a cup to his lips. Ardent bent over a sheaf of papers, scribbling as Serth raved. Annalessa's hand on Ardent's arm, trying to draw him into the warm sun.

And then the memories were gone. The Wiverwane took to the air, flapping wildly, trying unsuccessfully to gain height. Karny charged after it, shoving off Marrill's shoulder. He crashed into a pile of old tires, already scrambling.

The Naysayer plucked Karny free of the debris at the same time a rope dropped from the rigging directly into the Wiverwane's path. The creature clung to it gratefully.

Marrill cleared her throat as she toed a stop sign that had come to rest against her shoe. For a second, she thought of the message that had brought her here in the first place. She still had no idea who had sent it. But this sign was completely blank; it offered her no answers.

"So..." she tried, "what are the odds you'll show me the way down into the catacombs of Monerva?"

"'Bout the same as the odds you'll learn to mind your own business," the Naysayer grunted. "So none."

Marrill bit her lip. She had to get down there. And it would be much, much easier if she had help. "What if I told you the fate of the world was at stake?"

He seemed to consider it for a moment. It turned out to be a sneeze. "Didn't care last time. Don't care this time. Won't care next time."

Her eyes fell on a stack of tennis rackets. "I could show you how to use those?" she offered.

"Are you going to beat yerself unconscious with 'em?" he asked.

Marrill's shoulders slumped. "Fine. What if I let you take care of Karny while we're—"

"Done."

Marrill blinked. "Okay...so...how do we get into these catacombs?"

The Naysayer didn't smile. She wasn't even sure he *could* smile. But what he did was close enough to be particularly unsettling. "The more pertinent question is, how long can you hold your breath?"

++ + ++

Marrill stood next to the Naysayer inside the husk of an ancient ship, staring down at the pool of brackish water waiting below her belly. It wasn't glowing like pure Stream water, but there was still a soft sheen to it that lit up the bare timbers of the wreck.

How the Naysayer had found this place, she had no idea. But the ship must have run aground on an ancient part of the sinking city, because according to him, beneath the water, a flooded tunnel led straight down to the heart of the catacombs.

"How do I know it won't turn me into a topiary?" Marrill protested.

"'Cause I ain't that lucky," the Naysayer said. "And if you can't trust a Naysayer, who can ya trust?"

"Off the top of my head?"

But the Naysayer didn't hear her, because he'd already jumped. He hit the surface hard, sending up a splash that coated her legs. She winced, but when they didn't turn into a pair of lizards ballroom dancing, she pressed a hand against her shirt pocket where her Wiverwane huddled. If she wanted to save her world, she didn't have much of a choice.

"Here goes everything," she said, jumping.

For being brackish, the water at the base of the Wall was remarkably clear. She could see the Naysayer ahead of her, and she paddled after him, trying not to panic as her lungs squeezed. He'd promised her that it wouldn't be too far, but seeing how easily he stroked through the water with his four arms, she wasn't sure they had the same ideas about distance.

Just when she didn't think she could go much farther, a jolt of confidence shot through her. Memories flooded her mind: scuba diving with her dad in Indonesia, splashing in a frozen lake in Alaska, swimming across a roaring river in Colorado. The Wiverwane was drawing them out, giving her strength. She forced herself forward, kicking hard.

Two sets of hands grabbed her, pulling her through a short tunnel and past a valve. The Naysayer quickly closed it and the water drained away. A cool draft struck Marrill's face. She gasped, choking as she swallowed gulps of air.

"Thanks," she finally wheezed to the Wiverwane. A ripple of memory shivered through her—a bright moment of lying in the sun as a toddler. She guessed it was the creature's equivalent of a dog wagging its tail.

Nearby she heard a crack, and then a burst of blue light illuminated their surroundings. A surge of hope and energy flowed through her as she looked around.

Where she could see it, the ceiling wasn't much more than bare beams and the sheer bottoms of walls. The floor was a series of half-rotted planks with gaping holes here and there. "So these are the catacombs?" she croaked.

The Naysayer laughed. It echoed and boomed around them. "You wish," he said, holding up a glowing blue crystal; frozen-hope. At least now she knew where the light—and her sudden burst of optimism—was coming from.

He started walking and Marrill scrabbled after him, not wanting to be left alone in the darkness. The floor sagged and moaned under her steps. She cringed, expecting it to fall away at any minute.

In some places, it already had. The Naysayer reached a gap between thick floorboards and squatted by it. "Drop here," he grunted before disappearing. Marrill watched the blue dot of light fade, and a coldness swept in around her.

She quickly scurried after him. The Naysayer weaved his way from room to room, sometimes heading down flights of stairs and other times jumping through holes in the floor. It was like an intricate, three-dimensional maze.

Marrill found herself panting to keep up. "How do you

even know where you're going? I mean, you *do* know where you're going. Don't you?"

He tapped his forehead. "If there's stuff to be found and claimed, you can trust me to be the one findin' and claimin'."

Oddly, Marrill did trust that. But still, she had misgivings. "How deep do you think we are?"

The Naysayer thumped down a series of steep pedestals. "I figger the city's been sinkin' for about a hundred years, give or take a thousand. So...deep."

She glanced up, suddenly keenly aware of just how much was piled above her. The weight of generations of towers and buildings, all resting on the half-rotted timbers surrounding her. She placed her hand against one, to reassure herself.

It trembled under her touch. The vibrations grew stronger until she jerked away in alarm. A rumble came from far away, growing louder by the moment. "Um...that doesn't sound good."

The Naysayer glanced toward the ceiling. "Oh, fer jellying jigglefish. Again?" He let out a sigh.

"What?" Marrill asked, not sure she wanted to know the answer.

"You impervious to magic?" he grunted. Behind them the roar grew, the walls beginning to shudder.

Panic caused her heart to trip. "No. You?"

He shrugged. "Ish."

"How much ish?" she asked.

"I guess we'll find out." He pointed. "That way. Run!"

He led her across the room to a large decorative fountain. There was a gaping hole in the center of it. "This'll take you into the plumbing system. It'll get you to the catacombs eventually. A few left turns, then some right ones." He paused. "There's also some wrong ones but I wouldn't take those if I was you. Unless you have a penchant for spiderpillars?"

Marrill had no idea, but they didn't sound good. "No thank you?"

The Naysayer grunted. "Good choice." He shoved her into the fountain.

"But what about you? Aren't you coming with me?" Marrill cried.

"Nah. Someone's gotta block the pipe after you go." He patted a solid slab of dullwood large enough to cover the hole in the fountain. "Otherwise, what's the point?"

Marrill's throat tightened, her heart racing with panic. "B-but—" She swallowed, throat thick. She clung to two of the Naysayer's meaty wrists. "What will happen to you?"

"Same thing that happens to all Naysayers, I'd imagine." He dropped a couple of hope crystals into her hand.

That didn't answer her question. "Which is?"

He shrugged all four shoulders. And before she could stop him, he slid the dullwood slab across the opening, plunging her into darkness.

She closed her eyes, trying to keep the tears from escaping. She wanted to believe he'd get out. Because he was just ornery enough to do so. Either way, but for the Wiverwane, she was utterly and completely alone now.

More than anything else, she wanted to curl up in a ball, wrap her arms around her knees, and cry. She wanted her mom to rub her hand down her back and tell her everything was going to be okay.

But time was running out. The gears were already turning. Her world was already being sucked onto the Pirate Stream.

With a trembling breath, she cracked open a hope crystal. Its warmth infused her, chasing away her doubt and fears, filling her with optimism.

She could do this. She *would* do this.

Crouching, she held the crystal aloft to light up her surroundings. She'd landed in the junction point for what looked like seven pipes. One led up to the fountain above. The others led in six different directions.

"A few left turns, a few right turns and avoid the wrong turns." Her voice trailed off as she looked around. A terrible feeling grew in the pit of her stomach, strong enough that even the hope crystal couldn't beat it back.

"This is where you come in, little guy," she told the Wiverwane. "Let's hope you remember the way to the Syphon."

CHAPTER 26
The Syphon of Monerva

F in wound deeper and deeper into the salt-encrusted catacombs. They'd been walking for so long he had no idea how much time had passed or how much distance they'd covered. It felt like they'd gone far enough to make it all the way to the Wall.

"**Left here,**" the candle on his belt hissed. "**Now right. Straight for a while. That wall is really a door. That door is really a wall.**"

"Wow, you guys really didn't want anyone stumbling

onto this thing, huh?" Fin asked as he pried the salt off a trapdoor in the middle of a hallway.

"The Syphon can destroy worlds and grant wishes," said the Salt Sand King. "We could have just left it lying around with a Do Not Touch sign on it, but this seemed slightly wiser."

As they pressed deeper, glass piping filled with bright Stream water reached in through the walls. Raw magic to fuel the Wish Machine, Fin realized. He shook his head. "How much does it take to grant a wish?"

"That depends on the size of the wish," the King told him. "Already, the Syphon has sucked down enough magic to grant most any mortal his heart's desire. But that's not enough to satisfy the Master. He thirsts like I thirst. If the Stream were not endless, he would drain the whole thing dry."

Ahead, the salt-covered walls opened up. The pulsing of the air mixed with the dull roar of a distant waterfall. The whole hallway glowed with golden light.

"We're getting close now," the King told him. "When we reach the chamber, step lightly. The Master must not know we are here."

Fin took a deep, shuddering breath. He felt an ache in the center of his chest he didn't quite understand. He knew he should be happy—he was almost to the Syphon! He was going to get his wish!

And yet there was still something missing: Marrill.

Regret bit deep into him. Maybe he shouldn't have stayed behind on the Burning Plain after all. She wanted her wish as badly as he wanted his. And he wanted her to get it. Even if she had forgotten him.

He shook the thought from his head. She *had* forgotten him, though. If all went well, maybe he would be able to wish for her, too. If that didn't happen and she missed out, well, he'd feel pretty bad about it. But it was her own fault. Not his.

"Okay," he whispered to the light at his side. "I'm ready. What now?"

"I can feel the desire radiating off him," the King hissed. Fin noticed he was flaring a little higher than before, burning just a little brighter. "It's so strong I can barely stand it. His wish is nearly granted. All his attention is on it, and he won't be able to focus on you at all. Sneak in, grab the wish orb, and make a wish of your own, quickly."

Fin nodded. Sneaking, stealing, and wishing. The Salt Sand King was right—he'd been made for this.

Staying low, he stepped into a massive domed chamber. The floor was covered in white marble inlaid with red onyx in the shape of a dragon under a circle—the sigil of the Salt Sand King. Except here the circle was a great basin, a gaping open pit. And the mountains within it, Fin now realized, were the waves of magical water sucked from the Pirate Stream.

Above it, like an inverted mirror, Stream water swirled

in a torrent through a great glass funnel hung from the ceiling. It was a gigantic whirlpool, suspended in midair.

The Syphon of Monerva.

Six huge pipes, bent like straws at the top, ringed it, drawing water from the basin below and dumping it into the funnel.

Fin blinked, trying to take in the whole scene: the intricate network of delicate glass pipes filled with Stream water adorning the ceiling, the gears along the wall whirring as they pumped raw magic through the chamber, the elaborate pattern of red onyx inlaid on the floor.

But it was the center of the chamber that was most important. Because at the center of the room, the water spiraled tighter and tighter as it reached the tip of the funnel, until it poured out in a line so thin and delicate it was almost a thread. A thread that trickled down from the ceiling into a glass ball waiting on a pedestal below, filling slowly.

There was only one thing that could be, Fin thought: the wish.

But the pedestal stood on a platform that hung out in the air over the basin, suspended by brass struts anchored to the column-pipes. The only way to reach it was a set of stone stairs that led up from the rim of the pit. And standing at the top of those stairs, his back to them as he watched the glass ball fill, was a figure clad head to toe in armor: the Master of the Iron Ship.

Fin couldn't help the wave of fear that washed through

him. Even though he'd known the Master would be here, actually seeing him again was chilling.

Fin ducked back into the passageway. He closed his eyes against the uncertainty that flowed through him. For a second, he considered turning around. Maybe Marrill had been right. Maybe he *did* need Ardent.

But the flame in the lantern at his waist blazed, snapping him out of his thoughts. "The Machine is almost at full power," it hissed, the sound practically lost to the thunder of water gushing in. "Even now it sifts through the Stream, distilling down the very essence of possibility. Even now, that ball could grant most normal wishes. Once it is full, nearly anything will become possible."

Fin glanced back around the corner at the glass ball beneath the funnel. If the water flowing above was golden, what filled the orb was molten. A yellow so bright and intense it almost hurt to look at. Only the Master's dark shadow kept it from being blinding.

"There's no way past him," Fin whispered. "He'll definitely see me if I just try to walk up and grab it. I need a distraction."

The lantern flickered. The flame within had grown again, threatening to spill out. "Give me something to burn," it commanded.

Reluctantly, Fin tore free a scrap of cloth from his shirt and held it down to the fire. A spark floated up and landed on the fabric. There it smoldered, neither catching nor dying.

"Place it here," the King ordered. "Then make your way around, and be ready to grab the orb and wish."

Fin swallowed, preparing himself. He turned his wish over and over in his mind. *I want to be remembered.* "Just grab the ball and say it?" he whispered.

"Just grab the ball and WILL it," the fire instructed. "Leave the rest to me."

Fin did as he was told. He placed the scrap of cloth, still cradling its ember, just inside the chamber. Then carefully he crept around the edge of the room, trying not to draw attention. With each step, he grew more and more convinced that the Master would turn and see him at any second.

Just as he reached the point where he was confident he was in the Master's field of vision, fire exploded from the doorway. The Master turned slowly, deliberately. Fin caught a glimpse of his long beard, the only feature that showed he was human. Red lightning crackled across sharp metal fingertips.

Smoke billowed up around the fire, thick and black, drowning it until the flames were nothing but a dim orange glow. The cloud seemed to shrink and squeeze, tendrils of gray and white coalescing into the shape of a person. With a shuffle of cloth, a bandaged, crooked figure stood across from the Master. "So ready to strike down an old man, yunh?"

Fin recognized the opportunity. He danced across the floor, keeping his eyes on the ironclad wizard. Each step brought him closer to the golden orb.

"You never were much of a talker, yunh?" the Salt Sand King continued. "But you never needed to be. I can feel you wanting, yunh? So powerful I can scarcely control myself..."

Fin let his eyes skip away. Just a few yards ahead, one of the massive pipe-columns loomed; a brass support strut arched out from it, stretching across the empty air to the hanging platform. If he could shimmy up the pipe, he could scramble across the strut to the orb!

He was so close to his wish it nearly overwhelmed him. A spike of sadness drove through the hot desire, though— the feeling that all this was for nothing. That despite everything, he would fail.

"There is something cold here," he heard the Salt Sand King say. For one, the King sounded troubled. "Something here that doesn't want what it wants...how did I miss it?"

Fin pushed down the worry, swallowed the sadness. He needed to focus—it would all be over in a moment. He threw himself up the pipe, caught the lip of the strut with his fingers, and swung himself hand over hand across it, ignoring the pit full of Stream water below. If he fell into it, the raw magic would destroy him. But he didn't plan to fall.

A moment later, he dropped to the platform. The orb shone bright before him. So bright he could smell yellow, *taste* light. He reached for it, feeling possibility crawl on his skin.

"Oh, Fin," a voice murmured across from him.

He couldn't see its owner through the blinding light.

But he didn't need to. The quiver in that voice was one he'd never thought he'd hear again, but it was also one he'd never forget. An all-too-familiar shiver ran down the length of his spine.

A pale hand fell down to cup the wish orb. Its owner wore black robes adorned with white starbursts. The light of the wish glistened as it struck him, gleaming off his wet, black tears.

"The things one wishes when one knows they can't be granted," the cold voice whispered. It was so sad. Fin had forgotten how sad it could sound.

How sad it could make him feel.

"Serth." Fin's lips moved on their own, even as his mind grappled with the presence of what should have been a dead man. He couldn't tell if the weight in his heart was real, or if the wizard's dark magic was infecting him once more.

"Hello, Fin," the Oracle said. "I'm so, so sorry to see you again."

CHAPTER 27
The Reunion at Last

M arrill made the final turn in a sleeper's trance. The crusted salt columns were new, but the rest of this place was all too familiar, thanks to the Wiverwane memories. Every step was one she had made before; every stone was one she had fit into place. Just ahead, she knew, lay the chamber of the great machine.

The King, despite himself, let out a little gasp. For here the whole room was inlaid in white marble and onyx, surrounding a great empty basin. He smiled as he recognized a familiar pattern decorating the floor. "My sigil," he murmured appreciatively.

Gears turned on every wall, the glass pipes pumping the stuff of wishes into a massive glass funnel suspended overhead. It was impossible and marvelous all at once. And it was his.

"Behold," said the Dawn Wizard, "the Syphon of Monerva!"

As she neared the entrance to the chamber, a deep, welling ache spread through Marrill's chest, snapping her out of the borrowed memories. Tears pricked her eyes. It was a familiar sorrow. She'd forgotten how intense it could be.

Serth was here. Still alive. Already at the Syphon. Likely behind all of this from the beginning. After all, he'd seen the future.

Her mind flew to the Map in her back pocket. Even with the Key gone, it didn't matter. Serth didn't need it anymore. Map or no Map, Key or no Key, he could wish the Lost Sun free, and destroy the whole Pirate Stream, just like that.

If that happened, the Iron Tide wouldn't even be an afterthought. All this time, they'd been afraid of the Master, when he was apparently just a lackey. Serth was the real threat.

She couldn't help but envision his trembling hands smearing black tears into a message sketched on an old stop sign. Marrill swallowed hard, trying desperately to beat back the hopelessness that surged through her.

At the base of her neck, the Wiverwane tickled her with

one long finger, making her skin ripple. Familiar memories flooded.

"Don't listen to him!" Marrill cried, voice breaking from the cold. She couldn't see who she was speaking to; it was like someone had picked up an ink drawing with a wet hand, smudging just the one spot. Beneath her feet, the Black Dragon *strained to stay afloat.*

Serth's sadness wrapped around her, pushing its way into the empty spaces inside her and making them grow. His fingers were icicles against her skin. His breath was the north wind on her neck.

But inside her, warmth flowed. A warmth that melted the ice. A hope that defied the sorrow. She still didn't know who she was talking to, but she knew that together, this sorrow, this desperation, was no match for them. She pressed her thumb to her chest, in a sign the Oracle's power would never overcome.

Marrill's heart pounded. The same warm sense of strength and determination she'd had in the memory flowed through her once again. She'd stood up to Serth and fought back his tide of sorrow before. She could do it now, too. There was no other option.

"Okay. I can do this." She squared her shoulders. "You ready?" she asked the Wiverwane. It skittered off her shoulder to tuck itself into her pocket. "Okay, maybe not. But we're going in anyway."

She placed her hand against the door and pushed her

way into the massive chamber, ready for anything. A gout of fire roared past her. In a nearby doorway, at the source of the flame, stood the burning outline of the Salt Sand King.

Almost anything, she mentally added.

She jumped back, shielding her face, but the flames weren't directed at her. They shot across the room, breaking against an iron-clad figure. At the center of a raging inferno, the Master stood calm, one foot on the edge of a great pit, one on the stairs leading up to the platform suspended over it. His dark armor glowed from heat, but not even the unquenchable fire of the Burning Plain was hot enough to melt it. Even through the blaze, she could see the red lightning crackling around him.

The entire chamber vibrated with heat and energy. Behind the Master, an orb glowed impossibly bright, forcing her to look away. The wish.

The Wiverwane shrank deeper into her pocket. Marrill wanted nothing more than to do the same, but she forced herself forward. She didn't see Serth. But, with the Master and the Salt Sand King distracting each other, this might be her best chance.

She knew to keep her back to the wall and her eyes on the dueling foes as she darted around the edge of the chamber. Someone had taught her that skill, but at the moment, she just didn't have the time to remember who.

The Master stepped forward, pushing back the flames. The stairs were clear. **"Grab the wish orb! Now!"**

the Salt Sand King commanded, his voice echoing with the snapping of burning wood.

Marrill startled. But no, he couldn't have been talking to her. And it didn't matter. What mattered was keeping Serth and the Master from wishing, and stopping the Syphon from destroying her world.

She darted from the wall and sprinted toward the basin. Her legs pumped, carrying her as fast as she could possibly go. All her attention was on avoiding the Master; he was close enough now that she felt the heat still radiating from him. She hit the stairs so hard, she practically leapt up them.

And skidded to a stop, narrowly avoiding the frozen touch of the figure standing on the platform.

"Girl with wings." Serth's lips trembled; black tears cut down his deathly pale face. "I hate that you have to be here. I truly, truly do."

"Marrill!" another voice cried. It was a boy around her own age, with olive skin and dark, shaggy hair. He seemed to know her, but she had no idea where from.

"Leave her alone," he yelled, running at Serth. The Oracle turned and batted him aside with a toss of his hand. The kid flew backward, barely catching himself at the edge of the platform, his feet dangling over the Stream-filled pit. Marrill's heart lodged in her throat.

"Where were we?" Serth asked. He seemed genuinely unsure. Then he snapped his long fingers. "Yes! Right. You begin..." His eyes glanced past her. "Over there."

With a flick of his fingers, she went flying across the room, crashing heavily against the wall. She shook her head, trying to chase away the stars that suddenly floated in her vision.

"Marrill!" she heard someone cry. A moment later a hand fell on her arm. "You okay?" It was the shaggy-haired kid; somehow she'd completely lost sight of him. He rubbed one arm where frost clung to his jacket.

She pushed him away, jumping to her feet and raising her arms in her best imitation of Coll's fighting stance. "Who are you? How do you know my name?" she asked, bracing herself to strike.

The brightness of his eyes drained away, and his smile faltered. "I'm Fin . . . your friend?"

She shook her head, taking a step back to put more distance between them.

He sighed. "Listen, now's not the time. We have to stop the Syphon before it fills the orb. We can't let Serth or the Master make their wish." He smiled. "You know, defeat evil, save the world. As usual."

A smile tugged the corners of her lips. She didn't know if she could trust this kid. But right now, she didn't have a choice. "How?"

He glanced at where the Master squared off against the roaring fire of the Salt Sand King. "The King's got old Iron Boots. You draw Serth away, and I'll duck in and steal the wish."

Marrill narrowed her eyes. No way she was falling for

this. "Uh-uh. You want to help? *You* distract Serth and *I'll* snag the wish."

Even as she spoke, a wind picked up out of nowhere. Marrill held up her hand to shield her eyes. Just in time, too, because a roar like an inferno filled the chamber, and the whole room exploded in a flash of light.

The fire that had cloaked the room was gone. Little flames flickered across the floor and on the walls. They were all that remained of the Salt Sand King.

And then Serth stood before them.

"Blisterwinds," the kids muttered.

Overwhelming sadness tunneled through Marrill, icy claws grabbing at her heart. In her pocket she felt the Wiverwane trembling.

"The reunion at last," Serth said, choking on a sob. He wiped at his streaming eyes with the back of one pale hand. "Is it everything you hoped it would be, little lost boy? Or have you realized now that no one cares about you?"

Beside her, the boy flinched, his shoulders sinking under the weight of Serth's words. He fell to his knees, tears gathering in his eyes.

Marrill felt a stab of pity—no one deserved to be told such terrible lies. She clenched her hands into fists and stomped forward. "Everyone has someone out there who cares about them!"

Serth swept himself toward her. She sucked in a breath and crossed her arms over her chest, as though that could somehow protect her.

"Oh, do they?" he asked. He tilted his head to the side and black tears trailed along his jaw. "Even"—a sob broke through—"me?"

Marrill opened her mouth but couldn't find an answer. And then she felt the Wiverwane shifting in her pocket. A fingertip slipped out, tapping her arm. She was plunged into a memory.

The Oracle crouched in a corner, weeping, his arms wrapped around his legs as he rocked himself. "Dragons and whirl-pools...no, whirlpools then dragons..."

Annalessa knelt beside him. It broke her heart to see him like this. He had always been the strong one. He had always been the one who laughed when things looked hopeless. She wondered if she could possibly shoulder that burden.

Her hand wavered over his shoulder. It would hurt to touch him. Ever since he drank from the Stream, even the slightest brush was unbearable.

"Out of order, out of order," he mumbled. "Crow for comfort, light through water."

She put her hand down anyway. The cold seared against her skin like frostbite. "It's okay," she whispered. "We'll find a way to help you."

Marrill forced her way out of the memory. "Annalessa cares about you," she said. "She wanted to help you."

For a moment, Serth was silent. A fat black tear teetered on the edge of his eye, before tipping over and slicing way down his cheek. "Tell me, then," he whispered. "Where is she now?"

Pain and loneliness stabbed at Marrill's gut, but she fought against them. "She would be here if you'd let her. Ardent, too."

Serth laughed, a halting, gasping laugh. "*His* place in this I have never questioned." He spun away, fingers fluttering in the air. "But then, you would know about running away from those who love you, wouldn't you?"

A boy she didn't recognize appeared out of nowhere. "Don't listen to him, Marrill! He's trying to get in your head. He was wrong before. He'll be wrong again."

Serth reached out, ignoring the kid. One long blackened fingernail trailed lightly down Marrill's cheek, leaving a line of searing cold behind it. He clutched her chin. "Are you sure you really want to go back home?"

Her tears turned to ice as they trailed down her cheeks. "Yes," she whispered, her teeth chattering. Yet even *she* could hear how weak her response sounded.

He shook his head sadly. "But you worked so hard to escape."

"I didn't escape," she protested. "I...I c-came here because they n-needed me."

"They needed you or you needed them?"

"*Leave her alone!*" someone cried. The boy grabbed Marrill's hand and yanked her away, out of Serth's grip. She'd totally forgotten he was even there.

"Listen," he told her. "I'm a friend. You just don't remember. But before you forget again, do you think maybe we could figure out a way to stop those two"—he glanced from Serth to the Master—"from destroying the world?"

She looked at where the Master stood by the Syphon. Power radiated around him, crackling through the air like static electricity. At his command, the Pirate Stream gushed into the funnel overhead, frothing and churning, and spilling out over the sides.

The Syphon was going faster than ever. She had to stop them before they destroyed her world! She didn't know this boy or if she could trust him, but she couldn't defeat the Master and Serth alone.

She needed his help.

"Okay," she agreed. "You hold off Serth. I'll make a dash for the orb."

But Serth was already walking away from them, whimpering as he went. "Please don't bother," he told them. "My friend," he called to the Master, "help them not bother."

The Master of the Iron Ship looked down from the platform. Beneath his faceless mask, his cold blue eyes seemed to slice straight through Marrill. With a sharp cut of his hand through the air, an arc of power flashed upward, severing the lattice of pipes that lined the ceiling. Stream water rained down around the platform, obscuring it from view.

Serth's mouth twitched, something between a smile and a grimace. Then, as if it were nothing, he stepped straight through the glowing curtain of water.

Marrill gasped, expecting to see him explode into a school of minnows, or a demon howl, or *something*. But it didn't happen. He'd passed through as if it were nothing.

Despair swallowed Marrill. A rain of pure magic now cut her off from the heart of the Syphon.

"What am I going to do?" she whimpered.

Beside her someone cleared his throat. "What are *we* going to do. And here's a tip: If you could just leave a tiny little bit of your focus on my existence while you're trying to figure that out, it would help. Also, my name's Fin."

"It's impossible," she said. "We can't stop them. We can't reach them. There's no way."

The boy shook his head. "No," he said. "That's Serth talking, and I'm not going to listen. There has to be a way. There's always a way. I just…don't know what it is yet, that's all."

Marrill stared at the Syphon. From where she stood, she could just make out the shadow of the Master through the sheet of water, a dark blur commanding the Stream to pour in ever faster. Pulling her world closer and closer to destruction.

"Maybe if we could destroy the Machine," she said, thinking out loud. But she knew full well that wasn't possible. "Except we can't. Because what the Dzane made, nothing but the Dzane can destroy." Her knees wobbled. A gaping chasm of emptiness opened up in her chest.

She'd failed. She hadn't saved her mother or her world. She'd simply run from it all and then hoped she could wish her problems away. But of course it could never be that easy.

"That's it!" someone breathed. She raised her head to find a boy crouched next to her. "What the Dzane made!" He reached into a bag on his belt and pulled out a sun-shaped crystal knob. "And you have the Map."

She pushed away from him. "How did you get that?"

"Does it matter?" he asked. "We can use it to open the Gate."

All the blood drained from Marrill's face. "Are you kidding?"

"No," he replied. "We already know it'll work. Remember? Up on the top of Monerva? We opened the Gate accidentally, and it blasted through the Wall!"

Marrill narrowed her eyes. How could this kid know about that? He hadn't been there. On the other hand, he had a point. The light of the Lost Sun *had* blasted through the Wall. It had even severed one of the gears.

"Trust me." His voice sounded weak. Desperate even.

Marrill looked deep into his eyes. She couldn't help but think maybe she'd seen him before. Maybe he *had* been there.

Suddenly, something Remy said came back to her. *There's another kid. Plus One. Marrill, plus one.*

She grabbed the kid's hand so fast that even *she* was surprised. She had to trust her instinct. And her instinct said she could trust *him*. That he was a good person.

"Okay," she said. "Let's do it."

CHAPTER 28
Sunrise

Relief flooded through Fin. Even if she didn't remember him, *something* inside Marrill still cared. Something still trusted him. They could still work together.

Through the gushing water, Serth let out a wail of triumph. The Stream funneled in ever faster. Fin could see odd bits of Marrill's world coming down the pipes, changing in the magical flow even as he watched. He had no idea how much time they had left, but it wasn't much.

Marrill hesitated, Map in hand. "Okay," she said. "If we're going to do this terrible, stupid, very dumb thing, let's do it!" She unrolled the Map with a flick of her wrist, kneeling as she set it on the ground.

Fin crouched next to her, Key in hand. His fingers fit easily between the rays of the crystal sun as he lowered it. Already he could feel the parchment hum as it came alive.

"Wait," Marrill said before he could touch it to the surface. He looked up, meeting her eyes. "I don't remember you, but...thank you."

Fin laughed. "If you remembered me, you'd be yelling at me for getting you into this in the first place," he said, surprising himself. It wasn't like him to take responsibility when he didn't have to. Then he touched the Key to the Map.

The Map shook. Its surface buckled, just like it had on the Wall. Only this time, they *wanted* it to open. The ink thickened, the parchment morphed and grew. A long line split the paper in half. The arms of the crystal sun stretched, becoming handles.

The Gate was complete. And lying flat on the floor, staring up at them.

"If we open it, the rays are just going to blast the ceiling," Marrill pointed out. "Which will burst the rest of the pipes, dousing us in Pirate Stream water."

"And possibly turn us into wombats," Fin finished. "Looks like we're going to have to do a little more working together than I thought."

She looked him straight in the eye and nodded. Fin felt a flood of warmth rush through him. For the time being, at least, she saw him again.

Marrill moved around to the top of the Gate and crouched, slipping her fingers underneath the edge of it. "It's still light as paper!" Overhead, the sound of the Stream draining grew to a massive, overwhelming roar. "Get ready to open it," she warned.

He gripped the handle. "Got it." He held the Gate steady while Marrill lifted it high, bracing herself behind it until it was almost perpendicular to the ground.

"Okay," Fin said. "Here goes everything."

He yanked hard against the Gate's handle, feeling it buckle beneath his hands. As light as lifting the Map had been, opening those doors felt unbearably heavy. He planted his feet and pulled as hard as he could.

The Gate creaked. Rays of light sliced the air. Wherever they struck, metal bent, stone melted, glass simply ceased to be.

"Tilt it higher!" Fin directed. He tried to angle the whole thing with one hand while holding on to the door with the other. The Gate felt like bronze and pencil lead beneath his fingers. His skin tingled, nearly itching.

The light of the Lost Sun struck the gears of the Syphon and scattered, reflecting tiny beams that drilled holes in the walls around them. Fin's chest tightened as though grabbed by the Master's steely fist. It wasn't working.

But just as he teetered on the verge of despair, certain that not even the light of pure destruction could harm the Dawn Wizard's Machine, a wrenching shriek filled the air. The metal glowed hot.

Fin pulled harder on the Gate to let more light out.

As each beam struck it, the Wish Machine resisted, sagged, then finally gave way. Gears snapped free and bounded across the floor. Pipes vanished in bursts of bright sparks. One of the big brass struts squealed and tore in half. Another followed.

With two of its supports severed, the platform at the heart of the Wish Machine sagged and tilted to one side. Through the continued shower of Stream water, Fin could just make out Serth and the Master swaying to stay balanced. He smiled a grim smile. The Oracle hadn't foreseen *this*.

He tugged at the door, aiming the beams of the Lost Sun at another support. The deadly light sliced it in two and carved into the ceiling beyond, blasting a hole out to who-knew-where. The platform tilted further. The wish orb wobbled on its pedestal, a pendulum dangling from its thin golden thread.

"Quickly now!" Serth shrieked above the din. He held his arms out to either side for balance. A deep rumble sounded overhead.

Red lightning sparked through the air. The Master raised one hand, urging the tide to come faster. The other stretched out toward Fin and Marrill.

Everything moved in slow motion. "To the right!" Fin

cried. A long, cruel finger leveled at him; in a moment, they'd be dead.

He threw the Gate open, not caring how much deadly light he let free. A spear of brightness pierced the rain of Stream water and struck the Master of the Iron Ship square in his chest. For a moment, the ghost in iron simply stood there, struggling against the Lost Sun of Dzannin, as if his will alone could outlast its power.

His white beard burst into flames. His black armor glowed red, then white-hot. His boots started to melt at the edges, sliding him backward. The Master struggled to step toward them, but instead he slipped, toppled backward, and fell over the side of the platform, into the Stream-filled basin below.

"One down!" Fin hollered in triumph. "Serth, you're next!"

But the Oracle just shook his head wistfully, and stepped deliberately toward the light. Almost as if he *wanted* the light to strike him.

"What's he doing?" Marrill yelled from behind the Gate. "Is he crazy?"

The Lost Sun's rays smashed into the Oracle's porcelain skin, flowed over and across it, and seemed to sink into his body. The sound that came from him was neither a laugh nor a cry, not a howl of pain nor a victory shout, but somehow all of those things at once. It scraped down the back of Fin's spine and clawed at his stomach.

"Dawn, Sun of Dzannin!" Serth growled. "Light my

path!" He moved himself fully between the Gate and the nearly filled wish orb.

Fin gave Marrill an uncertain glance. "I'm going to open it wider!" He hauled against the Gate with all his might. It creaked, then gave way, slamming open. The full light of the Lost Sun blasted out into the chamber, blinding him.

"Fill me with your power!" Serth bellowed. The Lost Sun's rays poured onto the evil wizard, as if he were sucking it into himself.

"Uh-oh," Fin murmured. The Oracle, blazing with light, descended the stone steps toward them. At his back, the Syphon was a ruin of jagged metal and shattered glass. A last bit of Stream water drizzled into the wish orb, then the flow was no more.

The orb, no longer gathering magic, dropped from the air, bounced down the steps, and rolled across the chamber. Serth paid it no mind. As he reached the final step, the whole platform groaned and collapsed into the basin below.

"Behold the power of destruction!" he snarled. The light of the Lost Sun formed a halo around him. The air crackled. Stone smoldered where he passed.

Fin met Marrill's eyes. He could see his own terror reflected in them. He gulped. "I think we may have messed up."

CHAPTER 29
Lessons in Perspective

Serth raised a finger. "Get back!" Marrill squealed. She wobbled the Map hard to the right. Her new friend scrabbled behind the door as a ray of light seared past him.

So much for trying to close the Gate, Marrill thought. Apparently, the Oracle wouldn't allow it.

Serth continued toward them. Slowly. Haltingly. It was as if the Sun's light were a rope, and he was pulling himself hand over hand up it. Toward the Gate. And beyond it, toward them.

Helplessness crept over her. The Lost Sun couldn't kill Serth. Stream water couldn't kill Serth. He would reach the Map, bring out the Lost Sun, and destroy the Stream. He was unbeatable.

And she was all alone.

Just then, someone yanked on her sleeve. A boy—*the boy*—was looking at her, his expression fierce. "Fight off the sadness, Marrill," he told her. "We already took down one unstoppable evil wizard today. No time to give up just yet, right? We can do this!"

Marrill choked down the sorrow and stood tall. But now Serth was almost upon them. Each new step left a burnt crater on the ground. Energy coursed over and around him as he moved.

"We can do this together," Marrill repeated. She took a deep breath. And she *wasn't* alone. There were two of them now facing down Serth from both sides of the Gate.

Both sides. The memory of the Dawn Wizard came back to her. The key was to look at things from both sides. *The cost and the gain. The in and the out.*

Her jaw dropped. She had to think about the Gate *from the other side.* Because a gate works in *two* directions.

"The Gate goes both ways," she whispered. "The Lost Sun can come out of it—"

"—but Serth can also go *in!*" the kid squealed. "Marrill, you're brilliant!"

Time was running out. Serth closed on them, just a few feet away now. Already, he reached toward them. Already, the end was upon them. "Let the Prophecy be fulfilled at last!" he cried.

"It's no good," the kid groaned, barely audible over Serth's wailing and the crash of the broken Machine. "We can't touch him, remember? There's no way to push him in!"

Marrill had felt the searing cold of Serth's touch before; she knew he was right. The frame of the Gate wobbled in her shaking hand.

And then she remembered—the Map was made of *paper*. She laughed. "*Of course* there is!" she said. "Opening that door may be hard, but *moving* this thing is a cinch!"

"Come forward, Star of Destruction!" the dark wizard cried. He was mere inches away, his fingers stretching toward the opening. Ready to pull forth the Lost Sun of Dzannin. Ready to end the world.

Marrill caught the kid's eye. "On three?" Even though she didn't know him from anyone, Marrill *knew* they were thinking the same thing. *One,* she mouthed.

He crouched, grabbing hold of the bottom of the gate. She did the same.

"Come forward, end of all time!" Serth shrieked.

TwothreeNOW! she shouted.

As one, they lifted the edges of the Gate. As one they

hauled it forward, swooping it at Serth like a net at a butterfly. The dark wizard let out a startled shout as the Gate passed over him.

And as one, they heaved against the doors, straining to close them before Serth could escape. Deadly light sliced out from the narrowing gap. Something thumped against the other side, shoving them back and away. They moved together, ramming their respective doors with all of their might.

The Gate, at last, slammed shut.

"Quick, take the Key out!" the boy cried. Marrill grabbed for the crystal knob, struggling to wrench it free. The doors trembled and shook as Serth banged on them from the other side. If it opened enough to let out even a single ray, she'd be torn apart.

"Hurry!" the boy cried.

"Almost…" Marrill grunted. "Got it!"

She tumbled backward, the crystal Key loose in her hands. Before her eyes, the Gate faded to ink and paper once more. The banging stopped. Marrill fell to her knees, heart pounding.

The Map curled to the ground. A trail of footprints, seared into the red onyx of the Salt Sand King's sigil, marked the last place where the Meressian Oracle had stood—on the back of the dragon. The only sounds were the rushing of water, the groaning of the broken Machine, and the smoldering of motion metal.

She cupped her hand over her pocket, making sure the

Wiverwane was still okay. It wriggled beneath the fabric, and she gave it a comforting pat.

Around her, the chamber of the Wish Machine lay in ruins. Stream water dribbled from above, turning stone into sonatas as it did. Flames flickered on the scorched ground and burnt gears. One of the massive column pipes had sheared in half and lay tilted against the wall. Marrill's eyes followed the line of footprints back to the steps that had led to the heart of the Syphon of Monerva. The platform where once wishes had been granted was now gone entirely.

Nothing remained but rent metal, dangling in the air.

"Did we do it?" the boy asked. He turned the Map over in his hands, peering at it cautiously.

Marrill scarcely heard him. Over the dripping of pipes and the low flicker of the flames, a strange sound began rising. A bubbling and churning, like a pot getting ready to boil. And it came from the pit full of Stream water.

Marrill forced herself to her feet. Slowly, she walked toward it, one step at a time. When she reached the rim of the basin, she braced herself. This was where the Master of the Iron Ship had fallen. She'd assumed that took him out of the picture. But then, he'd already survived one dip in the Pirate Stream.

Cautiously, she leaned out and peered over the edge.

Down in the basin, the Stream water burbled and rose, like lava in a volcano, and it looked about to blow its top. Which would have been bad enough. But it wasn't the worst part.

The worst part was the black skim spreading across the surface of the water.

"Oh no," Marrill gasped. "Oh no!"

"What is it?" someone called from behind her. "It's bad, isn't it? Just tell me it's bad; my mind can fill in the rest."

The basin belched again. The gentle, golden hue of the Stream had gone. Now there was just the dull, unyielding gleam of iron.

The walls of the basin grew black and metallic. It crept up them, infecting everything it touched. Fear rose inside her like the black water rising slowly up the pit. The lines from Pickled Pate's Colloquy came back to her:

An I seen tha comin' at creepin' stride

O' tha doom whut fears me.

O' tha IRON TIDE

"It's the Iron Tide!" she screamed. "Run!"

She took off toward the tunnel entrance, dodging puddles of Stream water as she went. Panic surged through her. But just as she reached the archway leading out, a sheet of fire exploded to life, driving her back.

"Not yet," the popping, growling voice commanded.

Marrill turned away from the fierce heat. All around, the tiny flames that had flickered across the wrecked chamber now burned with life. Hot air slapped at her skin. It was like being in the desert all over again.

Her eyes lit on the glowing wish orb where it had rolled to a stop against the wall. The most precious thing in all the Stream, cast off and forgotten.

Fingers of flame licked up around it. As she watched, they gripped it, lifted it up into the air. Smoke billowed out around it. A figure stepped forward, outlined now in fire and soot. He closed in, carrying the wish toward her.

But his blue ember eyes were not looking at Marrill. She followed them to a strange boy standing beside her. The boy glanced at her, then back at the burning figure of the Salt Sand King.

"First, you wish," the King ordered. He held the wish out to the boy. "Then, my soldier, we will leave together. And all of the Pirate Stream will be ours for the taking."

CHAPTER 30
The Legacy of the Salt Sand King

Fin stared at the glowing yellow orb. It was nearly filled. And if the Salt Sand King was right, that was plenty powerful enough to grant anything Fin could hope for.

Anything he dreamed of could be his. Would be his. All he had to do was take it and wish. His palms grew sweaty, fingers shaking with the desire to reach out and snatch it.

"We have to get out of here!" Marrill cried, plucking at his shirt. Behind him the basin burbled. Wrought iron gathered on the rim of it, threatening to spread across the stone floor.

"What are you waiting for?" the Salt Sand King rasped, shoving the orb at him. **"Make the wish, and you will be free to leave."**

Fin looked to Marrill. He could see on her face that she still didn't recognize him. Even after what they'd just done, even after defeating Serth *again*, she didn't remember him. Which meant she probably never would.

It felt worse than when she'd left to go back to her world. At least then, he knew she was still out there thinking of him. But now...now she stood right next to him, and he was as a complete stranger.

"Wish and you can change that," the Salt Sand King hissed, reading his desire. **"Wish and everyone will remember you. Wish and you will be KNOWN."**

He wanted it so badly. This is what he'd come here to do. And yet, as close as he was, he hesitated.

"If you're going to do it, do it," Marrill sighed. Her eyes welled with tears. Her bottom lip trembled. "I... *we* have to get out of here. My world is safe, for now at least. I guess I don't get any more wishes than that."

Fin swallowed. Shouldn't he wish? Didn't he have to? He tried to focus on the look of recognition he would see in her eyes, in everyone's eyes from now on. But he couldn't. His mind kept going to Marrill here, in front of him. The

Marrill with tears in her eyes. The Marrill who couldn't fix her sick mom.

Maybe wishing was the only way for Fin to be remembered. Then again, maybe it *wasn't*. After all, he knew where he came from now, in a way. And he had a lead to find his mother. A few days ago, he would have stolen the world for as much.

"Your people are my army," the Salt Sand King reminded him. "Wish, and we can find them together. Wish, and you will finally belong!"

Behind them the basin let out a deep belch. Streaks of iron reached out across the marble floor. He had to do something soon.

He shook his head. He should wish. Marrill would *want* him to wish. He reached for the orb. If she could remember, he told himself, Marrill would want the best for him, just as he'd want the best for her.

His heart froze at the thought. He *didn't* want his wish, he realized. Not at the expense of hers. That's what friends did. They looked out for each other, no matter what.

He took a deep breath. Then he thrust the glowing orb into Marrill's hands. "The wish is yours."

Her eyes widened with surprise. "Mine? Why? You don't even know me."

He smiled, even though it made his heart ache. "Yes, I do. You just don't remember. We were best friends once." He looked past her to where the Tide crept closer. Everything it touched had turned to iron. "You have to hurry," he added.

"It matters not who wishes," the fire snarled. "Either one of you can set me free." The blue flame eyes guttered away from Fin, and toward Marrill.

"Sickness encircles you," the Salt Sand King hissed. His voice came like steam from a wet log. "Wish and she will be well again. I've made this possible for you. My soldier has given up his wish for you. Do it, and do it now!"

Marrill sucked in a breath, her entire being focused on the wish orb. Sweat glistened on her forehead as the Salt Sand King's flames grew hotter.

Fin hopped from foot to foot, anxious about the creeping Tide. "Don't forget to wish for a way back home," he reminded her, forcing a smile. "Oh, and be specific! You know how persnickety wizards are about the wording of things. That has to go triple for wishes."

Marrill's lips trembled, tilting up at the corners. "You're a good friend," she said. "I'm sorry I don't remember."

Fin looked down at his feet. There wasn't really anything he could say to that. It was the story of his life.

With that, Marrill slipped her hand into his. Then she squared her shoulders and took a shaking breath. Fin waited for her to wish.

"I'm not doing it, either," she told the fire.

"What?" Fin gasped. "But Marrill, your mom—"

"No." Marrill shook her head. "I wouldn't be a very good friend if I took your wish from you."

Fin sputtered. He had no idea how to respond. "But...I *gave* it to you."

She shrugged. "I'm giving it back."

"You don't even remember me," he protested.

She squeezed his hand. "But I trust you."

"**ENOUGH!**" roared the Salt Sand King. Flames burst over them in a wave, crashing down and encircling them. The heat alone threatened to cook them alive. "**One of you will wish!**"

A wind rose up, whipping the inferno into a coil that turned into a serpent of fire, twisting tighter around them.

"**For years, I've waited for this moment. For ages, I scorched my own lands, again and again, unable to bring myself to give up the power YOU hold so casually in your hands. All that time, trapped in this prison of a world, cursed to be deprived of my destiny!**"

Fin and Marrill threw their arms over their faces, stumbling back against the assault. But they could only retreat so far. Behind them, the Iron Tide grew. Tendrils of metal stretched out ahead of it, the ground itself petrifying into cold iron. A bolt of red lightning streaked from the basin to somewhere up above, bursting in a loud POP.

"**But I am ready now,**" the fire serpent hissed.

"I am a generous, giving King. You will have what YOU want, I will have mine. We will conquer the Stream together! Take your wish. MAKE your wish. And SET ME FREE!"

Fin fumbled for his thief's bag, snatching a pinch of the salt he'd stashed there. He tossed it at the threatening fire.

With a howl, it shrieked back, but just as quickly, it roared toward them again. Fin tipped his entire bag over, using the rest of the salt to draw a circle around them on the ground. The flames broke against it, raging and sputtering.

Fin let out a short breath of relief. It wouldn't last long, though, not with the Iron Tide rising so fast. But at least they had a moment to think without being barbecued.

He looked at Marrill. "So, here's the thing. If we wish, we set him free. And I'm starting to realize just how bad of an idea that is."

"Yeah, I get that, too" she said, nodding. "But what do we do?"

"**Wish!**" the Salt Sand King shrieked. His flames circled them, slashing the air and burning ever higher.

Fin gulped, glancing between the whipping flame and the ever-spreading metal. If they didn't wish, they were trapped. Dead. And if they did, the Salt Sand King would be free. No one would be safe from him. And Fin had no doubt that he would burn them all, just as he had the Boundless Plains.

They couldn't let that happen. Even if it meant being swallowed by the Iron Tide.

"No," he said firmly. "No wishing."

"YOU MUST WANT SOMETHING!" he demanded. "EVERYONE WANTS SOMETHING!"

Marrill looked at Fin. For a moment, he could see the sadness in her eyes. She was giving up the chance to have everything she wanted. He wondered if she could see that same sadness in his.

Then she smiled at him. "Nope," Marrill said to the blaze. "I think we're fine, actually."

"Thanks, though," Fin added.

"'Thanks, though'?" the fire mocked. The flames towered to a soaring height. They licked at what remained of the dome ceiling, cracking and cooking the Stream-filled pipes.

Even with the salt protecting them, the heat was unbearable. It threatened to bake them alive. A cracking sound broke through the chamber, but the Salt Sand King was so enraged he didn't seem to hear it.

"YOU are NOT fine." he ranted. "You are desperate, needy children. I can FEEL the desire inside you. I can FEEL you wanting, so bad it's almost unbearable. Let it out! Give in! TAKE WHAT YOU WANT AND WISH! YOU MUST WISH!"

"Psst," Marrill hissed, rolling her eyes toward the ceiling. "Check out the pipes."

Fin looked up. Overhead, just above the dancing tips of flame, a spiderweb of tiny black fissures ran along the pipes. As the King raged, the flames licked against the glass, and the fissures widened, leaking wisps of white vapor.

"Water expands when it turns into steam," Marrill whispered. "It's cracking the pipes as it boils!"

"And if we make it hot enough..." Fin trailed off. He met Marrill's eyes.

"We can burst them entirely!" she concluded.

Fin smirked. "Hey, Sandy," he called. "Here's an idea: Maybe you should build a machine that lets you wish for us to want to wish!"

The fire roared brighter, angrier. Flames crackled against the pipes overhead. "Be ready to jump for cover," Marrill whispered. She poked a thumb at the huge chunk of glass the Lost Sun had sheared from one of the column pipes. Fin nodded.

"You WILL wish!" the flames raged. **"You can't resist it! I can FEEL you WANTING!"**

A blast of heat seared Fin's eyebrows. For a moment, he wondered if taunting a creature of pure fire was a bad idea.

But when had he ever let that stop him?

He focused every fiber of his being on one thought: hoping the Salt Sand King would stay trapped here forever. "You can feel me wanting? Then what am I wanting *right now*?"

The air grew hotter, scalding him. The fire crackled with fury. And just when he thought he couldn't take it anymore, a pipe burst overhead. Directly above the Salt Sand King.

Bright water gushed out, spraying down on the fire. The first drops boiled instantly into steam. The fire flinched, giving Fin and Marrill just the opening they needed to dive for the glass chunk and slide beneath it. More and more water rained down. The Salt Sand King shrieked, fizzled, and popped.

They watched through the glass as the flames shrank back, struggling to survive in the rain, until only the thin, crooked form they'd met on the plain remained. The deluge of magical water slowed, each droplet cooling the Salt Sand King's molten surface to embers.

"Fire...hides." His voice was the last gasping flicker of a dying flame. "Desire...can sleep. But it never...dies. Someday, you will give in and wish. And when you do...I...WILL... be...freeeee..."

And then all that remained of the Salt Sand King was a man-shaped sculpture of ash. No other signs of fire remained. Cautiously, Fin crept from their shelter and approached the statue.

It was completely lifeless. No coals glowed in the dull gray eyes. No heat came from the body. He reached out. The moment his fingers brushed against it, what was left of the Salt Sand King collapsed in a cloud of ash.

Resting on the ground where the King had stood was a glowing orb of molten light: the wish. He crouched and plucked it free. It pulsed warm in his palm. With one thought, he could be the boy everyone remembered rather than the one everyone forgot.

He could be the boy Marrill remembered.

He shook his head and stood. "Here," he said, holding it out to her.

She shivered. "You keep it."

He nodded, shoving it into his thief's bag as he started for the exit. "We should go."

"Hey," she called. There was something different in her voice. He turned.

She stood behind him, smiling, with her thumb pressed to her heart. Their sign for friend. "Thanks, Fin."

And the next thing he knew, he was buried deep in a huge hug.

CHAPTER 31
Tied Together, Bound in Place

Marrill squeezed Fin with all her might. Emotions tangled in her chest: guilt, regret, sorrow. The realization that she'd hurt her best friend.

She had no idea how to ask for forgiveness. She wasn't even sure she deserved it.

A deep shuddering groan sounded throughout the chamber. Cracks splintered up the walls. Remnants of the Syphon crashed into the basin, sending a wave of molten metal up over the edge of it.

Half of the room had turned to iron now. And it was spreading faster. "We should really go." Fin whirled toward the door Marrill had come through, but she grabbed him.

"We can't go that way," she told him. "It's blocked—the catacombs flooded." She tried not to think of the Naysayer, and what might have become of him. "We have to go out the way you came in."

He was already shaking his head. "That'll just take us back to the Burning Plain. We'll be on the wrong side of the Wall. Also, you know, fire."

"Well, we can't stay here!" she urged. The Iron Tide crept forward, a spreading blackness chewing away at the marble floor. Another groan shuddered through them as a large fissure shot up one wall and across the domed ceiling.

The Lost Sun had done too much damage. It wouldn't be long before the entire chamber collapsed. If they were still here, they'd be crushed in the debris. At best.

"The Burning Plain is our only option!" She tried dragging him to the other door, but he dug in his heels. His eyes scanned their surroundings and then he smiled.

It was a familiar smile. One that tended to get them in trouble. "How're your climbing skills these days?"

"Fin—"

It was too late; he was already gone. He skittered across a fallen beam and hopped to a chunk of debris that was slowly turning to iron. In moments the entire thing would be consumed.

Fin held out a hand. "You trusted me before," he reminded her.

"Because I didn't remember you!" she protested. "I didn't know better!"

He waggled his eyebrows. "Probably a good call." Chunks of the domed ceiling began to crumble and drop. His expression turned serious. "I won't let anything happen to you, Marrill."

She let out a long breath. "I hope I don't regret this," she said, stepping carefully away from the creeping metal.

Fin laughed. "Oh, I'm sure you most certainly will at some point." He leapt to a broken gear and scrambled up a slab of fallen debris. "That second jump is tricky," he called back to her. "Make sure to keep your weight forward."

She did as told, grunting as her foot slipped, almost touching the line of iron. Another shudder rocked the chamber, sending more cracks up the wall. But she kept her focus on Fin, following his instructions until they reached the top of the dome.

He crawled through a hole the Lost Sun had blasted, pulling her up after him. From here she had an excellent view of the Iron Tide as it swept through the chamber.

It moved like liquid. But it didn't fill space. Instead, it was a line of creeping petrification, climbing across whatever it touched. In the heart of the chamber, the basin bubbled black, spilling out dark water. Marrill felt sure that wherever that water reached, the tide of iron would go with it.

"What now?" she asked, panting.

"Up." He pointed. Marrill's jaw dropped. Above them a forest of gears loomed. Some of them were broken, many were cracked. None of them moved.

"How did you know this was here?" she asked, stunned as she took it all in.

"I didn't," he said. He started toward one of the gears and started climbing. "But it's all one big machine. I figured it had to be connected *somehow*. From here, though..."

She felt something shift in her pocket. The Wiverwane skittered up to her shoulder. Softly, it tapped her neck. A memory of an image flashed in her mind, so quickly it almost threw her off balance. She grinned as she realized what it was: schematics. The Wiverwane had shown her the way out. "That way," she told Fin, pointing.

He took off. She scrambled after him, following his every move. He pulled himself over the teeth of one gear, then hopped to another, clambering ever upward.

As they went, she thought of what had just happened, in the chamber. How he'd refused to wish, offering it to her.

"Why didn't you wish?" she asked, kicking up onto a broken cog. "Why didn't you just use it?"

He pulled himself through a rather tricky spot and reached back to help her. "That's not what friends do." He said it so simply. Guilt spiked through her. How could she have forgotten him?

She cleared her throat and gestured toward a crack where

sunlight shone through high above. "We want to go that way—stay to the right, though. Oh, and avoid the silver gears."

He made it look so easy, climbing and leaping and crouching. It was like he grew up playing on the world's craziest jungle gym.

Except this particular jungle gym was in the process of collapsing. Chunks of debris broke free above them, crashing past them. A gear trembled beneath her feet, shuddered, and began to slip to the side.

Marrill scrambled desperately, hardly even looking where she was going as she jumped from one falling platform to another. Furiously they climbed, up and up, for what seemed like eternity, Marrill pointing the way and Fin figuring out how to get there.

Soon, her arms and legs ached; she felt sure she couldn't go much farther. Below, somewhere in the darkness, the Iron Tide climbed slowly, steadily after them.

But then, another jump, another struggle, and the bright slash of sunlight was finally within reach. She threw herself at it. Her fingertips caught the edge. Her feet kicked in the air. Her arms quivered, threatening to let go.

And then a face appeared in front of her. Hands fell on her forearms. She was so startled she lost her grip. But the hands caught her, held her tight. She nearly screamed. Then she recognized the white beard, the purple cap.

"Marrill," Ardent cried in relief. "It's you! I'd nearly

given up hope!" With a tug, he pulled her through the hole and out onto the other side of the Wall where a gear had fallen away.

Marrill brushed her cheek in thanks against the Wiverwane perched on her shoulder. It unleashed a flood of relieved memories before tucking itself safely under her collar.

Fin landed next to them a moment later. He slapped her on the shoulder as he caught his breath. "Nice climbing. That was a close one!" Marrill collapsed back against the broken surface of the Wall, beaming at the compliment.

Ardent looked at the two of them and shook his head. "Honestly, Miss Aesterwest, you make friends in the strangest places."

A shudder rumbled up through the stone beneath them. "We'd best be going," the wizard added. Ardent's voice trailed off as he looked past her, down into the gaping hole in the Wall. Even from where they stood, Marrill could hear the soft crackle of stone turning to metal, the trickle of water rising. Spreading. Threatening to spill out across the Stream.

"What in Falmore's feathers happened down there?" the wizard asked.

"Um...yeah, we broke the Syphon and started the Iron Tide," Marrill blurted. "It's coming. Fast!"

Ardent's face turned ashen. "Oh dear," he said. His eyes darted from the hole in the Wall out toward the Stream. "Oh...oh dear."

They stood on a tilted gear, not far above the Grovel. All around, chaos reigned. It wasn't hard to figure out why. A massive crack ran up the Wall, splitting it clear in half. Beetles clambered through from the other side, joining the teeming horde of Monervans dropping down from above. The city was falling apart.

Every dock groaned under the weight of escapees jostling for a spot on one of the waiting ships. The air was thick with shouts and the rumbling of the still-shaking Wall. "Shanks," Fin breathed.

"Yes, well, it seems like the tide has turned, if you will pardon the expression." Ardent pointed to the flotilla of ships already headed out toward a giant whirlpool waiting on the horizon. One reached the edge of it, and then just... disappeared.

"Wait, what just happened to that boat?" Marrill asked.

"Annalessa calls it the Boundary," the wizard explained. "The point where the bubble of Monerva ends and the way back to the Stream begins. Before, it was only one way— in—thanks to the pull of the Syphon. Now, it seems to have reversed itself. It appears all we have to do is sail out, and we should be returned right back to the Stream."

"Then we should go," Fin suggested. "Like everyone. We should all go. Now."

Ardent nodded. "Your new friend has a point." Without another word, he stepped onto a sinking beam and let it carry him to the docks, where he plunged into the crowd, pushing his way toward the *Kraken*. "Hurry, everyone, hurry!" he shouted as he went. "No good reason, nothing to be alarmed about, but seriously, *hurry!*"

Marrill chased after him, jostling through the mob. The creatures of Monerva packed the docks, clambering to abandon the doomed city. Ships cast off all around, striking out for the Boundary. She bit her lip, glancing over her shoulder. Was it iron or shadow that now darkened the hole she and Fin had escaped through?

"Look, the Wall!" a loud voice cried.

Sure enough, the darkness was growing. It spread out in all directions: climbing, creeping down; stretching fingers out across dullwood beams and tracing the teeth of gears. "The Iron Tide," Marrill breathed.

"The Iron Tide?" Another voice picked up the words, then another, carrying them around the crowd. Soon, they were on everyone's lips. A moment ago, no one here had ever heard of the Iron Tide. Now, with it moving like a sickness over the face of the Wall, none of them would ever forget it.

"The Iron Tide is coming!" a woman shouted. "You must stop it!" Marrill jerked her head up, swallowed in déjà vu. She knew that voice! She pushed through the chaos after it, running smack into a tall Monervan with a frog clutched in one hand and a long, rather pathetic flag on a pole in the other.

"Stop the Iron Tide before it spreads beyond the docks

and—oof," Talaba grunted as Marrill collided with her. "Hey, watch where you're—" The frog squirmed from her hands. "Oh, wait, my frog! Get back here, you little—" The Monervan scrambled away after it.

Marrill blinked. "No time to engage the locals," Ardent said, pulling her onward. The *Kraken*'s gangplank lay just ahead, and he ushered her quickly up it.

"Marrill! Plus One!" Remy launched herself toward them, pulling Marrill in with one hand and Fin in with the other for a fierce hug. "I was so worried about you guys! I'm totally hitting up your parents for hazard pay after all this." She herded them eagerly onboard.

Ardent stalked across the main deck with fierce determination. "Coll, make sail," he commanded. His voice was cold and flat. "No more waiting. Go, now."

The captain hunched over the wheel, expression fierce. Sweat beaded on his brow. "Finally," he rasped, rubbing at his throat. Above, the pirats scampered across the yards, untying knots and raising sails.

"He's not doing well," Remy whispered. "He won't tell me what's going on, but I think he really needs to get out of here."

"I think we all do," Fin said. He kept his eyes trained on the Wall. Black-stained water now trickled from the gap where they'd emerged. Anywhere it touched, the dull metal plague took root. And when it reached the waves of the

Stream below, it spread faster than ever. A chill stole down his back.

"Hey, look, it's the Iron Tide," the Naysayer snorted behind them, Karnelius tucked in the crook of an elbow. "And here I thought the literally thousands of stories documenting its existence would end up being a typo."

Marrill jumped at him, wrapping him in a huge hug. "Naysayer! You made it! You're alive!"

"Yeah, and now you're making me regret that circumstance," the cantankerous old creature grumbled. With two hands, he shoved her away. But if Marrill hadn't known better, she would have sworn a third hand gave her a light, friendly pat.

The moment didn't last long. Shouts erupted across the Grovel, as beetles, Monervans, and various creatures of all kinds shoved their way onto already-filled ships, threatening to capsize them in the rush to escape the creeping onslaught of metal. The *Kraken* jolted, throwing Marrill off balance. Above, the sails snapped full. The ship eased away from the docks and the thronging horde.

"Wait!" Marrill cried. Coll's face remained grim as he guided the ship out toward the open water. She couldn't believe he'd just abandon everyone like that. "What are you doing? We can't just leave! We have to do something."

"You said make sail," Coll croaked at Ardent. He drew

a labored breath. His hand clawed at the tattoo knotted around his neck. The ink ropes twisted into a hangman's noose.

Annalessa snapped her fingers. The sails eased, flapping uselessly in the wind. Marrill hadn't even noticed the wizard come up on deck. "She's right, Coll. We can't just abandon these people."

The sailor looked to Ardent. "Please," he wheezed. "I can't..." As Marrill watched, the ropes of his tattoo seemed to somehow squeeze even tighter. Coll stumbled back a step, then collapsed to his knees, gasping.

"Coll!" Remy raced to his side, helping him to sit. Her hand rested on his back, supporting him as he struggled for air. "Do something!" she shouted at the wizards.

Ardent's expression was strained. "There's nothing we can do. The ropes that bind him are powerful ones. If he stays in one place for too long, well...this happens. Being trapped here, outside of time, it's even worse." He knelt down by his friend and gripped Coll's forearm tightly. "They're right, Coll. We *must* stop the Iron Tide before we escape," he said softly. "Can you hold on just a little longer?"

Coll squeezed his eyes shut and nodded. "I will," he gasped. "Whether I can or not."

Ardent cupped the back of Coll's head. "Thank you, old friend," he whispered. Then he was up, striding purposefully across the deck. "We need to get these people out of here, fast, before the Iron Tide reaches them. And then get ourselves out of here before the currents trap us."

He pointed to the metal now covering half the Wall. Black water splashed up onto the docks, the Tide swelling and growing with every moment. "Because if we don't," he finished, "I expect we may be stuck in here, with *that*, forever."

CHAPTER 32
The Iron Tide

As Fin watched, the Iron Tide swept across the Wall, turning everything it touched to metal. Nothing in its path was safe. It coated gardens and terraces, cranes and the buildings they'd been lifting.

Beside him, Annalessa dragged her hands through the air. With each motion, another ship's sails jumped to life. All across the Grovel, the last of the vessels launched, racing to stay ahead of the creeping plague.

As the *Kraken* made its way through the marshes, the

iron covered the end of the docks. A dull, dark sheen coated the wood and the waves, growing faster with every second.

"It's no use," Annalessa murmured, as much to herself as to Fin. "So long as the ships can reach the Boundary, they can escape back to their own times. But the Tide will follow right on their heels."

A niggling thought grabbed at the back of Fin's mind. An idea that was so close he could almost feel it breathing on him. "Back to their own times..." he muttered. "As long as they reach the Boundary..."

Then it hit him. He jumped into the air with a clap. "Hey!" he said. "Aren't we all forgetting something?" Annalessa raised an eyebrow with confusion. "I mean something other than me? In all those old stories, sailors were fleeing the Iron Tide. But it never actually showed up on the Stream, right?"

The wizard cocked her head, running one long finger down the strong line of her chin. "You're right. Perhaps because the Iron Tide would also go back to where it came in. Which I assume would be where, or rather when, the Master and his Iron Ship came in."

Fin snapped his fingers, trying to hold her attention. "Right, we *assume* that. But what if it isn't true? I mean, the Iron Tide began in Monerva, with the Master and the Stream water, and even the Lost Sun all coming together. It could seep out any...when. But what if it doesn't? Because it doesn't *ever reach the Boundary?*"

Annalessa snapped her fingers, just as he had. "Of

course!" She laughed. "Monerva was always connected to the Stream by the flow of water coming in. Right now, that flow has reversed, but soon it will die off entirely, and the link between Moneva and the rest of the Stream will be severed. If we can keep the Iron Tide from escaping before that happens, it will be stuck here!"

She paced frantically from one side of the *Kraken* to the other. Fin struggled to keep up with her. "But how, but how…" she muttered.

A tall Monervan ship sailed by. Fin was pretty sure he could see Talaba on its crow's nest, hoisting up her rag canopy. "Still building to the end," he said, shaking his head.

"Now, there's a thought," Annalessa said. "Building! We could build something, to stop the Iron Tide…"

"A wall!" Fin and Annalessa cried at once.

With one finger, the wizard tapped the end of Fin's nose. "My goodness, you're not memorable," she said suddenly. "I'm so sorry for all the times I must have forgotten you. Not to mention all the times I will. Now let's go stop this Iron Tide."

Fin raced up to the front of the ship, calling for Marrill and Ardent. The wizard looked at him with unfamiliarity. "Man, Annalessa is so much more on the ball than you," he muttered. Quickly, he explained what they'd figured out about slowing the Tide. ·

"So if we can get the Monervans to work with us…" Marrill said.

"Then we can build a barrier to hold back the Tide!" Fin shouted.

Marrill beamed at him and his chest puffed up. "Fin, that's perfect! And I know just who to ask." She scanned the nearby ships and cupped her hands around her mouth shouting, "Elle!"

The snail was perched on the stern of a squat barge, which tilted precariously under her weight. At Marrill's call, she shot out a snail tail, wrapping it around the *Kraken's* mast to pull the ships together.

"Well, won't you look at that?" a familiar voice said as the ships drew closer. Slandy leaned over the railing, waving. "See, Brendel dear, it's that girl I told you about, the one from the party. Girl from the party, meet Brendel, the missus!"

Marrill nodded hello to Brendel before turning to Slandy. "We need your help," she explained. "We need to use the levator snails to build a barricade and stop the Iron Tide."

Brendel's mouth opened in an O. "Oooh, building again? Maybe we can snag the highest after all, huh, Slandy?" she said.

"I'm not sure that's what they meant, Brendel, my love," Slandy said, "but I think I've got the clue of it. Sure thing, young lady. If it'll help the situation, just tell me what you want and where you want it and we'll get it done. Won't we, girl?" she added, running a hand across Elle's shell.

Between them, Slandy, and Brendel, word spread quickly to the other ships. But Brendel wasn't alone in her reaction; apparently, the idea of building brought out the competitive nature of the Monervans. A number of snail-bearing ships volunteered immediately, each insisting they'd definitely be able to gather more junk, and better, than the others. In moments, what seemed like a surefire solution was falling apart to bickering and petty rivalries.

"This isn't about height," Fin tried to remind them. But already, the Monervans were piling debris into floating columns, leaving massive gaps between them as the Iron Tide washed closer. The Tide spread through the water faster even than it had across the Wall. Fin's shoulders pulled tight with frustration.

"Ugh," Marrill groaned, "how do we get them to stop wanting to be Highest so badly and just work together?"

"Perhaps I can be of assistance?" a voice buzzed from the side of the *Kraken*. Fin leaned over the rail. A curious sight awaited him at the waterline: a big brass bowl bobbed on ostrich legs, its large feet strapped tightly into makeshift skis. A black beetle stood inside of it, arms akimbo, the reins held loosely in one clawed hand.

"Say the word, and my brothers and I stand ready to help the Monervans focus. We beetles are, after all, experts in suppressing desire." Though his shiny beak was literally expressionless, Fin couldn't help but think that was self-satisfaction shining in his red, multifaceted eye.

Fin flashed a relieved smile. "That's perfect! Listen, everyone," he shouted as beetles clambered to join their Monervan counterparts. "We have to all work together. Build out, not up! In fact, the ship that listens to their beetles' instructions the best will become…" His mind scrambled. "Uh…Best-est. Which is better than highest. Trust me."

"We would know," Marrill said. "We totally met the Salt Sand King." The Monervans, impressed, fell into a chatter.

"…And we killed him," Fin quietly assured the now-chittering beetles. *Sort of,* he mentally added. Satisfied, the beetles, too, broke into conferring.

With the beetles to soothe their insane rivalries, Fin was amazed with what the Monervans accomplished. Their outward-pointing faces could spot prime chunks of debris all around them for the snails to snatch and anchor into place. Before long, the last piece of the barricade fell into place, blocking off the marshes just before the Iron Tide reached it.

A raucous cheer went up from the fleet. For a long moment, it seemed the Tide was contained. But then a dark spot appeared on the barricade. The iron was spreading, slowly petrifying its way through this new barrier just as it had the Wall. And when the line of creeping metal reached the water, darkness raced across the waves.

The Iron Tide was on the move once more.

Fin's shoulders slumped. "We didn't stop it," he moaned, feeling deflated. A shudder ran across the fleet.

But it seemed Marrill wasn't ready to give up just yet. "Maybe we don't have to," she announced. "Look: The Iron Tide moves way faster when it's in the water. If we can put up more barriers, we can slow it down long enough for the current to die and the Boundary to close. Keep building, everyone!"

The Monervans and beetles fell back into place, crafting another barricade out of junk, then another after that. The bravest moved to the front, holding the lines so the others could escape. One at a time, ships broke for the Boundary. Annalessa and Ardent took turns boosting them toward the horizon; she pulling on the wind, he pushing with the waves.

But as the fleet lost builders, the Tide came faster than they could stop it. It had already reached the second wall before they'd finished the third. In no time, the Iron Tide spread through the second barrier and onto the Stream. Fin held his breath as the wash of iron slapped against the third barrier.

"More, more!" cried Brendel. "You, snail, snag that piece over there! You there, Necarib! I see you hoarding it—send that window out to the front lines. And yes, the stupid pedestal, too!"

"Calm your ambitions," Rysacg urged. "Focus on what you achieve, not what you wish."

"There's little to grab, and no one left to do the grabbing," Slandy pointed out.

Fin looked around. Aside from Slandy's and Rysacg's boats, the *Kraken* was the only one left. All the others had made it to the Boundary and disappeared down the whirlpool. But as Fin watched the water spiraling into the whirlpool, the vortex seemed to wobble. At its mouth, the only exit out of Monerva flexed. It grew and shrank, like a hungry bird chirping for food. At the same time, the water swirling down it seemed to stutter and halt, just as it hit the rim.

Fin's pulse hammered loudly in his ears. The Boundary was collapsing. It was time to leave or be stuck here forever.

Annalessa seemed to have come to the same realization. "Come on, Ardent," she said. "Let's hold this barricade together just a touch longer." She planted her feet and held out her arms. A loose section of the final barrier stood suddenly firm.

"Way ahead of you," Ardent said, making little swatting motions with one hand. Each time he did, a new piece of flotsam jumped out of the water and onto the barricade, giving the Iron Tide another obstacle to spread through before it could reach the waves.

"I'm afraid we've done what we can do for you," Slandy shouted from the prow of her ship. "We'd best be on our way!"

"Oh, it's been such fun meeting you folks," Brendel added.

Marrill jumped and waved. "Bye, Brendel, bye, Slandy! Thanks for everything. Take good care of Elle!"

And with that, Ardent cut his hand through the air again, sending a wave to pick up the Monervans' ship and slide it down the whirlpool.

The beetle's ship pulled up along the other side. "I fear I, too, must be leaving," Rysacg buzzed. "We owe you all a great debt for tearing down the Wall. For bringing us back to our lost cousins. And for mastering your desires as my people could not."

Fin waved furiously, even though he knew the beetle

probably wouldn't notice him. Ardent shoved the air again, and soon Rysacg, too, was gone.

Which left the *Enterprising Kraken*, alone, against the Iron Tide that had devoured Monerva. The Wall was a cracked black slab, mired as if melted in the unyielding iron water below. The spires of the Highest now stood rigid, cold and dark. For once, the sinking city remained still.

The wizards both braced themselves, holding the final barricade in place with all their might. Remy gripped Marrill by the shoulders as the vibrating waves grew higher. All around, Fin watched pieces of the city and bits of Marrill's world wash out toward the mouth of the wobbling whirlpool.

"Ardent," Coll gasped. "The chop's getting too much. We have to go, now!"

Annalessa dropped her hands. One of them, though, she slipped around Ardent's arms. "We've done it," she said to him. "Come now. Let's go, dear."

The wizard bit his lip. Fin could tell he was straining, trying to hold on until the last possible second. And for that moment, it was almost as if his will alone was a perfect match for whatever force propelled the Iron Tide.

But then he, too, let his arms fall and nodded. Coll gave an audible sigh of relief and yanked the wheel sharply. The *Kraken* turned. Behind them, the final barrier groaned.

Then they were full about, heading away as fast as they could. The bow of the *Kraken* crashed through the waves, her course set for the shrinking whirlpool . . . and home.

CHAPTER 33
Full Circle

"Hey, check it out!" Remy pointed as they neared the whirlpool. "Isn't that all junk from home?"

Marrill caught sight of a balding tire floating through the water along with an old, rusted train caboose. Even Roseberg's, the empty store from the abandoned strip mall, bobbed a few dozen yards away.

"You know, it seems really unfair that all that stuff's still intact, while my car's probably mounted on some pirate's wall as a trophy by now," Remy grumbled.

"Different currents," Annalessa pointed out. "With your world practically touching the Boundary, these objects are likely caught on a brackish current."

"What'll happen to it all?" Marrill asked.

"It'll get sucked through the whirlpool just like the ships." Annalessa shrugged. "According to everything we know, it should go back to where it came from as though nothing happened."

"Wait." Remy pushed to her feet, face draining of color. "Does that mean that *we* could go home, too? Like, if we were in that store when it crossed back into our world, it would take us with it?"

Annalessa ran her finger down her nose as she considered the question. Marrill's pulse skittered. It hadn't occurred to her that getting home could be so easy.

"Theoretically, it's possible," Annalessa finally pronounced. "We know everything will return to its own *time*, but we always just assumed everything would be going back to the same *place*: the Shattered Archipelago. That store, though, is crossing directly into your world. It's hard to say *when* you would show up, but it's quite reasonable to think you could, essentially, ride it home."

Marrill grabbed the rail to steady herself. A way home. But how could they be sure? If Annalessa was wrong, they could end up doggy-paddling in Stream water.

She stared across the short distance to where Roseberg's floated past. Something moved, somewhere inside of it. She squinted. If she didn't know better, she would have sworn there was a frog hopping along one of the shelves.

She sucked in a breath as the revelation hit her. It was the speakfrog—the one Talaba had lost just minutes ago. The same one she had found days ago, in the gully by her house.

Or rather, would find.

She closed her eyes. Ardent was right. This whole time business *was* tricky.

But it didn't matter *when* the frog ended up in Arizona. What mattered is that it *did* end up in Arizona. Which meant she could, too. So it was true: Roseberg's was her ticket back.

Home was only a few yards away.

"The speakfrog rode it home," she said. "We can, too."

Remy looked at her, eyes wide. "So I guess that means..." She bit her lip and glanced down at where Coll hunched over the wheel, still wheezing. She swallowed. "We should go?" But the babysitter didn't move.

Marrill stared at the abandoned store, feeling strangely empty. Yes, she'd be going home, and her parents would never even know she'd been gone in the first place. But her mom would still be sick. Nothing at all would have changed.

"Would we be able to come back?" she asked, chest squeezing tight.

Ardent and Annalessa exchanged a glance. "I don't know," Annalessa said.

Marrill nodded. "And if I don't go now...will I be able to get home later?"

Again the two wizards exchanged a glance. "I don't know," Annalessa said again.

Ardent cleared his throat. "You'll have to do it soon, before the store hits the whirlpool."

She glanced over at Fin. He stood with his arms crossed and his shoulders braced, waiting for their inevitable good-bye. He blinked back something that looked suspiciously like tears. A spike cut through Marrill's heart.

He stepped forward then, holding out the yellow wish orb. "Take this—you can use it to make your mom better."

Marrill stared at it. It was tempting. Deeply, severely tempting. But she couldn't. The risk was too great. She shook her head. "Remember what the Salt Sand King said: If we wish, he'll be freed, and the whole Stream could go up in flames."

"Okay. Marrill," Remy called. She'd made her way up to the quarterdeck. Her hand lingered lightly on Coll's arm. "It's time. We gotta go if we're going."

Marrill met Fin's eyes. He cleared his throat and jerked his chin toward the floating store as it grew closer and closer to the edge of the whirlpool. "You should hurry." But as she started toward the railing, his hand shot out, stopping her. "Why did you remember me, back in the catacombs?"

She swallowed. It was the same question she'd been asking herself. Now she thought she might have the answer. "Before all this, back when we first met, I think I remembered you because I felt like you needed me," she said. "And I forgot you because you didn't need me anymore."

She stopped herself. "That's not true. I forgot you because I took you for granted. That's what really happened."

She chewed her lip. "But now...now I remember because I care about *you*. It's because I can't forget *you*, no matter what happens, no matter what you or I do, no matter how things go. You're my best friend."

He looked back at her. "You said that before, you know," he reminded her.

Marrill hung her head. "I know," she said. "And I took *that* for granted. I shouldn't have."

Fin glanced away and then back at her. "I did the same thing," he confessed. "I put what I wanted ahead of you. And I don't want to ever do that again." His voice cracked as he spoke. "But...how do we know this time is different?"

More than anything else, she wanted to reassure him. But how could she know for certain? Whatever made him forgettable was far beyond anything she comprehended.

All she could tell him was what was in her heart. "We don't." She lifted a shoulder. "But isn't that the way it always is with friends? You just have to trust they'll be there for you."

He thought this over for a moment. "That's pretty scary."

She felt the sides of her mouth lifting into a smile. "Yeah. It is."

"Will you do me a favor?" he asked. She nodded without hesitation. "When you get home, will you make yourself one of those sail scraps with my picture on it like the ones you made last time? To remind you of me, just in case?"

Marrill felt tears burn in the back of her throat. "I'll make a hundred of them," she told him.

He smiled. She waited for him to crack some sort of joke. But instead he just said, "Thanks."

Marrill took a deep breath as she searched the deck for Karnelius. She had been here before. On the verge of leaving everything, with nothing to take back but memories. Serth had been right, she realized. She hadn't just come back to the Pirate Stream to help Fin and the others. She'd come to run away from not being able to help her mom.

And yet, here she was now, on the Pirate Stream, where magic flowed like water. Where wishes came from machines. Where else *could* she find a way to help her mom.

So why was she leaving?

As she was wrestling with the thought, the Wiverwane, forgotten in her pocket, crept out and skittered across her bare arm. A flood of memories filled her. Some from home. Some from the Stream. Some from an ancient time, from a small, golden, whiskered little thing, a being of immense, incredible power, but so, so lonely, she could scarcely even imagine. The Dawn Wizard, last of its kind, building a machine to grant wishes. Wishing for the friends it had left behind.

Marrill rubbed her palms against her shorts brusquely. "You know what?" she told him. "I'll do you one better. I'm not going."

Fin opened his mouth. Marrill held up a hand. "At least, not yet, anyway." She jerked a thumb at the store. "Counting that thing, I've found my way home twice already. I can do it again. And this time, when I do go, I won't regret not doing what I could for the people I love."

She smirked and put her hands on Fin's shoulders. "I'll be able to *do* something when I get home. *And,*" she said, her resolution growing as she spoke the words out loud, "I won't leave you to get forgotten again. We're not giving up on my mom *or* yours. We're going to find her. Together. So yeah. I'm staying."

Fin looked away for a second. She could see him trying to figure out how to screw up his face so it didn't look like he was getting teary. She pretended not to notice.

"Then I'm not going back, either," Remy announced.

"But, Remy—" Marrill protested.

The older girl cut her off. "Like I said, Arizona's best babysitter doesn't lose a kid." Her eyes flicked to Coll and then away. Two bright spots of color appeared on her cheeks. "Besides, maybe I've got my own reasons for staying."

A broad grin devoured Marrill's face. And when she looked back down, Fin was shoving the wish orb into her hands. "Okay," he said. "But keep this." He looked her dead in the eye and winked. "At least you'll *know* you can go home, if worse comes to worst."

She threw her arms around him. "Thanks, Fin," she whispered in his ear.

"Aw, ain't I proud," the Naysayer mocked. "I knew one day,

if you tried *real* hard, at least one of ya could make a friend. Now wrap up the snuggle-huggin' and the cheerleadin' and get us out of here before the world collapses, how 'bout?"

"I told you," Remy shot, "I'm *not* a—" Before she could finish, the deck tilted and she scrambled for purchase.

The Naysayer was right. The vibrating waves had grown to a fever pitch. The whirlpool yawning before them wobbled unsteadily, ready to collapse at any second. Behind them, iron spotted the surface of the barricade. If they didn't get out before the Boundary collapsed, they would be stuck here with it.

But still, Ardent didn't give the command for the ship to leave. Anguish wrinkled his brow. And suddenly it dawned on Marrill as to why.

She turned to Annalessa. "If everything goes back to where it came from, what will happen to you?"

Annalessa glanced at Ardent, her eyes watery. "I'll return to my own ship and time."

"So you'll go back to the past," Fin said. She nodded. He frowned. "But you know the future now. Doesn't that mean you can change it?"

Ardent stepped toward her, taking her hand. "You can, you know—change the future." His voice held so much pain that Marrill's heart ached for him. "Go back to see me again," he urged. "I'll listen this time. I promise."

She laughed softly, but it was marred with sorrow. "But I can't, Ardent. Because I didn't. My future is already your past. What I've done—it's all been written and set. There's no changing it."

The *Kraken* pulled to the edge of the ever-shrinking whirlpool. Behind them, the final barrier crackled as the Iron Tide consumed it. "Guys!" Remy called. She sounded on the edge of panic. "It's coming! And Coll's getting worse!" She crouched next to him as he struggled for air, his fingers clutching his neck.

Ardent pressed his lips together until they disappeared into his beard. "Ropebone," he called, his voice flat. "Take us in." Rigging snapped tight, the sails filled as the *Kraken* turned toward the center of the swirling whirlpool.

Annalessa placed a hand against Ardent's cheek. "Goodbye, Ardent Squirrelsquire."

He placed his hand on top of hers. "I'll never stop looking for you, Annalessa. I *will* see you again, though all of the Pirate Stream should stand in my way."

The *Kraken* wound tighter and tighter, the bowsprit almost piercing the center of the vortex when Annalessa smiled and stepped toward Ardent, as though about to kiss him. But before her lips could touch his, she vanished.

"My stuff!" the Naysayer cried. "What's happening to all my stuff?!" As the *Kraken* passed into the whirlpool, pile after pile of junk began to disappear. He dove onto the remaining bits, pawing pieces aft in a desperate—and pointless—effort to save them. Karny skittered after him, batting at the loose scraps as they bounced free and evaporated into thin air.

Marrill started to laugh. But it caught in her throat when an octagonal plate of bright metal came skittering across the deck to rest right at her feet.

Almost in a trance, she picked it up and flipped it over. STOP, it said in white letters, glaring against a bright crimson background.

For a moment, Marrill thought about writing a message to her parents, telling them not to worry. Telling them that she had returned to the Pirate Stream, and would be back once she'd found a way to fix her mom. Under her feet, the deck pitched upward. The *Kraken* was falling. There was no time. Frantically, she searched through her pockets, pulling out the hunk of charcoal she'd snagged on the Burning Plain.

And in the end, she knew exactly what she had to write. The very words that had gotten her here in the first place:

Because it was the truth. Just not the way she'd first understood it. She was needed to stop the Iron Tide. But not just that. Fin also needed her. To be his friend. To help him find his mother. And if she was honest, she needed herself to be here, too.

She'd just finished drawing the sigil of the Salt Sand King when the stern of the ship plunged into the whirlpool. A second before it disappeared, Marrill whipped the stop sign out into the air. Knowing, without a doubt, that it would find its way home.

CHAPTER 34
Promises to Keep

Fin let out a long whoop as the *Kraken* rocketed down the swirling funnel of water, swooshed through the hairpin turn at the bottom, and shot upward once more. Behind them, the tunnel collapsed in on itself, creating a massive tidal wave. But Fin wasn't worried. Because after everything they'd been through, there was no way they were dying now.

Up ahead, the churning water gave way to bright blue sky. The wave lifted them from behind, raising the ship up and out of the whirlpool. "Whoa, bwah, whoa!" he yelped.

"All hands, brace yourselves!" Coll shouted.

"Floating islands ahoy!" Ardent called as they moved through the heart of the Shattered Archipelago.

"My stuff!" the Naysayer wailed. "Why did it have to be my stuff? Why couldn't it be the cheerleader!"

"IIIII AAAM NOOOOT AAAA CHEEEER-LEEADEERRR!!!" Remy shrieked.

The *Kraken* surfed the magical wave as it crashed through broken islands. Some of them vanished, turning into a flock of butterflies and the taste of butter on a hot roll as the wave consumed them. And then, finally, slowly, the wave subsided. The ship drifted down onto now-calm seas. No hint of the whirlpool remained.

Fin braced himself for the crack of red lightning, the punishing roll of thunder. But they didn't come. Above, the sky was a brilliant blue, the Stream an endless expanse of emptiness. There were no other vessels in sight. "But the Iron Ship—it was right here when we went through the whirlpool. If we came back at the same time we left..." He trailed off.

Marrill finished the question for him. "Where is it?"

"Um, isn't it a good thing it's not here?" Remy asked. "Besides, I thought you said you guys took him out with that magical death-star thingy."

Fin caught Marrill's eye. "We did, it's just..."

Coll stepped forward and took a long, deep breath. His tattoo no longer wrapped around his neck but snaked down his arm instead. "It's just that for now, we're okay. Why don't we enjoy it for a while before looking for more trouble?"

The captain had a point. Fin collapsed on the deck, exhausted. Marrill pounced on his chest, making him groan and laugh all at once. "We did it!" she shouted. "We made it!"

A second later, Remy dog-piled on top of them. "I can't believe you talked me into staying here, young lady!" she chided. "If you think for a second we aren't getting back in time for my exams, you've got another thing coming." But her voice was anything but unhappy.

Karnelius let out a contented purr. Marrill's Wiverwane flexed its fingers happily on the sunlit railing. Even Coll laughed. Loud enough that the rumor vines along the stern took up the sound, amplifying it across the Stream.

It took Fin a moment to realize that the only one who hadn't joined in, other than the Naysayer, was Ardent. The wizard stood at the bow, staring off toward the horizon, his face drawn and anguished.

Fin slipped free of the celebration and made his way toward him. Being forgettable had a few advantages; sometimes folks preferred to open up to a stranger. And it looked like Ardent needed someone to talk to.

"You'll find her, blood," Fin said quietly, joining him.

Ardent sighed. "I don't know that I will."

Fin had never heard him sound so weary. "Why wouldn't you?"

"Because she never found me." Ardent shrugged. "Either she doesn't want to, or something's happened and she can't."

Fin thought about that. "Maybe she was just waiting for you to come back from Monerva. Maybe she didn't want to interfere with what she knew had to happen there."

Ardent laughed, but it was a hollow sound. "You mean she's like Serth—already knowing the future and trying to make it so."

"You can't give up hope." Fin almost laughed at the number of times he'd had to remind himself of the same thing.

It was so long before Ardent answered that Fin started to wonder if he'd been forgotten. "When I used the Map to find her, it was blank," the wizard said. His voice was so devoid of emotion it caused a chill to scurry down Fin's spine.

"What does that mean?" Fin asked.

Ardent squeezed the railing tightly. "I don't know. But I promised her I'd scour the Stream for her, and I intend to do just that." The wizard kicked aside the hem of his robe and strode toward his cabin.

For a moment, Fin stood staring at the indents Ardent's fingers had left in the wooden railing.

"Ardent?" Fin called after him. One thing still bothered him.

The wizard turned, looking at him absently. "Hmm?"

"We still don't know who the Master was, do we? Or why he was helping Serth?"

Ardent sighed. "No. If anything, we know even less of him now than we did at the start of all this." He shook his head gravely as he rejoined Fin, staring out at the Stream. "But that, too, I intend to change. Before, I was willing to let it stay a mystery, to be one of those secrets the Stream alone gets to keep. Not anymore."

"Serth called him an old friend," Fin pointed out.

Ardent nodded, thinking about this for a moment before pushing back from the railing, determination spreading across his wrinkled features. "Then I suspect the Master may be an old friend of mine as well."

Fin blinked. "Wait, what? You think you may *know* him?"

"The Master is clearly a wizard of great power," Ardent explained. "A wizard of that caliber, and an old friend of Serth's? I can only think of a few and they were all members of the Wizards of Meres, as were Serth, Annalessa, and I.

"There weren't many others, as you can imagine." Ardent continued. "Though what could have turned one of them into *that*, I cannot say. But we were all dedicated to exploring the mysteries of the Pirate Stream itself...and look what that did to Serth..." He trailed off into uncomfortable silence.

Fin stood for a moment, certain the old man had forgotten him. But just as he moved to slip away, Ardent sighed. "I have a feeling none of this is over." He still stared across the water. "I will not make the mistake of assuming the Meressian Prophecy has ended this time."

Fin gulped. There would be time enough to think about that, but not now. Not on this beautiful, sunlit day, when they'd beaten back the forces of evil and saved both Marrill's world and the Pirate Stream. Today, that was something worth celebrating.

"Hey, Plus One," Remy called behind him. "What are you doing up there all alone?"

"Yeah, Fin," Marrill cried. "Get back here!"

Even Coll didn't threaten to throw him in the brig for once.

Laughing, Fin took one last look around before running back to join them. From horizon to horizon, the Stream sparkled like diamonds in the sun. An endless sea of possibility. And now, he had his best friend here to sail it with him.

He couldn't have wished for more.

ACKNOWLEDGMENTS

Climbing the Wall of Monerva has been a long and spectacular journey. It took a strong team and a steady hand to help us reach the summit, and many more to keep us from falling right back down again.

Our deepest thanks to Deirdre Jones for never losing sight of us or letting us drop, no matter how high the Wall seemed or how fast we were slipping. A very special thank-you to the one and only Victoria Stapleton, who we have no doubt is a wizard of the highest order (if humbler than most wizards we know). Thanks also to Andrew Smith, Kristina Aven, Jenny Choy, Emilie Polster, Annie McDonnell, and everyone else at Little, Brown Books for Young Readers and Orion Children's Books for making sure we had all the necessary tools for the journey.

Of course, climbing is always easier if you can fly. We are eternally grateful to the wonderful Merrilee Heifetz, who seems to sprout wings every time we're about to slip. Also to Sarah Nagel, Cecilia de la Campa, and the entire team at Writer's House for their unerring support.

But for the imagination of Todd Harris and the steady hand of his wife, Rachel, we would be lost and blind to the wondrous creatures and places of the Stream. Red @ 28th provided a welcoming base camp, and our fellow mountaineers supplied necessary advice, wisdom, and friendship: Thanks to Kate Sullivan, Rose Brock, Sarah MacLean, Beth Revis, Diana Peterfreund, Ally Carter, the folks at Bat Cave, as well as all the folks at FDWNC, for their continued support and tolerance of many skipped lunch breaks. And of course, our wonderful families continue to encourage us in expeditions such as these, no matter how far we go or how distant it takes us.

Finally, but foremost, to our fearless readers. There are no fires without fuel, and no stories without hearts to burn in. Thank you for climbing with us. The view from the top of the Wall is so much sweeter with you by our sides!